Off the Bench

A Sports in the Sunshine State
Rom-Com

Tiffany Noelle Chacon

WRITE HORSE
Publishing

Copyright © 2024 by Tiffany Noelle Chacon

All rights reserved.

No part of this publication may be reproduced, distributed, or transmitted in any form or by any means, including photocopying, recording, or other electronic or mechanical methods, without the prior written permission of the publisher, except as permitted by U.S. copyright law. For permission requests, contact Write Horse Publishing at tiffanynoellechacon@gmail.com.

The story, all names, characters, and incidents portrayed in this production are fictitious. No identification with actual persons (living or deceased), places, buildings, and products is intended or should be inferred.

Book Cover by Care Hibaya

Edited by Joyce Bloemker

Contents

Dedication	VII
1. Austin	1
2. Dani	7
3. Dani	15
4. Austin	20
5. Dani	24
6. Austin	30
7. Dani	35
8. Austin	38
9. Dani	43
10. Austin	50
11. Dani	54
12. Austin	56
13. Dani	59
14. Austin	61
15. Dani	64

16.	Austin	72
17.	Dani	77
18.	Austin	81
19.	Dani	88
20.	Dani	91
21.	Austin	95
22.	Austin	99
23.	Dani	107
24.	Austin	110
25.	Austin	115
26.	Dani	118
27.	Austin	122
28.	Dani	125
29.	Dani	130
30.	Austin	135
31.	Dani	138
32.	Austin	142
33.	Dani	145
34.	Dani	151
35.	Austin	159
36.	Dani	165
37.	Austin	167

38.	Dani	176
39.	Austin	182
40.	Dani	190
41.	Austin	194
42.	Dani	197
43.	Austin	202
44.	Dani	204
45.	Austin	206
46.	Dani	210
47.	Dani	216
48.	Dani	223
49.	Austin	226
50.	Dani	229
51.	Dani	232
52.	Austin	238
53.	Dani	242
54.	Austin	248
55.	Dani	253
56.	Austin	255
57.	Dani	258
58.	Austin	260
59.	Dani	262

60.	Austin	265
61.	Dani	267
62.	Dani	271
63.	Austin	275
64.	Dani	277
65.	Austin	282
66.	Dani	284
67.	Austin	288
68.	Dani	291
69.	Dani	298
70.	Austin	301
71.	Dani	305
72.	Dani	313
73.	Dani	318
74.	Austin	321
Epilogue		324
Epilogue		326
Bonus Scenes		329
What's coming next in the Sports in the Sunshine State Rom-Com series...		330
Many Thanks To...		333
About Tiffany		335

Dedication

Googolplex: A number so vast it's virtually incomprehensible, represented as 10 raised to the power of a googol (which is 1 followed by 100 zeros). This number far exceeds the total number of particles in the observable universe.

For my football-loving guys: Ty, Finn & Justus. This one's for you.

I love you a googolplex.

1

Austin

Undrafted Free Agent (UDFA): A player who is eligible for the NFL Draft but is not selected. After the draft concludes, these players are free to sign with any team.

It's a nerve-racking day for college football players all over the country. But not for me.

It's NFL draft day—which is actually a three-day event, not just one day. Over two hundred talented athletes will get picked to join NFL teams. Some of my friends might be among the lucky ones. I know a few guys who are in New York City right now, attending the draft. Roger Goodell, the NFL commissioner, will call their names, and they'll walk to the stage, posing with the team owner who just drafted them. They'll get a new hat with their team's logo to go with their fancy, flashy suits.

Meanwhile, I'm in my basketball shorts and Cincinnati Bearcats shirt, legs stretched out over my mom's coffee table. My dad is on his recliner, two of my siblings on either side of me on the couch. Olivia, my Irish twin—born almost exactly one year after me—is in her Bearcats sweatshirt, her legs tucked beneath her as she bites her lip. My little brother, Will, is taking up too much space on his side of the couch with his long limbs akimbo, his hair swooping into his eyes.

"Shouldn't you be in New York?" Olivia asks, her hazel eyes darting from the TV to me and back. "Isn't that, like, a thing on your draft day?"

"It's not my draft day, Livvy."

"You don't know that," her soft voice chides.

"I do," I say quietly. My family has their hopes up far more than I do.

Our oldest sister, Emily, sweeps into the room carrying a tray of pigs in a blanket. She shoos my feet off the coffee table and sets the food down in the middle. "Maybe if you'd gone to the combine it would be your draft day," Emily says with a huff. She's my older sister, but she fancies herself a second mom, which is why she thinks I should have been invited to the NFL combine—a showcase event where top college athletes are evaluated through drills and tests by pro coaches and scouts.

"I wasn't invited to the combine," I say, keeping my voice level.

"Trevor said if you'd hired an agent like he suggested then you would've been invited to the combine."

I shrug, looking away from her. Her lawyer boyfriend *Trevor* thinks he knows so much about everything. In this particular instance he's not wrong, but I wasn't about to seek out an agent. It's just not my style.

I've never had delusions of grandeur.

In fact, it feels wrong to even be watching the draft with my family—like I'm sending the wrong signals to them about my prospects. My pro day was a disaster. My athletic measurables—the forty-yard dash, broad jump, bench press, and so on—were in the lowest 20th percentile for my position as quarterback. I've always had the right feel for the game and pinpoint accuracy, but I've never been an elite athlete.

And I never will be.

So here we are, watching as my fellow collegiate athletes get called up to various NFL teams, while my family's hopes are poised to be dashed. Even though I've prepared myself for this, watching my friends get called up still feels like watching the ship sail away while I'm stuck on the dock.

"You know," Emily says, squeezing between Will and me onto the couch. "When you were little you always wanted to be a garbage truck driver. If you don't get drafted, you could still do that." She waggles her eyebrows at me as she pops a piece of hot dog into her mouth.

"You would always rush us out of the house to watch the garbage truck drive by," my dad says.

"I also wanted to be a dinosaur, but that didn't pan out either," I say, smirking at Em.

My mom hurries into the room as the Browns are about to name their first pick, carrying a plate of buffalo wings with a large bowl of ranch dressing. She places it beside the pigs in a blanket and then turns to me, placing her hands on either side of my face and kissing the top of my head. "No matter what happens today, we are so proud of you, Austin."

"Thanks, Mom."

It's painful to watch my family—all of them leaning forward in their seats, bated breath, as I lean back against the couch we've had since I was a kid. Sure, I've let myself imagine what it might be like to play in the pros—not least of all what it'd mean for my family. Getting my parents new furniture, a spa day for my mom, a car for Liv and one day for Will too. But as fun as it is to dream, I know it's just that—a dream.

My phone pings with text notifications. I pick it up to see a group text with Omar and Caleb, my two best friends.

> Yo, how's it going? Any word yet?

> Nothing yet. Not looking good.

> Dude, even if you don't get drafted, teams still pick up players after the draft. It ain't over till it's over!

> Yeah, UDFA is still a thing. Keep your head up!

I sigh at Omar's reference to being an undrafted free agent. He's right, but I don't even want to entertain the thought.

> Appreciate it, guys. Trying to stay realistic here.

> Realistic schm-ealistic. You've got skills, man. Someone's gonna notice.

> And if not, there's always Bucky's Used Cars. You'd be the worst used car salesman ever but they'd use your ugly mug in their commercials. 🏈

Omar

> Can you imagine Austin trying to sell a used car? He couldn't sell hand warmers to an Eskimo.

Caleb

> He couldn't sell water to someone dying in the desert.

Me

> You're hating on my skills as a salesman but I fleeced you last year in our fantasy football trade.

Omar

> Good point. Maybe you could become a full-time fantasy football player since you can't do the real thing.

We both laugh at Omar's jibe and Caleb sends a burn GIF in the thread.

Caleb

> Hey man, even if you don't get drafted today, I'll select you as my last pick in our league out of solidarity.

Omar

> You got this, man. 🏈

I chuckle at my friends' messages, feeling a bit lighter. Their support means a lot, even if I'm not holding my breath for a miracle. And I know better than to dream too much.

2

Dani

As of 2023, women hold less than 2% of data analyst positions in the NFL.

If I were a man, I'd be playing in the NFL right now. But I'm very clearly a woman, so instead I'm on the data analysis team for the Tampa Bay Buccaneers. Growing up, when people would find out that I'm obsessed with football, they assumed I'd want to be in broadcasting. I get it, I've got a pretty face, so that means I should use it. But it turns out I also have a pretty sweet brain too. And I'd much prefer to use that.

It's draft day for the NFL. This is my first season with the Bucs, and I'm trying to show what I've got. I know my analysis is spot-on—but I'm the newbie in the room. I've interned with other NFL teams, but this is my first full-time analysis position after finishing my masters degree at MIT for data science with a concentration in sports analytics.

This is my dream job and I'm ready to shine. However, it's the third round and I haven't said a peep except to debate back and forth in whispers with my co-workers.

We're in the draft room at the Bucs' headquarters inside the AdventHealth Training Center. Today, the massive room is packed with every scout, analyst and member of the coaching staff. Live coverage of the draft is playing on a mounted television at the front of the room. The scent of stale coffee and the buzz of hushed conversation between colleagues fills the space. We're on a conference call with our representatives at the draft as well as the Bucs' owner, Mr. Beaumont. Everyone is eagerly waiting to see who the Philadelphia Eagles will select. We have the next selection, so the Eagles' pick could greatly affect us.

My rival, *ahem*, counterpart, Ethan Driver, thinks they'll pick up Drake Blythe, a quarterback from Florida State, but my money's on Lorenzo Mattias. He's a running back from Michigan and the Eagles' new coach loves his run game.

The problem with the Eagles' picking Mattias is that *we* are planning to pick him up next.

My phone buzzes in my pocket and I sneak a glance. It's a text from my best friend, Claire Beaumont. Her dad owns the Bucs and we've been connected at the hip since her dad hired mine as the General Manager almost a decade ago.

Claire

> [GIF of a cat typing frantically] How's the war room?

Me

> Total chaos.

> **Claire**
>
> Have you given any of your suggestions yet?

> **Me**
>
> <rolling eyes emoji>

> **Claire**
>
> Dani! You're the smartest, most knowledgeable person EVER. Like, you should get an award for knowing so much football stuff. OPEN YOUR BEAUTIFUL MOUTH!!

I press my lips together to hide my smile as I tuck my phone away. Even though her dad owns the team, Claire knows as much about football as a toddler. But she believes in me, and I could really use some of her faith right now.

Roger Goodell steps up onto the stage to announce the Eagles' pick. "For the 2024 NFL draft, the Philadelphia Eagles select—" he glances down at the paper in his hand, though I'm certain he already knows the name written there "—Lorenzo Mattias."

Beside me, Ethan narrows his eyes, but I don't dare move a muscle. I can't afford to gloat, not now—and possibly not ever. Being a woman in this man's world, I have to be above it all. It's exhausting but so, so worth it.

Despite the fact that most of the people in the room are wearing casual clothes, I'm in my typical attire: a tailored suit. Today I'm sporting a black suit with tapered pants and a soft ivory blouse. I never, ever wear skirts or dresses. EVER. I do, however, allow two nods to my femininity: stellar high heels and long braids that I almost always wear down. After almost a decade of wearing my hair in a severe bun for ballet—thanks to my stepmom—I've opted to wear my hair down.

Ethan, on the other hand, seems to always be in a Bucs shirt that's been washed too many times and is losing its color. He's got a dark beard, perpetually smudged glasses, and what our boss Mark calls a "gamer bod." We're essentially a study in opposites.

Today I'm rocking a pair of Dolce & Gabbana heels with a pointed toe in a bright red to match the Bucs colors. My braids, which hang halfway down my back, are decorated with tiny red braid cuffs. My makeup is simple and, other than the braid cuffs, I don't have on an ounce of jewelry or perfume. When the men in this room look at me, I don't even want their brains to register that I'm a woman. I want them to only think I mean business. Because I do.

The moment Goodell announces the Eagles' pick, the draft room erupts in chaos. My dad, the Bucs' GM, Darius Marshall, takes his place at the front of the room. If he weren't my own father, Darius Marshall would be terrifying. Heck, he's still kind of scary, and I know he's got a soft spot for Italian anise cookies and his fluffy white Pomeranian, Fifi. He's six foot three inches, well over 250 pounds, with a perpetual scowl and a bald dome that seems to always have beads of perspiration gleaming off his dark skin no matter the temperature.

A white board hulks behind my father, who's frowning at the names written on the board. He crosses off Mattias's name from our list as I shuffle my papers and do the same. "Ten minutes on the clock. Should we take Yelenski? You have two minutes to convince me otherwise," my dad says in his booming voice.

Since the running back, Mattias, got snatched from our hands, Yelenski's the next best option for a running back. But with his talent level, he should go in the sixth round, not the third.

We also need a backup quarterback since we traded ours away. Though the odds of our backup QB playing are slim to zilch—our current starting QB just signed a massive four-year $180 million deal with us with a $50 million signing bonus and $100 million guaranteed—you always need at least one backup, preferably two, in case all your hopes and dreams burn down with an ACL tear or rotator cuff injury.

"Yelenski's got the speed we're looking for," Uncle Clive—excuse me, *Coach* Clive—says as I fidget with my braid cuffs, twisting the metal between my fingers, wondering if I should bring up my alternative option.

"Since the Eagles didn't take Drake, it's worth looking at," Ethan says. My dad points his dry erase marker toward the analysts: Mark (the lead analyst), Ethan, and now, me.

"Give me his numbers," he says.

Mark starts rifling through his papers and Ethan's scrolling on his computer for the data, but I cut in. I may not remember where I put my car keys, but football numbers stick in my mind like they're made of superglue. And Claire's admonition for me to open my mouth hits home. "His last season, Drake had over 3,700 yards and 37 touchdowns. His completion percentage is 65% but he threw fifteen interceptions." It's the first time I've spoken in this entire draft, and I can feel everyone's eyes on me. Assessing.

"And his combine stats?" I can't tell if my dad is testing my memory or if he actually wants to know.

"His forty time was 4.4 and he has a thirty-eight-inch vertical." His stats make him a standout option, but I have strong misgivings.

I'm trying to summon the courage to speak them when Ethan cuts in. "He should've been picked up in the first round. We're getting a steal if we grab him now. He's the most talented player on the board."

"There's a reason he didn't get taken in the earlier rounds: he makes bad decisions on and off the field. He's a huge liability." My words are strong, my tone is firm, and yet my insides are quaking like an off-the-Richter earthquake. I've been in meetings like this since my mom died when I was eleven and my dad had to drag me along. But this is the first time I've ever spoken in one. Even when I was interning with the Jets, I was a sit-in-the-back-and-take-notes kind of intern. Not the speaking kind. And certainly not the opinionated kind. "I've developed a new metric called the CHOICE score. We all know that in any given game a quarterback makes hundreds, if not thousands, of decisions. Should we run or pass? Is the defense blitzing? Should I shift the line? Should I hot route that receiver? And those are just the decisions before the snap. After the snap, the quarterback has to reread the defense, go through his progressions, and throw it to the right receiver. All within a few seconds. What you want in a QB is someone who consistently gets that right. I've charted Drake's decision making, and in a word, it's bad. His athleticism has overcome some of those decisions, but it won't work in the NFL. If we're going to draft a backup quarterback, we should draft Austin Taylor. He was the highest scoring quarterback that I charted. He always gets the offense into the right play, has a great feel for what the defense is trying to do, and makes the right choices time and time again."

"Thanks for the football lesson, chica." One of our scouts, Orlando, says with a not-so-discreet eye roll. "But draft day isn't the time to be experimenting with untested theories. There's a reason almost every NFL team has Drake graded above Taylor. You think you really know something that the entire scouting community missed?"

"All I know about Taylor is that he runs like a newborn giraffe," Ethan says, and the rest of the room chuckles.

My dad gives me a look and says, "I appreciate the outside-the-box thinking, sweet—" he clears his throat, stopping himself from calling me sweetheart and I try not to cringe. "—Danielle. But with Nolan Reese as our starting QB for at least the next four years, we have plenty of time to develop Drake into a much better decision maker. What do you say, Coach?"

Coach Clive looks at his computer and then back at my dad, nodding. "Let's draft him."

My dad barks into the phone to draft Drake Blythe, and I lean back in my chair. Beside me, Ethan has pulled up a picture of Austin Taylor from a Google search. He glances at me, then back at the picture. "He's easy on the eyes, I'll give you that, Marshall."

I clench my jaw, turning away from Ethan without a word.

We don't draft Austin Taylor.

In fact, no one does.

End Zone Report ✓
@endzonereport

Drake Blythe was drafted in the third round by the Tampa Bay Buccaneers.

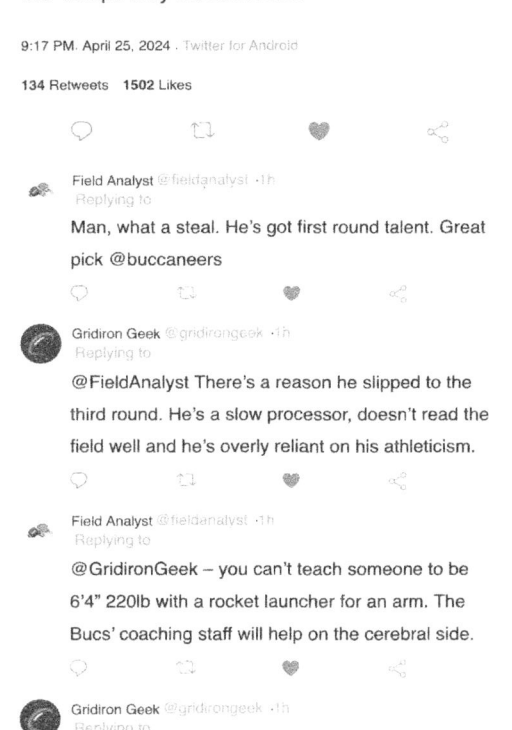

9:17 PM. April 25, 2024 · Twitter for Android

134 Retweets 1502 Likes

Field Analyst @fieldanalyst ·1h
Replying to

Man, what a steal. He's got first round talent. Great pick @buccaneers

---

Gridiron Geek @gridirongeek ·1h
Replying to

@FieldAnalyst There's a reason he slipped to the third round. He's a slow processor, doesn't read the field well and he's overly reliant on his athleticism.

Field Analyst @fieldanalyst ·1h
Replying to

@GridironGeek – you can't teach someone to be 6'4" 220lb with a rocket launcher for an arm. The Bucs' coaching staff will help on the cerebral side.

Gridiron Geek @gridirongeek ·1h
Replying to

@FieldAnalyst – Bucs coaching staff will have their hands full teaching him to stay sober. The playbook will be their last concern.

3

Dani

In any given year, 90% of undrafted free agents that are signed by an NFL team end up getting cut by the team before the season starts.

The moment the draft ends, my dad sends his scouts out like soldiers into the world to sign any key players who weren't drafted. We're hoping to score a couple linebackers, a backup tight end, and a defensive end. I wait my turn to speak with him as the room clears out.

Finally, his gaze settles on me, his scowl softening an iota. "Danielle," he says.

"Austin Taylor," I say, cutting to the chase. "We should sign him."

He sighs heavily, his massive shoulders drooping with the exhaustion of the draft. I draw myself up even taller, though I'm still a solid few inches below my dad's height, even in my four-inch heels.

"We've been over this," he says. "The scouts don't like him."

"The scouts are wrong. I like him."

"Even if I wanted to sign him, I don't have any scouts left to send."

"I'll go myself."

His eyebrows raise, his dark eyes assessing me.

"I haven't pushed any player," I tell him. "But I believe in this one. I've watched every snap he took in college. I know him."

He closes his eyes, his fingers going to the bridge of his nose. Fatigue lines his face and for a moment, I think he's going to say no. "Fine, but with the salary cap, we can only offer him the minimum."

"Understood," I say, trying to keep the glee out of my voice. I gather my laptop bag with my binder of stats, player profiles, and notes. "Well, I'll be on my way then."

"You're going to go tonight?" he says, incredulous.

"I have to get to him before someone else does."

"You know he'll probably get cut after camp." He puts his hands in his pockets, fixing me with a look that screams 'I am the voice of reason.' "And even if he manages to stick it out, he's going to ride the bench the rest of his life."

I give my dad a small smile. "We'll see."

I don't have many vices, but my Twitter addiction might be one of them—and no, I'll never get used to calling it X. Since I started grad school, I've masqueraded as @GridironGeek as a way to blow off some steam and tell people my thoughts about football, without having any connection to who I really am. Most of the people I interact with probably assume I'm a guy.

Including @FieldAnalyst, a fellow football nerd that I often chat with on Twitter. We're debating over Drake Blythe and I smile to myself as I shoot off another tweet at him.

It's all in good fun. I enjoy being able to debate others in a space where people don't seem to care or even consider who I am or what I look like. I've just got a football logo as my icon, and no one's ever asked my real name.

It's refreshing to be so free in what I say.

I make it to the parking lot without anyone talking to me, but now I have the misfortune of running into Ethan in the parking lot. "Heard you're on your way to nowheresville, Ohio," he says to me when he looks up from his phone. "You're wasting your time."

I clench my teeth. Word must have gotten out about me going to pick up Austin.

"Look, I get it," he says. "We all have those picks we get excited about—but trust me, Austin Taylor is a dud. He was a dud in college and he'll be a dud in the NFL."

I square my shoulders, looking Ethan dead in the eye. "One day, you'll see. I'm not wrong about this. The *numbers* are not wrong about this." I fish my keys out of my purse. "And when that day comes, you'll owe me an apology for being so patronizing."

Ethan smirks like I'm an amusement. "The numbers don't tell the whole story."

"You're right, Ethan, they don't," I say as I unlock my car and get inside.

"Nice wheels," he says, eyebrows raised as he looks at my car with unabashed longing. "Did Daddy get this for you too?"

I slam the car door, everything within me straining to not scream in his face. Instead, I turn on the car, put it in reverse, and squeal out of the parking lot, leaving Ethan in my dust.

Growing up in a football family and then going into a career that's predominantly male, I'm used to men. They stare, they whistle, they holler. As an absolute rule, I ignore them. Ever since I set myself the boundary of never dating an athlete at the age of eighteen, I've never come close to wavering on it. It only took one football player to ruin the allure forever.

I'm not one to fawn over men—even devastatingly handsome, famous men. I've met many of them over the years. My best friend, Claire, or my cousin, Portia, are the ones who would gush over some guy's strong jaw or ripped abs. That's just not my style.

After my football player, Jared, used me up and spit me out, I've stuck to the harmless geeks. The ones no girl would bat an eyelash at, but the ones who would be respectful, kind, and—if I'm being honest—boring. It's one of many reasons I haven't had any serious boyfriends—no one could keep my attention more than my football stats. Even my sweet nerds don't love getting blown off when I'm in the zone charting players.

As I'm flying to Cleveland from Tampa, a guy across the aisle on the plane is making eyes at me. I roll mine in response, taking out my notebook to keep working on some plays. Some would say that it's audacious for a girl to think that her plays would make it into an NFL playbook. But I'm not just some girl. I'm

Dani freaking Marshall. I dare you to find a man my age who knows more about the game than I do.

"You writing football plays?" the guy across from me asks, leaning halfway into the aisle to look at my notebook.

"Yes." I don't glance up.

"That's hot."

I lift my eyes to him, assessing. He's objectively handsome, with fresh locks, perfect skin, and a goatee edging a nice smile. I am unmoved. "You found your football coach hot?" I say with an eyebrow raise. "Good to know."

He scoffs, clearly offended. I turn back to my plays, my pencil scratching on the paper. Some people play Sudoku or scroll Instagram to relax—but for me, it's writing football plays. As I hurtle toward Austin Taylor in an oversized bullet, I lose myself in the Xs and Os, the sweep of the arrows and the motion of the play unfurling in my mind.

I sketch out a clean pocket for Austin, visualizing the protection holding steady. He's got time. His footwork is perfect and his reads are sharp. It's a short drop, just enough for him to launch a bullet of his own—a deep corner route that takes advantage of his accuracy and quick release. This play is designed for him, maximizing his strengths as a pocket passer, giving him the time and space to make magic happen. I press my knuckles against my lips, hiding a smile, as I picture the play unfolding in my mind's eye.

But one thought keeps coming to me, no matter how many plays I write: I just hope Austin Taylor doesn't sign with someone else before I get there.

4

Austin

> Ride the Pine: A term for a player who is not a regular starter and spends most of the game sitting on the bench.

I seem to be the only one *not* shocked that I didn't get drafted. Omar and Caleb practically kidnap me to take me to Omar's bar, The Hail Mary, to grieve. Except I'm not really the one grieving—they are. I think they wanted me to be in the NFL even more than I did. I'd come to terms with my limitations way before tonight. Watching the draft made me feel like a benchwarmer in my own life, waiting for a chance to play but knowing it might never come. I'm glad it's over—and I'm glad I don't have to struggle any more with unrealistic hopes.

Our table is loaded with every appetizer Omar offers—five types of wings, nachos, loaded potato skins, artichoke dip, and some kind of meat on a stick. Caleb is eating his feelings like he normally does, while I casually munch on the potato skins and nurse the IPA Omar recommended on tap. It's bitter, with a hint of citrus. It's good, but not quite as good as the IPAs Omar's experimenting with creating himself.

Once we move past all the "ah mans" and "they're missing outs," my friends are blessedly silent. It gives me time to look around at the changes Omar's made to the place. It was only two years ago that Omar made a deal with the previous owner to pay him in installments for the next ten years for the bar. It used to be one of those dark and sticky places that you went to because there wasn't a better option. But Omar has cleaned the place up, giving it an edgy, modern vibe with polished concrete floors that reflect the exposed, overhead light bulbs in funky metal fixtures. There's the traditional sports memorabilia on the walls, focusing on local legends—and yes, there's a signed Bearcats jersey by yours truly—and the TVs broadcast various games. In the center are tables for patrons as well as industrial-looking stools at the bar. But Omar's elevated the sports bar by having plush seating around coffee tables so people who want to sit and watch games for hours have a comfortable place to sit. Instead of pool tables lining the back wall, he has a ping pong table, foosball, shuffleboard, and corn hole. A huge chalkboard hangs on the far wall, announcing the standings of the various fantasy leagues Omar runs—including our legacy league that we've been a part of since we were ten. A list of champions keeps its permanent place on the board, where my name can be found for our fantasy football league for 2017, 2020, and 2022.

As I peruse the new photographs he's fixed onto the exposed brick wall, my eye catches on a girl walking into the bar. She's tall and elegant, gliding as if she's not even touching the ground. I find myself taking in every detail of her, because I can't help it. Her braids are caught in a twisting bun at the top of her head. Her almond-shaped eyes are assessing the room, as if she's looking for someone. Her dark cheekbones shimmer with a mesmerizing blend of girl magic that I don't understand. I admit I linger a little too long on her full lips. Her long neck reminds me of a dancer—she's as graceful as a ballerina. I've only gotten to her shoulders when Caleb notices my perusal.

"Ask her to come over here," he says, mouth full with chicken wings.

I force my eyes from her, feeling greedy for more. I push my IPA away, wondering if the pull I feel toward her is more a product of the alcohol rather than some kind of supernatural tug she has.

"I'm not going to go just talk to some random girl who's clearly here to meet someone else."

"Maybe she's here to meet a hunky football player," Omar says with a smirk.

I snort, but don't speak the words that come to my mind: *I'm not a football player anymore.*

And it's the first time since the draft ended that I've felt a deep twinge of grief. I may have convinced myself that I'm content with how things worked out, but I've been a football player my whole life. I don't know how *not* to be a football player. I sigh and half-heartedly dip a chip in the artichoke dip when I realize Caleb and Omar are still looking at me expectantly. "Guys, I'm not going to go talk to her. It's just not who I am."

"Tell me, exactly, what you are, man. Because I don't get it." Omar's got that fire in his dark brown eyes that always makes me a little uncomfortable, like he's about to start a fight. "From where I'm sitting, it seems like you're just someone who lets opportunities slip from his fingers without a fight."

"Dang, bro, chill," Caleb says to Omar as he reaches for more nachos.

"It's fine," I say.

Omar plants his hands on the table, standing. "It's not fine." And then he walks away.

"Who got his panties in a bunch?" I mutter.

"He's overcompensating for your lack of feelings over the draft thing," Caleb says in a fleeting moment of insight. I grunt and return to my IPA. But I just about spit it out when I realize Omar's gone over to talk to the girl. I mutter under my breath as I set the IPA back on the table, where it sloshes over the edge, getting beer all over my hand. I scramble for a napkin, keeping my focus on wiping up my mess as I sense Omar and the girl walking over to our table.

When she's beside us, I finally glance up. Looking at her up close takes my breath away, and I'm pathetically speechless.

"Austin Taylor?" she says as I'm momentarily distracted by the mesmerizing way her lips move. Then I'm confused about how she knows my full name.

"Uh, yeah?" I'm struck next by how closed off her features are. This girl didn't come over here to flirt with a guy—and the realization cuts almost as deep as my football future.

Then, she says the craziest words I've ever heard: "My name is Dani Marshall and I'm here to sign you to the Tampa Bay Bucs."

5

Dani

Less than 2% of undrafted free agents (UDFAs) become starters in their rookie season in the NFL.

I've watched hours of footage of Austin Taylor quarterbacking the Cincinnati Bearcats. I've seen photos of him online. But none of that could have prepared me for seeing him in person. To say that he's a gorgeous specimen of a man is like saying Pi is just an irrational number—vastly understating a fundamental beauty that underlies the very fabric of our universe. When God first took a handful of dirt to create man, He had this end goal in mind: Austin Taylor.

He's a masterpiece, drawing me in with eyes that seem to shift between green and gold, beckoning me to name their exact shade. His dark blonde hair, tousled and untamed, hints at countless hours spent under helmets and in huddles. I imagine that when he puts his helmet on, a curl or two will escape around the edges. His eyes are framed by a smattering of freckles that tell tales of sunny days spent on the field. They hold a depth and intensity, reflecting a mind as strategic as it is spirited. His build, honed from years of discipline and determination, speaks of power and agility rather than mere physical strength, embodying the grace of a player who moves with purpose and passion.

I'm so distracted by this man that it takes me several long moments to realize he hasn't responded to me.

"Why don't you sit down," his friend, Omar, says when Austin still hasn't said anything.

"Right, yes, of course." Austin seems to snap to, pulling out the empty chair beside him and gesturing for me to sit. "I'm sorry, this was . . . unexpected."

I sit, turning my attention to him and immediately I realize my mistake. I'm sitting far too close to him. I'm instantly aware of the magnetism of his body pulling at me. Clasping one hand on the far edge of my seat to anchor myself in place, I ask, "Really?" wondering if he truly hadn't expected scouts to come poach him the moment the draft was over.

"Well, yeah. I thought I was done playing ball."

I scoff. "Mr. Taylor, you threw for 3,300 yards and 30 touchdowns with a very subpar receiving core. I'm sincerely shocked you weren't drafted."

He blinks a few times, long eyelashes glinting in the golden overhead lighting. "You've done your homework."

I shrug, trying to seem more casual than I feel. If this guy knew how much time I'd spent pouring over his film, he'd be embarrassed for me. It's not that I'm a fan of his per se. It's more that I'm a fan of his play style and decision-making. That's right, I'm not a football *player* fan, I'm simply a fan of the game who's also a numbers girl. At least . . . that's what I'm telling myself.

"Tell me more about what I'd be signing up for," Austin says.

I explain that he would be our third string quarterback, behind Nolan Reese and the newly drafted Drake Blythe. He nods, taking it all in calmly. There doesn't seem to be an ounce of arrogance in this guy. Most athletes would bristle at the idea of being third on the depth chart, but he's taking it in like I just told him I ordered him a burger at the bar. Across from us, his buddies are silent, without so much as a crunch of nachos coming from either of them.

When I tell Austin the pay, his eyes widen—for a moment, I think he's going to be disappointed, but then he chuckles. "That's how much you'd pay a guy for never playing a single minute?"

Maybe it's his complete lack of hubris or perhaps it's the sheer allure of him, but I find myself leaning in and saying something I probably shouldn't say: "I'm 36.2 percent sure that you'll be a starting quarterback within three years."

Those hazel eyes widen again, and I'm so close that I can see his pupils dilate. He smells like Tide and something masculine and intriguing. It takes everything in me not to turn into one of those airheads in a commercial taking a deep sniff of clean clothes. I come to my senses, backing away from him.

"36.2?" his redhead friend, whose name I didn't catch, says. "That's, like, your exact number?"

"Who *are* you?" Omar says, ignoring his buddy, his dark eyes leveling me.

"Dani Marshall."

"You know what I'm asking." He leans back, crossing his arms over his chest. "If you're legit, we'll sign," his friend says.

"Dude," his other friend says.

"Are you his agent?" I ask with a raised brow. I can feel the protectiveness of Omar coming off of him in waves.

"Just a friend," Omar says. "You don't seem like a typical scout. Maybe I'm wondering why they sent you."

"I'm a sports data analyst for the Bucs." I leave out the 'junior' part . . . or the part about me being GM Darius Marshall's daughter. Or that I charted all of Austin's numbers myself for his past two seasons. I know more about Austin Taylor's stats than he does. A fact I'd proudly tell my dad, but I would *not* announce in front of Austin himself.

"Do all analysts look like you?" Austin's other friend, who I'm starting to think of as Red, asks as he crunches on a chip with artichoke dip. Omar reaches over and smacks his friend on the back of his head. I feel Austin tense beside me.

"You don't ask that kind of stuff, *idiota*."

"It's fine," I say, waving a hand. "But no, most analysts are way nerdier than me."

"Right on," Red says with a goofy smile.

"Don't get me wrong, I'm as nerdy as the worst of them." I reach out for a nacho covered in jalapeños. "But I keep my nerd hidden."

"Must be pretty deep," Austin says under his breath.

"You're not into nerds?" I say in a tone that comes across as way more flirtatious than I intended.

Austin leans in close enough for me to catch his clean scent and to see the tiny pinpricks of his five o'clock shadow. "You know, I didn't think I was." He smiles, revealing a dimple on his perfectly chiseled face.

Okay, time to abort, my inner protective sirens sound repeatedly. "Well, it's been a pleasure," I say, pressing my hands on the table as I stand. "I hope you'll consider the Bucs' offer." I'm careful to say "the Bucs" rather than "my offer." I sense Austin's eyes on me as I reach into my purse and grab a card to hand him.

"I'll be staying here tonight, flying out tomorrow. So if you want to sign the contract before I leave, let me know."

Austin takes the card, fingertips brushing mine and I have to steel myself so that I don't melt at the touch. Before I can morph into someone who is very unlike Dani Marshall, I bolt to the door, leaving behind Austin Taylor and his stupid dimples.

As I escape through the door, I turn my head slightly to look back at Austin's table once more, and I find Austin's eyes still on me as I exit. Once I'm in the parking lot, I glance through the window and find Red standing on his chair, twerking as he chants, "Tampa Bay! Tampa Bay!"

End Zone Report
@endzonereport

Austin Taylor, QB from University of Cincinnati, signs to the Tampa Bay Buccaneers as a UDFA.

4:40 PM. April 28, 2024 . Twitter for Android

184 Retweets   534 Likes

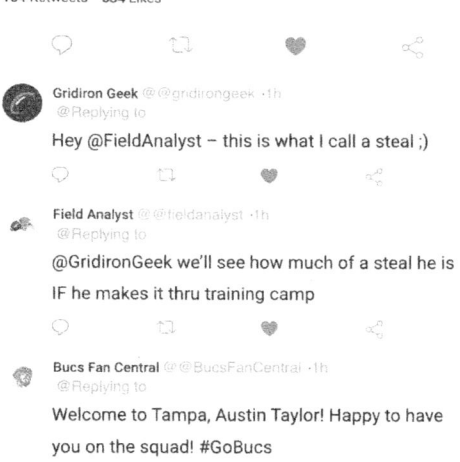

Gridiron Geek @@gridirongeek ·1h
@Replying to

Hey @FieldAnalyst – this is what I call a steal ;)

Field Analyst @@fieldanalyst ·1h
@Replying to

@GridironGeek we'll see how much of a steal he is IF he makes it thru training camp

---

Bucs Fan Central @@BucsFanCentral ·1h
@Replying to

Welcome to Tampa, Austin Taylor! Happy to have you on the squad! #GoBucs

6

Austin

> Pocket passer: A quarterback who primarily operates from the pocket, the area behind the offensive line, and relies on throwing rather than running to advance the ball.

I proved myself enough at training camp to not get cut. My first victory in the NFL.

But apparently I haven't proven myself enough to get hazed by the team. I know that sounds ridiculous, but in the days and weeks since training camp wrapped up, I've watched each and every rookie get pranked by the other players. Except for me. I'm beginning to wonder if maybe I'm too irrelevant to haze.

It's a few weeks until our first preseason game. Since training camp finished, I don't see any snaps in practice. I get a few minutes of the quarterback coach's time when he's done with Nolan and Drake—we practice my footwork and my throwing action, but I can sense his lack of conviction as we go through the motions. Mostly I stand on the sidelines and watch Nolan during practice, making notations on my clipboard about the various plays that they run.

Nolan Reese is an incredibly entertaining quarterback to watch—the guy is like a frigging gazelle. Or whatever a manlier version of a gazelle is. He's swift and agile, with almost supernatural footwork. So many times I've thought he's about to be sacked by our defense—and somehow he gets out of it. He seamlessly orchestrates our offense, keeping the defense guessing at every turn. When he executes a bootleg, it's like watching a magician perform a sleight of hand trick, leaving defenders grasping at thin air as he rolls out of the pocket with finesse.

However, despite his prowess on the move, Nolan's weaknesses become apparent when he's confined to the pocket. Nolan's more prone to throw picks if he's forced to throw from a tighter space. It's a personal strength of mine to be a pocket passer, delivering accurate throws under pressure from the defense.

Nolan responds to the defense by running. I typically respond by finding a receiver and throwing, even if it means I get hit by a defender.

It's a different style of play, but the Bucs obviously prefer the run style over my pocket passing.

I'm fine with it. If they want to pay me a ridiculous amount of money to sit on the sidelines and watch Nolan, I'm good.

At least, that's what I tell myself.

Some of the other backups stand with me and the topic of conversation always seems to revert to what it would take for one of them to get in on the action and become a starter. "Just sayin'," says Derrick, a backup tight end who's third on the depth chart. "They put me in, with Nolan dropping dimes like that and I'm going for glory."

"Dude, like ten people have to get injured before Coach would even think about putting you in," a backup lineman says.

"Coach wouldn't even know your name to throw you in," says Brick, a defensive tackle.

"Hey, at least we got a shot at a Super Bowl ring—whether we play or not, that ring is ours if the team wins," Derrick says.

They glance over at me and I nod like I really care about getting a ring I didn't fight for myself.

"If it comes down to you, though, Taylor, we might as well pack it up and call it a season," Brick chides.

The laughter that follows is good-natured, but it stings all the same. I force a chuckle, shrugging it off. "Guess I better keep practicing my clipboard skills then," I say, smacking him with my clipboard.

After practice, we shower and watch film. In the afternoons, I work out with one of our trainers and spend some time memorizing our massive playbook. This repeats over and over again, with the addition of team meetings, quarterback meetings, offensive meetings—all in which I'm essentially irrelevant. I sit in the back, alert but silent.

Don't get me wrong, I absolutely love being here. I love being a Buc and I love that I get to be on an NFL team. And I'm definitely not complaining about how much they're paying me. But it's difficult to feel a little ... purposeless.

At the end of every NFL draft, the very last player drafted is given the nickname of "Mr. Irrelevant." They even get a jersey with that emblazoned on it.

But what do you call the guy that's even more irrelevant than Mr. Irrelevant himself?

By the time I get to our locker room to get suited up for practice on Tuesday, it seems like all my teammates are there. I check the time on my phone to see if I'm late, but I'm not. It's a little strange since I'm usually one of the first ones in here. As I pull on my pads and jersey, I swear it feels like everyone's eyes are on me. I cringe as I don my uniform—all of it is still wet from our grueling outdoor practice in the Florida humidity yesterday. Even though I mostly sat on the sidelines, I still sweat enough in my pads for them to be soaked the next day.

Once I'm dressed, it feels oddly cold against my skin—a fact I chalk up to the wet equipment combined with the frigid A/C that seems synonymous with Florida indoors.

That is, until it all starts to burn.

I notice it first in the very region you *never* want to feel a burn. It quickly spreads down my legs, across my torso, over my back, until my whole body is tingling with fiery pins and needles. Frantic and confused, I tear off my jersey and my pads, shucking my pants and the rest of my equipment in an attempt to flee from whatever is causing this burning sensation that's all over me. It takes all of my self-control to not scream in discomfort—but I'm not about to do that in the Bucs locker room, even if I were actually on fire.

I'm looking around frantically for something to put me out of the misery that is flaming across my body. I scramble to the first thing I see that can help me: a Gatorade cooler filled with the ice-cold drink. Without thinking, I chuck the lid and pull the cooler onto me, the startlingly cold liquid pouring over my blazing skin.

The temporary relief brings with it a return of my sanity.

I still can't quite make sense of what's happened to me, until I turn back to my teammates, where I see one of the linebackers filming me as the rest of the team looks on, laughing hysterically. One of the defensive ends is behind him, holding up an empty jar of Icy Hot. My jaw drops when I realize *that* is what's all over me, making me feel like a million fire ants are on my you-know-what.

Even so, for the sake of the team and the fact that I'm finally "in," I crack a smile and call over my shoulder, "Nicely played, guys," as I run to the shower.

7

Dani

On Super Bowl Sunday, Americans consume about eight million pounds of guacamole and 14,500 tons of chips. (Which is approximately how much my dad and I consume in one football season.)

It's Sunday evening and I'm at my dad and stepmom's house, watching a preseason game. Even though it's hard for me to be here at times, I do relish these moments with him. It's not often that we get to hang out and watch a game together. And since the Bucs had their first preseason game on Thursday, we're free to watch the other games together all day today.

My dad married Heather less than three years after my mom passed—way too soon, in my opinion. Heather's nice, but she's decidedly very different from my mom with her blonde hair and Ann Taylor vibe. I miss my mom's lilting Jamaican accent and her beachy coconut scent. Heather smells like a Lancôme counter exploded on her.

It feels like my dad created a whole new family—one that does not look like mine anymore.

Not even a year after they married, Heather and my dad had twins: Lucas and Layla. I'll be the first to admit they're strikingly beautiful kids, with their golden-brown skin and hazel eyes. But the age gap between us, and the fact that we're only half related, makes me feel more like an aunt than a sister to them.

They're also really not into football—so there's not much to discuss with them. What else could I talk about with a seven-year-old? I don't know anything about Disney princesses or dinosaurs. Lucas is in tae kwon do and Layla is in gymnastics. They both play soccer. Things I've never done nor had any interest in.

I try to take them to get ice cream every couple weeks, and during the off-season, we have weekly family dinners. I'm hoping as they get older we can connect on more topics, but I'm not holding my breath.

It's a treat these days to get to watch a game with my dad. Heather seems to sense that and respect it—she made us our standard fare of nachos with the works and has kept the twins occupied doing whatever it is they do so we can watch unhindered.

It's glorious.

By the second game, most of the nachos are gone and my dad's working on his second beer—a rare splurge for him. The glow of the TV casts a warm light over the living room as I settle into the couch beside my dad with a fresh La Croix. Their dog, Fifi, curls between us, looking like a ball of white fluff. The preseason match between the Cowboys and the Steelers is in full swing, and I can't help but analyze every move.

"Watch number 88," I murmur, leaning closer to Dad. Number 88, Marcus Hill, was picked up by the Cowboys in the second round—this is his first time on the field in the NFL and he's one to watch. "He's been slipping through the coverage all night."

Dad nods, his eyes narrowing as he follows the player on the screen. "Good catch, Dani. Let's see if the defense adjusts."

The snap comes, and number 88 bolts off the line, a blur of speed and agility. My heart races in tandem with the action on the screen. The quarterback releases the ball and it slices through the air. Hill reaches out, fingertips grazing the leather. For a moment, it looks like the ball will get past him—until he grasps it, seemingly with his pinkies. And then he's off, darting past defenders. The crowd's roar fills the room, and I stand, hands going to my head while my dad goes, "Ooohh!"

"What a steal!"

"That was incredible," he says, patting Fifi.

I can't help but grin at the excitement coursing through me. Even though it's not the Bucs, the game is electric, a reminder of why I love football so much.

Dad leans back, a thoughtful expression on his face. "The Steelers' secondary is young this year. They're talented, but inexperienced. Hill is exposing them. They need to tighten their coverage and communicate better."

"Makes sense. They're playing off coverage and giving him a free release at the line. A decision he is making them pay dearly for."

Dad smiles, a glint of pride in his eyes. "Exactly. It's those little details that can make or break a game."

The warmth of his approval mingles with the thrill of the game, and for a moment, everything feels perfectly aligned.

8

Austin

Film Study: The process by which players and coaches analyze game footage to evaluate their own performance, understand their opponents' strategies, and develop game plans.

It's strange living in a house all by myself—my entire life has been spent living with my very large and loud family or in the college dorms at Cinci. The silence of my little historic bungalow in South Seminole Heights overlooking the Hillsborough River could not be more deafening. The house isn't overly large, but it feels ridiculous for just me. I suppose I got this place thinking I'd have space for when my family or Omar and Caleb visit, but I haven't filled it with enough furniture for guests quite yet. And with the season about to get started, I don't know when I'll find the time.

I go to bed early and wake up early. About a week and a half before our first regular season game, I find myself blinking at my digital clock at five in the morning. I shower and get dressed in an Under Armour shirt with the sleeves cut off and a pair of athletic shorts. Coming from Ohio where we had frigid days for almost half the year, I'm resolved to never wear pants as long as I can help it. That's gotta be one of the biggest pros about living in Florida—I can wear shorts year-round.

I head to the Bucs' AdventHealth training facility, even though no one will be there. I've made a habit of getting there early to watch film and work out before anyone else arrives.

I've been in Tampa Bay for over a month and I've yet to see Dani Marshall again. And not for lack of trying—I've been caught by various members of the organization while lurking in parts of the building I have no business being in. But no Dani. I've started to think of her as 'The Elusive Dani Marshall.'

I wander the halls of the facility, peeking in the darkened weight room and the trainers' room. No one's around. But when I duck my head into the film room, I'm surprised to find game footage rolling. My first instinct is that someone accidentally left film on all night long—it's only six a.m. But in the light of the screen, I find her.

I don't know if she's glowing because of the light from the projector or if that's just what Dani Marshall does. She turns in her seat, her almond-shaped eyes assessing me. Maintaining eye contact, she pauses the game.

"You're up early, Taylor," she says as if we see each other all the time and this is normal.

"Hey, it's the Elusive Dani Marshall," I say because I'm an idiot and that's what popped into my head.

Two adorable lines form in between her eyebrows, indicating her confusion.

I shrug, trying to remain cool, even though this girl makes me feel as uncool as the towel boy that I am right now. "I guess when you signed me, I thought I'd see you all the time, but . . .

" I trail off, waving a hand to encompass the fact that this is the first time I've seen her.

She gives a half-laugh, half-snort. "Data analysts. We're like the ghosts of professional sports. Better to not see us or hear us. Our intel just magically appears in your inbox. They don't even love seeing us at coaching meetings."

"That's hard to believe." When I look at her, I wonder how anyone could *not* want to see her as frequently as possible. I shake my head, as if to clear the thought. "What are you watching?"

"Prepping for our week one game against the Panthers. I'm charting how likely they are to run certain coverages when they see certain formations."

I don't even ask her if I can join. I circle the couch and take a seat on the far end—inexplicably, I want to be near her, but not so much that it freaks her out. She gives strong mile-high-wall vibes. "You're in my seat," I tease.

She turns around, making a show of inspecting the couch. "I didn't realize it had your name on it."

"It doesn't yet," I tell her. "But that's where I've been sitting every morning, watching film."

"I usually watch in the analysts' room but the TV wasn't working this morning."

"I'll let you have my seat this time," I say, wondering if I'm doing this flirting thing right or if I'm failing miserably.

"Good," she says, waving her hand around her space—she's got her computer, mouse, several print-outs, a binder, and a notebook. "Because I wasn't planning on moving."

I chuckle, leaning back onto the couch. I notice she's written lots of stats in her notebook rather than her computer. "You prefer to chart the game by hand?"

She nods, her braids rustling over her shoulders. "I find that it helps me remember them this way. After I chart them, I put them in the computer, so I'm touching the numbers multiple times."

Touching the numbers. As if they're tangible things that would benefit from a graze of her fingers. "It's a good strategy."

"Works for memorizing plays too."

"You know this from experience?" I ask with a smile.

She doesn't quite smile back. Something about her demeanor makes me wonder if she has the whole playbook committed to memory. Without really responding, she presses play again.

"The Panthers check to cover two almost every time they see eleven personnel," Dani says as she replays part of the game. "What would you do if you saw that?"

"I'd look the safety off and hit the tight end on a seam route."

I'm not sure, but I think I see the hint of a smile tugging on Dani's lips. We continue watching, exchanging insights as we see them.

"Same time tomorrow?" I ask when the game finishes and Dani's completed her final notes.

She opens her mouth, then closes it, clearly hesitant to answer.

"I get it. You like your alone time," I say, holding up my hands in understanding.

"It's not that—"

"It's alright. You gotta stay true to form. The Elusive Dani Marshall wouldn't be so elusive if I knew where she was all the time."

I give her a smile and walk out before she can say anything else. I just hope the analysts' TV stays broken forever—because however ghostlike Dani Marshall is, there's something drawing me to her as surely as the moon pulls the tides.

9

Dani

36% of Americans believe that the ideal way to enjoy art is with a drink and a snack in hand. (And Claire Beaumont is one of them.)

My best friend, Claire, owns an art gallery downtown, about a block from the Hillsborough River. Our other friend, Isabella—who works as a sports reporter for the Tampa Bay Times—and I make a point to visit once a week for our weekly dose of estrogen. Being surrounded by football-crazed men all week long leaves me stuffed to the gills with testosterone and in need of a girly fix. Isabella is similarly starved for femininity, to which we turn to Claire.

Before you picture a stuffy art gallery imbued with the cold distance of a stoic critic, let me stop you. Claire's art gallery is about as opposite of that as you can get. It's feminine and light and airy. Cozy.

When I step inside, the familiar scent is breezy and floral. Gauzy curtains line the floor-to-ceiling windows, and a rope bench swings in the corner with a soft throw blanket hanging over it just so. Sure, art decorates the walls, but it's all woven into Claire's aesthetic. It's comfortable here—a place you'd want to sit and stay awhile. Every few feet there's some kind of comfy seating arrangement: wicker egg chairs stuffed with pillows, a rustic hand-painted bench, a loveseat with a ladder of blankets beside it.

The ceiling is decorated with living clouds—puffs of cotton with LED lights hidden within them. When it storms, Claire turns on a setting where the clouds light up as if the lighting were inside too.

Claire is chatting up a customer as she stands behind a bar cart on wheels. Like everything in her store, it's in a different place each week. This week, she's right in the center, with an extra-large mason jar of strawberry lemonade beside a platter of cupcakes. Claire's addicted to baking—she's a fine-bred Southern woman who popped out of the womb with a whisk in one hand and the Bible in the other.

Her life's plan was to finish college, get married, and have babies the moment she could. But when things didn't quite pan out that way, she decided to open this gallery, where she gets her homemaker fix by selling art and hosting parties.

When she sees me, she squeals like she hasn't seen me in ages. "Pardon me, Miss Dee," she says to her patron, "but this is my very best friend." She throws her arms around me, her Dior perfume wrapping around me with its floral and fruity notes. I'm not one to give a lot of affection, but I accept Claire's with the grace of a pageant queen. Or at least, that's my goal.

After releasing me from her death grip—I mean, hug—Claire finishes her conversation with Miss Dee, an older woman with a bob of bright red hair, while I polish off one of her cupcakes. A zesty lemon cupcake with strawberry buttercream frosting—sweet and tart, light and summery.

"Don't you just love these?" Claire exclaims when her customer leaves. She watches me with bright blue eyes as I lick the rest of the frosting off my fingers.

"Amazing."

"I'm trying to soak up the dregs of summer."

"Ugh, *why*?" Summer in Tampa is so gross. Humid and unbearably hot—I can't wait for fall. For more reasons than one.

Claire shrugs, the tie strap on her little sundress falling down her shoulder with the motion. "I always feel sad about every season when it's about to pass by. I'm afraid I've taken it for granted until it's almost over."

I snort-laugh. It's so typical of Claire to think that way. I can't say I've given much thought to any season other than football season and . . . not-football season.

Isabella arrives, her wild curls frizzing in all directions. She's wearing her typical jeans, heels, and blazer, looking sharp but, well, *hot*. She huffs in, using her notebook as a fan. "It's brutal out there, people," she announces, giving us both a sweaty cheek kiss in greeting.

After Claire pours us strawberry lemonade, complete with a sprig of fresh mint, we take our seats in a corner of the gallery with Claire and me on a loveseat and Isabella in a wicker chair, shucking her blazer as she sits.

Claire hands me a blanket from the ladder, tosses her strappy leather sandals off, and tucks her feet beneath her. We talk about our days, with Isabella telling us about her boyfriend's contract negotiations with Tampa Bay's hockey team, the Lightning. She's biting her nails in between recounting the back-and-forth between Elliot, the star center of the team, and the management.

"It's just nerve-racking because if he doesn't stay with the Lightning, I don't know what that will mean for us." She sighs, chewing on the skin around her thumbnail. Claire reaches out, putting her hand on Isabella's arm—and I'm not sure if it's for comfort or to stop our friend from making herself bleed. "It's just so new and I just got this job with the Times."

We talk about Isabella's dilemma for a few minutes—though Claire and I are in two different camps: Claire is in the 'love will always win' camp and I'm firmly in the 'put your career before the man' camp.

At the end of the conversation, I'm not sure if Isabella is comforted or more disheartened. She's in a tough spot, but I know she'll land on her feet no matter what happens.

The girls look to me next and I tell them about my latest disagreement with Ethan after our game two win against the Jets. The guy gets under my skin like no other.

For some reason I can't quite pinpoint, I don't tell them about Austin Taylor crashing my film-watching the other day, even though I can't stop thinking about it.

Claire then regales us with her latest dating woes. She's moved past trying to meet men in bars and has gotten creative. Her latest venture: going to dog parks. Claire didn't own a dog prior to this idea, so she went out and got a dog that is the antithesis of who she is: a mastiff. He's big, slobbery, and masculine-looking. Preferably, the man she attracts will be the same—minus the slobber.

Oh, and she named the dog *Gronk*.

Gronk, who is currently drooling and snoring in the corner of the shop on a fancy dog bed, is apparently failing epically in his quest to bring his human a husband.

"I'd prefer to just meet someone online," I say, cringing in Gronk's direction.

Claire looks at me, aghast. "Whyever would you say such a thing, Daniella?"

I roll my eyes at her over-the-top reaction. "I like to analyze my prospects before emotions get involved. Chemistry and good looks can take a back seat."

"Oh but darlin' the chemistry is where all the magic presides. What if you meet them in person and there's no chemistry? Then all your data," she waves a hand like "data" is a strange term, "would be useless."

I shrug, flipping my braids over my shoulders. "The chemistry thing can be overcome."

Claire gasps, clutching her chest. "No, my dear, it cannot!" Have I mentioned my best friend is a touch dramatic? She waves her hands in front of her face like she's about to faint, then quickly recovers, leaning forward to clutch my knee. She's finally ditched her Southern belle accent and says to me in her normal voice, "I think you're only saying this because you've never experienced real chemistry firsthand."

Even Isabella is nodding sagely, like she's discovered chemistry too. Ugh.

But my pesky heart flutters at her words because unfortunately, the first thing that pops into my mind is Austin freaking Taylor, with his obnoxious dimples and crazy weird magnetism. It's been a few weeks since I've seen him, and yet I can still feel his pull on me like he's dark matter and I'm caught in the gravitational field of his unseen presence. "Whatever," I mumble under my breath to cover up the fact that I spaced out there for a second. If I told the girls about Austin, they'd absolutely freak.

But I don't date athletes—a boundary Claire and Isabella don't quite understand. Claire would totally fall for someone like Austin, and Isabella is dating the hockey superstar she fell in love with while writing a piece on him. (Okay, okay, to her defense, they'd known each other since high school. But still. Conflict of interest, much?!)

I glance over at my best friend, with her shiny blonde hair, her cute little upturned nose with a sprinkle of freckles across it, and her blue eyes that shift tones based on what she's wearing. She's got a knockout body and even better personality—to say she's a catch is like saying Tom Brady's a decent quarterback.

I could introduce her to Austin Taylor. They'd have perfect, blonde, model-esque babies.

For some reason, I find that I can't quite bring myself to introduce them. Not yet, anyway.

At least, that's what I tell myself.

End Zone Report
@endzonereport

Drake Blythe, backup QB for the Tampa Bay Buccaneers, was arrested early this morning for a hit & run where he fled the scene. When he was arrested, he was charged with a DUI as well. Given the NFL's new 'No Tolerance' policy, Blythe is facing a massive fine & 10 week suspension.

1:23 PM · Sep 20, 2024 · Twitter for Android

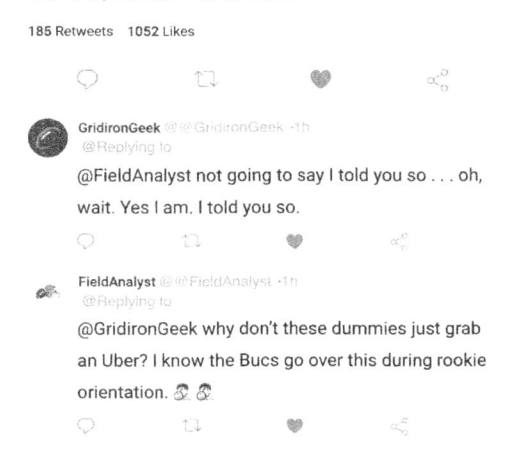

185 Retweets 1052 Likes

GridironGeek @GridironGeek ·1h
@Replying to

@FieldAnalyst not going to say I told you so . . . oh, wait. Yes I am. I told you so.

FieldAnalyst @FieldAnalyst ·1h
@Replying to

@GridironGeek why don't these dummies just grab an Uber? I know the Bucs go over this during rookie orientation. 🤦 🤦

10

Austin

> Depth Chart: a hierarchical listing of players at each position, ranked by their playing status. It indicates the starters, second string, and other backups.

News of Drake's arrest, NFL suspension, and court-mandated rehab rippled through the team as quickly as it did on Twitter. No one was shocked necessarily—it's not the first time this has happened to an NFL player and it certainly won't be the last—but it always hits a certain way when it happens on *your* team. And, of course, it has a particular impact for me. I'm no longer third string. It's entirely possible that during Drake's ten-week suspension and rehab, I'll play a snap or two. However, because of when Drake's arrest happened, I'll go into our game tomorrow afternoon without taking any practice snaps. It's Saturday and all we have today is a walk-through.

The thought leaves me feeling equal parts excited and queasy. My expectations when I signed with the Bucs were low. I knew my place—I *still* know my place—but it's moved up slightly. For a short time.

It's made all the worse by the fact that I haven't practiced with our starting offense since training camp. It's typical for the starting QB and even the backup to get snaps in practice, but not the third-string QB. Nolan is as healthy as ever and we've crushed our first two games, so I'll probably continue to be a statue on the sideline.

My mom is the first to stumble upon the news—apparently, a friend from work forwarded her the story. After calling me three times during our pregame walk-through, she resorts to sending a text to our family thread.

Mom
> My baby boy is a second string QB in the NFL!!!!!!

Emily
> Whhhaaaattttttttt?!? No way!!

Will
> [GIF of football player doing a touchdown dance]

Will
> Dude, that is sick nasty.

Mom
> Is Austin sick? Is that why he's not picking up my calls?

Olivia

> No, Mom, he's not actually sick.
>
> Congrats, Austin. Happy for you.
>
> Does this mean we get season box seats?

I shake my head as I send a quick text back and then put my phone on silent so I can keep studying the playbook after our walk-through. Even though I know our plays, before today, it was all just hypothetical—now I'm only one injury away from playing football in front of millions of people. So I study late into the night until all of the play names, colors, and positions blur in my mind.

But a distant voice in my head whispers that this could be my time to shine, my chance to prove myself. The problem is: do I even have what it takes to succeed in the NFL? The night before our first game without Drake, that question weighs heavy in my stomach, like I've swallowed a stone.

It's our third regular season game and the energy in the locker room is buzzing through my veins like a drug. Music pounds from the overhead speakers. It's our slot receiver Malik's turn to pick the playlist, and he's got a rap song reverberating through the room. I learned that a couple years ago there were some serious scuffles over the music choice, so they created a way to keep it fair. There's a list of who gets to choose the music and when. But you have to be a starter. Not that I care to pick the music—too many opinions for my taste.

Once we're padded up, Coach Clive comes in to give his pregame speech. He gives a few details of how to defeat the Cowboys then launches into his inspiration to us: "I don't need to tell you what's expected—if you're in this locker room, you already know." He looks around the room, making eye contact with each and every one of us. It takes a while because there's more than fifty players. I admire his dedication, even if the adrenaline pumping through me is screaming to be out on that field. "Intensity, integrity, and intelligence. Play hard, play smart, and play together. Who's ready?"

"We are," the team shouts.

"Who's ready?" he yells again.

"WE ARE!"

"Bucs on three," Coach shouts, the deep timber of his voice echoing into my chest. We all stand, putting our hands in the middle. "Bucs on three, one, two, three . . . BUCS!"

11

Dani

NFL teams that win the coin toss and defer to the second half have a 52% win rate.

I'm watching the home game in the staff box seats, perched high above Raymond James Stadium, offering a panoramic view of the entire stadium. The indoor, air-conditioned seats are strategically positioned to provide a perfect vantage point for analyzing the game. Plush, leather seats are arranged in rows with tables in front to hold our laptops, notebooks, and other equipment. Behind us, team memorabilia adorns the walls, along with several TV displays broadcasting the game from different channels. The buzz of the crowd outside is a constant backdrop—muted, but still present. Inside the sounds are more subdued, with the soft hush of rustling papers and fingers clacking on keyboards. I sit at the end of the row of data analysts—Ethan to my right and Mark on the other side of Ethan. Mark has a travel mug in front of him that reads "Behind Every Great Team is a Data Analyst with Coffee."

Mark, as the lead analyst, has a headset that connects him to Coach Clive down on the field. He feeds relevant stats to Coach to help him make decisions during the game. One day, I want to be the analyst in the Coach's ear—it's a lofty goal, since there's never been a female analyst in that position—but I want it.

Against the back wall, there's a table of food and refreshments that we've already picked over, with fruit, turkey wraps, cookies, and bottled beverages. Ethan has several small plates packed with food in front of him, with crumbs dusting the front of his Bucs t-shirt.

There's the coin flip on the field. We win and defer—so we'll start on offense in the second half. Our kickoff team takes the field. "It's game time, people!" our offensive coordinator calls out and a little cheer ripples through the staff.

I smile, fingers poised on my keyboard, ready.

Let's win this thing.

12

Austin

Snap: The action where the center passes the football between their legs to the quarterback to start a play.

We're crushing the Cowboys 27-10 with two minutes left in the first half. In the last drive, our top receiver, Malik Washington, caught a gorgeous pass from Reese for a sixty-yard touchdown. The crowd is going nuts, their screams thunderous. It feels good to be a Buc. I'm a minute away from donning an eye-patch and a captain's hat and shouting "Fire the cannons!" with the best of them.

And then it happens.

Reese takes the snap, steps back, looking down the field where Jordan Ellis is double covered. He pivots to search for his second option, and two defensive linemen break through our line at the same time—one on Reese's right and one on his left. They hit him simultaneously. The guy on the left hits him in the shoulder while the guy on the right slams into his legs.

Even in the roaring of the stadium, I hear his guttural shout as Reese goes down. And I know something's wrong. From a distance, I can tell that his leg isn't positioned in a natural way. Once the linemen come off of Reese, he stays on the ground, writhing in pain as he holds his leg.

That's when I see it—and from the sounds in the stadium, that's when we all see it.

Reese's leg is at an unnatural angle, and the pain on his face says it all. Blood stains his skin, but it's the way his leg looks that sends a chill through me.

There's a collective gasp throughout the stadium. Then sheer silence. The kind of quiet that worms its way into your breath, holding you captive so you don't make a sound.

Both teams immediately take a knee as the medics race onto the field. Silence stretches on, and the only sounds that are heard are the medics loading Reese onto a stretcher as he moans.

I'll remember those groans for the rest of my life. I imagine that's what a man might sound like when he's felled on the battlefield—helpless, out of control, in pain so bright and blinding that you don't care who hears you.

The quiet elongates even after Reese is wheeled off the field. It stretches for a minute, two, until there's murmurs about what we'll do next. There's only thirty seconds left in the first half.

Coach Clive approaches me, a hand clasping the back of my jersey. "We're going to knee it out till half," he says, and I swear he glances at the back of my jersey to remind himself of my name. He goes on to inform the rest of the offense that we're taking a knee to run out the clock.

I jog onto the field—the sensation entirely familiar from a lifetime of football games, yet the situation completely alien.

The stadium is eerily quiet as I line up to take the snap—all of the energy from earlier seeped away after Nolan's injury.

I call the hike and our center snaps me the ball. I take a knee and then we jog off the field for halftime.

Our team shuffles into the locker room. More unbearable silence. Because now they're all looking at me.

Me. The backup quarterback.

Me. The one who was never supposed to play a snap in my life.

Me. The third-string guy who wasn't even important enough to take any snaps in practice.

Our defensive coach, Coach Martinez, leads our team in a prayer for Reese. And then I'm whisked away by Coach Clive and our quarterback coach, Trent McAlister, to a side meeting room so we can go over a few key plays. We've got fifteen minutes for halftime and we'll need every second of that to prepare me. Because one thing is for certain: this was never part of the game plan.

13

Dani

The likelihood of a team that loses its starting quarterback mid-season going on to win the Super Bowl is only 3.2%.

Even though I'm enclosed in glass and separated from the crowd at Raymond James, I can still feel the grief hanging over the Bucs fans. It's spreading through the air we breathe, infectious and lethal. Killing our spirit and our hopes.

Nolan Reese, our franchise quarterback with the $180 million deal, is definitely out for the season—if not longer. A quick Google search for the recovery time of open fractures like his revealed some haunting results. I cover my phone, tucking it under my leg.

It feels surreal when our team takes the field again—it's almost unnatural, like they should have stopped the game completely. But the show must go on, apparently.

The TV announcers have cycled through all of the talking points on Reese's injury already—their Googling was even more robust than mine—and now they're turning their attention to the one player everyone is wondering about: Austin Taylor.

"Who is number 7?" one of the commentators, Bill Metzos, asks. "Ladies and gentlemen, we're looking up information about this player right now, give us a moment."

"We're getting word now that this is Austin Taylor," the other commentator, Julian Pelts says. "He was an undrafted rookie who was signed as the Bucs' third-string quarterback. He played for the University of Cincinnati."

Bill Metzos laughs, throwing his hands up. "And that's the extent of our knowledge of Austin Taylor."

"Look, Bill, this is what I know about Austin Taylor: Nolan Reese had already won this game for the Bucs. This Taylor guy just needs to not screw it up."

14

Austin

> Sack: When a quarterback is tackled behind the line of scrimmage before they can throw a forward pass, resulting in a loss of yardage.

For the first time in my life, I'm walking out onto an NFL field to play a game.

It's not the best of circumstances, but here I am.

I feel my pulse rocketing through me, my breath coming in short spurts even though I haven't run a single step.

I snap my helmet on and adjust my wristband, which is already collecting sweat. My teammates huddle around me as I tell them the play. I look them in the eyes, trying to make contact with each and every one of them like my quarterback coach taught me to do in college. But what I find staring back at me isn't heartwarming: it's terrifying.

I see cynicism, defeat, mistrust, and disdain. I may not be the one who snapped Reese's leg, but it sure feels like I'm the one stealing their Super Bowl hopes right now.

We're about to break when one of the offensive linemen, a huge Pacific Islander, number 56, named Mosi Tuiasosopo, goes, "What's your name again, kid?"

A nervous chuckle breaks out of me. "Austin Taylor."

"Alright, Tay-Tay, let's see what you got."

We've run the ball almost every single play—which means, I'm essentially an overpaid delivery boy, handing off the ball each snap. It's obvious that the coaches hope we can just run the clock out and milk our lead without me having to throw any passes. The few times I've dropped back to pass, I've been sacked before I even have time to think. And each time, I try not to think of what Nolan's leg looked like after he got tackled.

The Cowboys' defense is abundantly aware of what we're trying to do. They're loading up their defensive players as close to the line of scrimmage as possible, which is making it impossible for us to move the ball.

By the fourth quarter, we've punted four times without getting a single first down. The Cowboys' offense has rallied with the shift in tide and now the game is 27-20. Their defense is getting through our offensive line so quickly, I barely have time to hand off the ball, and even when I do, I'm still getting pummeled.

Getting hit by a defensive lineman in the NFL is not at all like getting hit by a defensive lineman in college. If getting sacked in college is like getting pummeled by a wave, getting sacked in the NFL is like being caught in a tsunami. I'm getting walloped before I can even blink. I'm certain there's at least three dudes who tackled me—except when the dust clears, there's only one guy there.

"Welcome to the NFL, baby," the lineman cackles in my face.

15

Dani

In the NFL, the average quarterback is sacked 2.5 times per game. However, rookie quarterbacks are sacked an average of 3.2 times per game.

Watching Austin Taylor in his first game is akin to watching a paper boat get tossed around in a hurricane. The poor guy is lost and defenseless. Anger is boiling beneath my skin because our offensive linemen don't even seem like they're trying to protect him. He's getting sacked over and over again. And when he's not getting sacked, he's handing off the ball to our running backs, Landon Mitchell and Isaiah Roberts, and they're getting hit before they even pass the line of scrimmage.

My heart races as I glance at the live stats streaming on my laptop, synced with the players' wearable sensors. Austin's heart rate is spiking—understandably so. And so is mine. I fought to pick up this guy and now *my* reputation's on the line along with his. I find myself praying every prayer I can think of that Austin Taylor will perform the way I hoped he would.

"Dani, I need to know at what rate they're blitzing," Mark says, his voice steady despite the chaos.

I quickly pull up the data, fingers flying over the keys. "Since Taylor's gotten in there? 92% of the time. Basically, they blitz every play, except when we're punting."

Mark relays the information to Coach Clive. I glance at the field, where Austin lines up for his next play. The Cowboys' defense is formidable, their front line poised to pounce.

Austin is sacked twice on the next drive, struggling to find his rhythm. I jot down the play outcomes in our tracking software, noting the pressure points and defensive setups. My eyes flicker between the field and my screen, capturing every detail.

I've got a headache from clenching my teeth so hard as I watch our offense take a beating. With Nolan Reese as our franchise QB, our plays are designed for a dual threat. Not a traditional pocket passer. And of course Taylor is the epitome of a pocket passer—and unfortunately he's not even close to being a dual threat. I cringe as Taylor attempts to run the ball. Ethan wasn't totally incorrect when he said Taylor runs like a newborn giraffe. I will him to be faster, just this once, but he gets tackled from the right and goes down hard.

This whole situation is rough on so many levels: not only is our playbook designed for the opposite of Austin's strengths but Drake Blythe getting arrested right before our game meant that Austin didn't get any reps in practice this week.

The Cowboys get the ball back and throw a touchdown so we're tied up at 27-27. We haven't even been past the fifty-yard line since Austin took the field and it's the end of the fourth quarter, with a minute and a half on the clock. If we can get within field goal range, we could still win the game and salvage Austin's reputation.

The Cowboys kick the ball off and it goes through the end zone, resulting in a touchback. We have the ball on the twenty-yard line and need to make it to the Cowboys' forty to have a chance at a field goal. Given the score and time left in the game, we have no choice but to play out of shotgun and go no huddle—Austin's specialties.

"Dani, what defense do the Cowboys run against a two-minute offense?" Mark calls out.

"86% of the time, the Cowboys run a cover four prevent-style defense," I say, not even needing to refer to my stats. "That defense is vulnerable behind the linebackers but underneath the safeties. But Taylor will know that."

The offensive coordinator swivels in his chair, squinting at me. "Next time, just give me the stat without the commentary." Then he barks into the headset at Austin. "Look for the Cowboys to come out in cover four so we're going to run Trips Right Gun 62 Double Smash Z-Shallow Cross Y-Dig."

And just like that, Austin Taylor comes to life. He drops back, glancing down the field toward the Cowboys' safety, drawing him toward the sideline. Then, he pivots and uncorks a fast ball fifteen yards down the middle to Jordan Ellis, over the linebackers but underneath the safeties—just like I knew he would. Ellis gains twenty yards and for the first time since Reese was carted off the field, the crowd is energized.

The next few plays, we go no-huddle and Austin's dropping dimes. The team is coming into a rhythm and we're working our way down the field—five yards, ten yards, until we pass midfield and we're on the Cowboys' forty-six-yard line.

There's nineteen seconds on the clock and all we need is six yards to be within field goal range.

Our center snaps the ball, Austin steps back, scanning the field, and I sense the moment he decides to throw.

Every single staff member in the box seats is holding their breath. In fact, I'm certain every Bucs fan in the stadium is holding their breath as Austin Taylor launches the ball into the air.

I recognize the play immediately. Jordan Ellis is supposed to run a deep post, Malik Washington, a slant across the middle, and Mike Donnelly, a seven-yard out to the sideline.

I stand, my hands going to my head as the ball cuts through the air. A perfect spiral. My heart is pounding a relentless rhythm in my chest. "C'mon, c'mon, c'mon." But as the play unfolds, I see Donnelly veer off his route, running toward the middle instead of cutting to the sideline. And the Cowboys' corner, a wily player named LeMarius Bruss, snatches the ball out of the air, with a clear path to our end zone.

"No!" every single person in the box yells.

As soon as Austin sees what happened, he takes off toward Bruss—along with every other Bucs player on the field. One by one, players miss the tackle as the Cowboy's corner speeds past. Austin is sprinting with all his might, chasing down one of the fastest players on the Cowboys. But before he can even attempt a tackle, Austin's feet get tangled, and he goes sprawling onto the field, nowhere close to stopping Bruss.

A collective groan ripples through the room.

Everyone sitting in the box seats beside me is either hanging their heads or staring down at the ground. The only sound that can be heard is the echoing of the announcer's commentary as they re-play Austin Taylor's pick-six.

Like some sort of recurring cancer, Ethan's leaning into my workspace, shaking his head in a way that feels like he's mocking me. "Can't believe this guy's going to be responsible for ruining our season."

I can't even summon the energy to scoff or roll my eyes. "One pick does not a quarterback break."

He turns to me, his lips puckering to the side. "'We coulda been contenders,'" he says in a weird accent that sounds like an attempt at being a New Yorker. "'We coulda been somebody. Instead of a bum.'"

"What are you even saying?"

"Marlon Brando? No?"

I continue to gaze at him as if he's lost his mind—or maybe this is a bad dream. A really, really weird and bad dream.

"We're still contenders, Ethan."

He meets my eye, then purposefully looks up at the TV screen, where they're recounting all the ways Austin Taylor is, quite literally, dropping the ball. "It happens to the best of teams at the worst of times," he says philosophically. "And it's happened to us."

"Austin Taylor is a good quarterback, he'll adjust and so will the rest of our team. I'd bet my salary on it."

An evil twinkle shines in Ethan's eyes when he says, "Really? Your whole salary?"

I sit up, squaring my shoulders. "You have a bet in mind? You know I'll put my money where my stats are."

"Oh I know." He runs his fingers over the edge of his beard. "I'm just trying to decide if I'm bold enough to take advantage of that fact." He squints into the distance, considering. "Yep, I am."

"What do you have in mind?" I ask, knowing I'll have the advantage if he throws out the first line. Then I'll know how to counteroffer.

"We're stuck with pretty boy Austin for the next nine games. If he wins seven of the next nine games, you win. If he loses six or more games, I win."

"That's utterly ridiculous. I wouldn't make that bet even if we were discussing Nolan. The line should be four games, max."

"Six."

I cross my arms, leaning away from him. "What are we betting?"

"You said your salary, but I'd settle for your car."

I bark out a laugh. "My car?" Ethan doesn't need to know that the car was a graduation gift from my dad when I finished my master's at MIT—and it costs more than my salary.

"Oh, now you're skittish?" He raises his eyebrows, taunting. "Can't stand by your stats?"

"I can stand by my stats. Look, I can't give you my car." I pinch one of my braid cuffs between my fingers, thinking. "But I could trade cars with you for the offseason." The pure glee on Ethan's face tells me my offer is a good one—he didn't really think I'd bet my car, so this is a favorable line for him. "What will you offer me when I win?"

"*If* you manage to pull off a miracle, I'll give you my office."

I feel my nose scrunch before I can tame it into submission. To be fair, Ethan does have one of the nicest offices in our department, with a little window that faces the practice fields. And I'm in a cubicle, so it would be a big upgrade. But he has something else I want even more.

"When I win, you bring me on your podcast. Publicly declare that I was right about the Taylor pick on draft day and give me ten minutes of airtime." Ethan's podcast, *The Fantasy Playbook*, is a go-to resource for fantasy football enthusiasts who want to gain an edge in their daily fantasy leagues. He gives in-depth statistical analysis, expert interviews and insightful picks each week.

Ethan's mouth twitches at the corner—a hint of a smile. He wasn't expecting this, but in a way, it's a stroke to his already massive ego. I'm telling him that I think his podcast is valuable—and it is. With a listener base of over 100,000 followers, he has a lot of ears on him each week. *The Fantasy Playbook* consistently ranks in the top ten sports fantasy podcasts on Spotify and Apple podcasts. He's never had a woman as a guest speaker—and I'd love to be the first. "Five minutes of airtime and you got a deal."

"Five games?"

"Six."

I school my features into a neutral facade. Six games is a steep bet. It would be incredible for any rookie quarterback to have a win-loss ratio over 66%. But Ethan's right: can I stand by my stats? If I'm right about Austin and his scores are really as high as I charted them to be, he has the potential to go buckwild on the NFL.

I sigh and hold out my hand. "You got a deal."

End Zone Report ✓
@endzonereport

Third string QB for the Bucs, Austin Taylor, took to the field when QB1 Nolan Reese broke his leg during the game. Taylor went 6/14 for 63 yards and threw a pick six to seal the game for the Cowboys.

10:17 PM · Sep 23, 2024 · Twitter for Android

93 Retweets 832 Likes

FieldAnalyst @fieldanalyst · 2h
@Replying to

@GridironGeek Hey look, it's your "steal" 😏

GridironGeek @gridirongeek · 1h
@Replying to

@FieldAnalyst Let's see how he does with a week to prepare instead of being thrust into the middle of the game with zero practice snaps.

FieldAnalyst @fieldanalyst · 1h
@Replying to

@GridironGeek I won't be holding my breath.

16

Austin

Press Conference: A media event where players and coaches answer questions from journalists about games, performances, and other related topics. (And, often, the goal is to make the player in question feel as dumb as possible about his mistakes.)

I'm still reeling from the game as I step into the press conference room. The fluorescent lights are harsh, making everything feel even more surreal. My legs are heavy, each step a reminder of the brutal hits I took on the field. The noise of the room—reporters chatting, cameras clicking—hits me like a wave, but I try to steady myself.

I find the podium and grip its edges like a lifeline. The room goes quiet as I face the sea of expectant faces. I can see the judgment in their eyes, the unasked questions hanging in the air.

"First NFL game, Mr. Tyler," someone from the back calls out. "Not the debut you were hoping for, huh?"

I swallow hard, trying to keep my voice steady. I don't even bother correcting my name—what's the point? "No, definitely not. It's . . . it's a tough loss. We fought hard out there, but I made some mistakes that cost us the game."

Another reporter jumps in. "Austin, walk us through that pick-six in the fourth quarter. What happened there?"

I resist the urge to flinch. I knew this question was coming. "It was a miscommunication." As in: Donnelly was supposed to run his route and he didn't. "I take full responsibility for that. I should have seen the defense shifting and adjusted the throw or just threw it away."

Another question hits me like a punch. "Austin, can you talk about what it was like seeing Nolan Reese go down with that injury?"

The image of Nolan's twisted leg flashes in my mind, and I feel a wave of nausea. "It was . . . it was really hard. Nolan is a leader on this team and seeing him get hurt like that . . . it was devastating. It's something you never want to see happen to anyone, especially a teammate."

The room is stifling, and my shirt sticks to my back. "How are you handling the pressure, being thrown into the starting role so unexpectedly?" A reporter from the front row leans forward.

I take a deep breath, but it feels like my chest is tightening. "It's a challenge, no doubt. The pressure is intense. But I've got to stay focused and learn from my mistakes. Today was a tough day, but we'll keep pushing forward."

More questions come, but I answer them on autopilot. My mind is still on the field, replaying every hit, every missed opportunity. The weight of the coaches' expectations—or lack thereof—presses down on me. I know they don't fully believe in me. And as the press conference wraps up, even I'm drowning in doubt.

It's my brother, Will, who first figures out that I'm a GIF.

Will

> Dude!! You're a GIF!!

Will

> [GIF of Austin Taylor tripping over cleats]

I watch in horror as I fall to the ground, my helmet smacking against the grass.

Over and over again.

Mom

> Oh honey, you were out there giving it your all. That's what matters. Remember when you tripped in that peewee game and still scored a touchdown? You'll bounce back!

Dad

> Keep your head up, son. Everyone has a rough start. It's how you get back up that counts. Proud of you for stepping up.

Emily

Austin, seriously. You're living the dream, no matter what! Also, you know Will is going to use that GIF for eternity now. 🗙

Olivia

Don't listen to them, Austin! You were amazing just for being out there. Plus, it's kind of a badge of honor to be a GIF, right? 🗙

Will

Totally. You'll be the most famous rookie in no time!

Olivia

I think his fame isn't the problem here.

Emily

Well, let's hope next time you're a GIF it's for something... good.

Mom

Exactly. And you know what? We all believe in you. Just keep working hard, and everything will fall into place.

Emily

And just think, years from now when you're winning games left and right, this will be a funny story to tell.

Emily

> A REALLY funny story.

> Olivia

> Also, maybe you need new cleats? ❌

> Will

> Yeah, I don't think Nike will be knocking down your door anytime soon for an endorsement.

> Me
> Thanks, guys. I really appreciate the support.

I sigh, flipping my phone onto my bed. My very first game of the NFL, and I'm already a GIF.

I mean, it can only go up from here, right?

17

Dani

Rookie quarterbacks in the NFL have a combined win rate of just 40% in their first season.

The Tampa Bay Bucs coaching staff is making my bet with Ethan very difficult to win. In our next game on Sunday afternoon against the Falcons, the coaches clearly don't trust Austin to throw the ball—the very thing he's best at. He hands off the ball or runs the ball himself. Each time he runs, I can't help but cringe. He's slow. It's undeniable. Watching him lumbering across our home field, he looks like he's moving in slow motion.

A handful of times, they allow him to make little five-yard dumps, but honestly a middle schooler could make the throws he's making. They're not allowing him to show his capabilities.

Wednesday afternoon, I knock on Coach Clive's door when I know he doesn't have any meetings. I find the coach at his desk, squinting over a notebook of plays. Coach Clive Howard is the yin to my dad's yang—where my father is intense and scary,

Clive is jovial and welcoming. With his huge smile, massive jowls, and a belly that would befit someone who lives in the North Pole, Clive gives Caribbean Santa Claus vibes. After my mom died, we spent every spring break at "Uncle" Clive's house in Gainesville when he was the head coach of the Florida Gators. He and my dad played together back in the 90s for the Gators and then again for a short time when they both played for the Chargers.

Clive isn't technically blood related, but he and his wife, Roxanne, and their kids are the closest thing to a real family we have. They opened up their home and their arms to us during a time when we needed it the most.

Back then, we lived in Chicago and I have so many memories of escaping to Florida during their balmy spring weather. We spent afternoons in the Howard's pool, and my dad and Clive always took me on a tour of the hallowed Ben Hill Griffin Stadium. My dad has a framed photo of the two of us standing on the field of the stadium when I was eleven years old with "This is the Swamp" emblazoned on the stadium behind us. This was before Heather was introduced to my dad—or my hair—so I look like a hot mess in the picture, with all of my baby hairs fuzzing around my head—but I'm happy. And I want to say that my dad was too, but now I'm not sure.

Coach Clive glances up, smiling at me over his reading glasses.

"Hey, Coach."

He gets up and envelopes me in a hug, and I accept it, if a bit stiffly. We're at work and I'm supposed to be his employee, not someone he views as a niece.

"To what do I owe the pleasure of this visit?" he asks, shifting a bowl of peanut M&M's between us as he sits back down. I lower myself onto the seat across from him, sitting on the edge of the chair.

"I want to discuss Austin Taylor."

The light in his eyes slips away at this. "You and everybody else," he grumbles. He scoops up a handful of M&M's and funnels them into his mouth.

My relationship with Clive is close but we've never discussed a player like this before. My heart hammers against my ribs and my mouth is suddenly dry. "Our playbook isn't doing him any favors," I force myself to say.

"Danielle, there ain't a playbook in the whole NFL that would do that boy favors."

Despite his words, his tone is playful and it gives me the courage to keep going. "I've watched over eighty hours of film on Austin Taylor in college. He excels in a spread offense where he's in shotgun and he gets to read the defense presnap. He especially does well going no-huddle. As you know, your read-option plays are designed for a mobile quarterback. And that's not his strength."

Clive snorts. "That's putting it nicely."

"The times you are putting him in shotgun, you're not allowing him to make checks at the line of scrimmage."

"I'm not letting a rookie who's only real pass was a pick-six change my plays before the snap. Between you and me, I don't trust the guy." He grabs another paw full of M&M's, shoving the entire thing into his mouth.

"Well that much is obvious." I put my hands flat onto the desk in front of me, steadying myself as I gaze directly at Uncle Clive. "But, Coach, can you trust me?"

He sighs deeply, crossing his arms as he assesses me.

"We gotta play the cards we're dealt, right?" I say. "God didn't give you Mahomes or Lamar Jackson. He gave you a cerebral pocket passer like Brady or Joe Burrow."

Clive chuckles, his typical light returning to his eyes. "Oh, heavens, Danielle. From your mouth to God's ears, let Austin Taylor be the next Tom Brady." He guffaws now, a full belly laugh that jiggles his sizable midsection. "Heck, I'd settle for half a Kirk Cousins at this point."

"I'm telling you right now, Coach, Austin Taylor has Kirk Cousins's energy but he's got a Brady mind."

He shakes his head, but he's smiling. "I must be crazier than a pack of hyenas to listen to you, but I'll think about what you're saying."

"That's all I'm asking."

We shoot the breeze for a few minutes before he has to take a Zoom call and I head back to my office, grabbing a handful of M&M's on my way out the door.

18

Austin

Blitz: A defensive strategy where defensive players, typically linebackers or defensive backs, rush the quarterback in an attempt to hurry or sack him.

After a second devastating loss to the Atlanta Falcons, I feel like a piece of meat that's been hammered within an inch of my life. I'm sore in places I've never even thought of before. During our practice and team meeting today, the normally jovial Coach Clive ripped everyone to shreds, from our defense to our special teams, and everyone in between. I feel like a punching bag with my seams ripped open and my stuffing spilling out.

And, of course, Dani Marshall is waiting for me outside of the locker room.

As much as I've tried to find her lately, she's the last person I want to see right now. But when I see her leaning against the wall, one heeled foot propped against the concrete, her braids falling forward like curtains hiding her face, I forget why I'm frustrated with football. She's staring intently at her phone, completely unaware of the chaos she's causing in my chest. It's like seeing a rare animal in the wild—beautiful and elusive—making my heart seize momentarily.

She looks up, her sharp eyes zeroing in on me, and I'm caught in her gaze. What day is it? Where was I going? Who am I? I have no idea. All I know is that Dani Marshall is standing in front of me, taking up my whole brain.

"Uh, hey," I say eloquently.

"Taylor." She unfurls from the wall, pocketing her phone. "Where you eating? I'm treating."

My eyebrows raise, and Dani must sense my confusion—or my desire—because she quickly clarifies, "For *business* purposes."

"Ah." I'm trying to think of a classy place to eat—someplace that will fill the calorie deficit that this practice just took from me while still coming across as a reputable place to eat with Dani Marshall. However, my brain is malfunctioning and the only eating establishment I can think of is one of the most disreputable places in the world. "Waffle House," I say because, why not tank my reputation completely? As if I hadn't already hit rock bottom with the memes of me tripping over my cleats.

Dani's eyes widen, but she doesn't say anything about my restaurant choice. "The one off Columbus near Dale Mabry?" I nod like a dufus. "I'll meet you there in ten."

And that's how I find myself sitting across from Dani Marshall at Waffle House, with food filling every inch of our table. "You ever been to Waffle House before?" I ask with a mouthful of eggs like the classy guy that I am.

"My uncle would bring us here during spring breaks. My dad calls it 'Awful House.'"

I groan, running my fingers through my still-wet hair. "Awesome. Your dad's first impression of me is officially tanked. I took his daughter to Awful House."

She laughs. "Fortunately—or unfortunately, depending on how you look at it—this won't be his first impression."

"Oh no, is he a Bucs fan?"

Dani cocks her head to the side. "You don't know who my dad is?"

"No?"

"My dad is Darius Marshall."

I'm silent for one heartbeat, two. I vaguely hear my silverware clatter to the table. "Darius Marshall, as in the GM of the Bucs? Like, my *employer*?"

She nods, an amused twist on her pretty mouth. I quickly stand, gathering a wad of cash and throw it on the table. "C'mon, we're getting out of here."

"And going where?" She doesn't budge.

"I dunno, to Bern's or-or," I throw my hands out to the side as I think, "just, someplace way nicer than Awful House."

She tilts her head back and laughs, her graceful neck on full display. "Austin, sit. Finish your food."

When I give her a skeptical look, she insists. "I want to finish my food. I like Waffle House. Who cares what my dad thinks?"

I refrain from saying that I care—deeply—about what her father thinks. In more ways than one. But I sit back down, sighing as I survey my half-eaten meal. "Fine, but if he asks, I wanted to go to Bern's and you insisted on Waffle House."

A grin tugs at her lips as she scoops hash browns into her mouth. "Deal."

"So . . . you said this was for business?" I sit back, my meal suddenly less appealing. "You're not firing me, are you?"

"I don't have the authority to fire you. And I wouldn't even if I could."

"You must be alone in that opinion." She shrugs, but I notice she doesn't disagree. "If you're not firing me, then what's this business meeting about?"

Dani takes a final bite of her eggs and then pushes her plate away. She folds her hands in front of her and levels her gaze at me. "I need your help."

I can't quite fathom what she could need my help with, but I say, "Okay." Because, let's be real, there's something about this woman that makes me want to say "yes" regardless of what she asks. I take a sip of my orange juice to not seem too eager to help.

"I need you to win your next six games so I don't lose my car."

At her words, the orange juice gets stuck in my throat and I'm choking. In an instant, Dani's on her feet, pounding at my back. The confusion in my brain seems to be spreading to the rest of my body—I don't even know how to swallow a sip of juice.

Once I've got my breath back, I splutter, "You think I'm *trying* to lose these games, Marshall?" I expect a smirk from her, but her face is completely impassive as she settles back into the bench seat across from me. "Also, what's your car got to do with it?"

"There's another analyst in my department and let's just say . . . he's kind of arrogant. Needs to be knocked down a few pegs." She tucks a stray braid behind her ear, suddenly looking sheepish. "And, well, we made a bet on you."

I narrow my eyes, trying to piece together what she's telling me. "You bet your car that I was going to win six games in a row?"

She waves a hand, like losing her car is no big deal. "It wasn't six games *in a row* originally, but you had to go and lose the game against the Falcons."

I tap my fingers on the edge of the table. "I'd like to think I didn't single-handedly lose that game."

"No, you didn't." She shakes her head definitively.

"What makes you think I'm capable of winning at all?" I ask, genuinely interested.

She shifts in her seat, her gaze sliding down to our empty plates. It seems like my question has made her uncomfortable for some reason. It takes her a long moment to answer the question. She finally says, "That pick-six wasn't your fault."

In the short time I've known her, Dani Marshall has said a lot of surprising things to me. But this might top them all. "Another opinion you're likely alone in. But, humor me. Why do you say that?"

"Donnelly didn't complete his route. He wasn't where he was supposed to be. If he ran his route like he was supposed to, he would've caught your ball and it wouldn't have been picked off."

The air in my lungs suspends at Dani's words. She's right, Donnelly didn't complete his route and it led to the interception. Has anyone mentioned that on the team? Of course not. It's easier to lay blame at the feet of the rookie QB rather than the star receiver who inexplicably didn't finish his route. But it's not like the media knows our playbook—no one outside of the offense and coaching staff knows Mike Donnelly's route.

So, why does Dani Marshall know?

I lean forward, like we're sharing a secret, and ask, "How do you know that?"

She fiddles with the silverware next to her plate before meeting my eyes. "Because I wrote that play."

My breath whooshes out of me as I fall back into my seat. She can't be serious. What twenty-something-year-old woman is writing plays for an NFL team? Better yet, what NFL team is *using* plays from someone not on their coaching staff? I mean, sure, there's the infamous story of the Steeler's janitor writing plays and the team using them. But that's the stuff of legends. What Dani's suggesting is a little far-fetched.

And yet, for some reason, I believe her.

How else would she know about Donnelly's route? That's not part of her job description.

Dani's suddenly giving off nervous energy, her long fingers adjusting everything on the table—moving from empty plate to cup to silverware, not really moving anything, just keeping busy. "That needs to stay between us."

"Does Coach know?"

She shakes her head.

"How . . . ?"

"I slip them under his door in the mornings. I come before everyone else arrives."

"And they make it into the playbook?" I chuckle, running a hand through my hair. "That's pretty epic, Dani."

At this, she finally looks at me and gives me a tiny smirk of pride. She holds eye contact with me for a long moment and something crackles between us. A shared secret? Chemistry? Magic? Whatever it is, I *really* wish we weren't in Waffle House. I'm imagining Dani in a stunning dress—red, to match the hue she seems to always incorporate into every outfit—her arm tucked in mine as we walk into Bern's. Or, really, anywhere but Waffle House.

"So," Dani says, breaking through the image in my head. We are very much *not* on a date. Dani Marshall is all business—and now that I know her dad is my GM, I realize with a sinking feeling that she's very much off limits. "I want to discuss how we can elevate your game."

"One more question: what do you get out of this bet if you win? The other analyst gets your car, what do you get?"

"A spot on his podcast, a public apology, and five minutes of airtime."

"A public apology?"

Her eyes flick toward me and then away. "I, uh, thought we should pick you in the third round instead of Drake Blythe. He gave me a hard time about it."

My brows raise of their own accord—she thought I should be picked up in the third round? Heck, I'd give her a hard time about it if it wasn't, well, *me*. But I can tell she feels awkward about it, so I let it roll by.

"And he gets your . . . car? That doesn't seem like a fair trade." Not to mention that winning six out of nine games seems completely and totally unreachable at this point.

She lifts a shoulder as if, again, losing her car isn't that important. "It's more about pride than anything else. Although I really don't want to explain to my dad why I lost my car."

I laugh, hearing the undertone of nerves in the sound. "Well, what do you have in mind to keep that from happening?"

Dani smiles at me and I swear it lights up the entire Waffle House, somehow overpowering the fluorescent lights. "I thought you'd never ask," she says.

19

Dani

Quarterbacks and their analysts who work closely together can improve their performance by up to 20% due to better communication and understanding of play strategies.

I can't tell if Austin is more amused or surprised as I lay out plans for our NFL takeover—*ahem*, winning the next six games. He seems grateful when I offer to help him memorize the playbook but balks at the idea of going to yoga with me.

"Look, what can it hurt?" I ask. "It'll only improve your flexibility and strength. It's good for injury prevention."

"But bad for my dignity," he says as he crosses his arms over his chest.

I laugh. "We'll see about that. It'll be fun."

"For you, maybe."

"Oh, definitely for me." I give him a little smirk, and this feels like it's bordering on the line of flirtation so I quickly get it under control. "It might help with your speed." I try not to grimace, but I'm not sure I succeed when I say, "You really need help with your speed. Your ten-yard split is 1.8 seconds, we gotta get that closer to 1.6."

He laughs good naturedly and it's this quality about Austin that makes him so likable: he's humble. Self-deprecating but not in an insecure way. "You just keep those numbers about me in your head?"

My face warms and I find myself scrambling to explain why I know all of his numbers so readily. "I'm the QB analyst," I tell him, though that's not the full truth. I didn't know Nolan Reese's numbers nearly as well.

"Ah, makes sense," he says, and I'm relieved when he doesn't bring up how well I know his numbers anymore.

We pay for our meal—rather, Austin pays for it, even though I insisted on paying since this was a business meeting—and then walk out to our cars. "Wait a second," he says when I unlock my BMW. "*This* is your car? This is what's at stake?"

I bite my lip, debating whether to tell Austin the full truth—that I'll only lose my car for the offseason. But I really need him to buy in completely, so I nod. He moans painfully, his hands going through his hair and resting on top of his head. I train my eyes on his forehead so that I'm not tempted to stare at his biceps, which are peeking out of the sleeves of his shirt. (Who am I kidding? I'm still tempted. And I am *never* tempted.)

"Dani," he groans my name and something about it sends a shiver down my spine. "Can you back out of this deal? This is a really, really nice car."

I step closer to him, pretending it has more to do with bolstering his confidence than the inexplicable magnetism this man exudes. "Austin Taylor, you are winning this bet for me," I say, poking at his massive chest for added emphasis. "Look, I charted stats for every single QB eligible for the draft last year. And you had the highest CHOICE score of all of them. You make good decisions on the field, Austin. If you'd played at Alabama or Florida, you would've been a Heisman winner."

Austin's golden eyes gaze down at me, soft and welcoming. Every part of me wants to lean in even closer to this man. "I don't know if I share your faith in me," he says softly.

I shrug, backing up before I can do something I'll regret. "Sometimes you just have to borrow other people's faith in you. And I've got plenty to share." I scurry around to the driver's side of my car before Austin can draw me into his orbit anymore. When I'm safely on the other side of the car, I look back at Austin, whose eyes haven't left me. I can't quite interpret his gaze, but I also don't want to. My feelings are confusing enough as it is.

I open my door, fidgeting with my keys. "See you tomorrow to watch film. Six a.m.?"

Austin nods. "Just don't take my seat this time," he says with a wink.

As I drive away, I can't help but feel like I'm walking a very thin, very dangerous line with Austin Taylor.

20

Dani

Research shows that spending time together and sharing personal goals increases the likelihood of developing romantic feelings by 30%. (I will not be part of this statistic. I will not be part of this statistic. I will NOT be part... oh crap.)

I really thought this whole Mission: Impossible Bet to Win action plan was a really good idea. That is, until Austin Taylor showed up the next morning looking impossibly stunning. His ash blonde hair is darkened from a shower, the scent of whatever musky magic is in his body wash floods the room. My very unhelpful heart pounds foolishly, making me question why I thought scheduling time with Austin—*alone*—every day this week was a good idea. And, to make matters worse, it's a bye week so we penciled in even more time for studying and watching film.

Regret fills me to overflowing.

He's wearing a red dri-fit Nike shirt that clings to him in all the right places, and black athletic shorts that make my mouth go dry. As if that's not enough, the glint in his eyes tells me he *knows* I'm checking him out.

Awesome.

He's carrying a box of Dunkin' Donuts—with enough doughnuts to feed an army. Or a football team.

"I brought breakfast," he says. His easy smile has my stomach swooping in a way that makes me wonder if I somehow body-swapped with boy-crazy Claire overnight. I surreptitiously glance down, catching sight of my familiar brown skin. I'm still me, but I certainly don't feel like me.

Chill, girl, I tell myself when Austin sits beside me, his hefty body making the cushions sink so that I tumble a little into him. He drops the Dunkin' box into his lap, righting me with his hands on my bare arms—which might as well be the same as striking me with lightning. All of my nerve endings are on fire, my pulse is erratic, and it seems like all of my brain cells have fled the building.

What is happening to me?

An alarm sounds somewhere in the back of my mind: this man is dangerous. He threatens to break down my boundaries, to force me to throw out all my logic and well-built reasoning that have kept me safe throughout college and grad school. All I want to do is sink into his warmth, burrow into him, and never come out.

I clear my throat and straighten, needing distance from this man.

"Doughnut?" He opens the box casually, like my brush with lightning didn't affect him at all.

"Thanks," I mumble, grabbing a Boston creme. But when he goes to take a chocolate frosted doughnut with sprinkles, I smack his hand. "What are you doing?" I say, finally finding my voice—and a few brain cells.

"Eating a doughnut . . . ?" he says slowly.

I shake my head, my braids shifting with the movement. "Austin, your doughnut-eating days are over until the season ends."

He stares at me, his hazel eyes wide and incredulous—as if I just told him he was being cut from the team. "But, I, these—"

I take the box from him, hiding it under the couch. "No more junk food, Austin."

"But, *you're* eating a doughnut," he says, gesturing to my Boston creme, as if he just won the argument.

"Yes, but I'm not a professional athlete," I say as I sink my teeth into the doughnut. And I can't help but laugh as Austin groans.

Our first yoga session takes place the next day after Austin is done with practice. I figured it would be a good way to cool down and stretch out his body. I take him to the yoga studio just a few blocks from my Riverwalk condo. The studio is decorated in soft greens and earthy browns, potted plants and bamboo accents frame the space, and the air is scented with a subtle blend of lavender and eucalyptus. Natural light floods the main yoga room through the floor-to-ceiling windows that give a view of the Hillsborough River. The far wall has a painted mural of a river scene that makes it seem like a continuation of the view outside.

"This is going to be a bloodbath," Austin grumbles in a faux-grumpy way—the guy's probably never had a truly moody day in his life—as we set up our yoga mats at the back of the room. I'm normally a front row kind of girl, but Austin's so big, he'd block everyone's view if we stayed in the front.

"C'mon, it can't be that bad," I say. "Can you, like, touch your toes?"

Austin rears back, eyes wide in a mock surprise. "What self-respecting NFL player can do that?"

I can't help but smirk at him. "Tom Brady can do that," I tease.

"I'm not Tom Brady."

"Not yet you aren't."

He barks out a laugh. "Dani, one day you're going to realize that you picked the wrong guy to be your pet project."

"And one day you're going to realize that the numbers are never wrong. And since I'm always on the side of the numbers, I'm never wrong."

"You really should do something about your low self-esteem," he teases. "It's really holding you back."

I swat at him, my hand momentarily connecting with a veritable brick wall of abdominal muscles. I'm tempted to let my hand linger. But when I glance up at Austin, he's got a confident smirk on his face. I snatch my hand away, face heating.

"I'm not the only one with a self-esteem problem," I mutter as I busy myself with rearranging my mat and my props while Austin laughs.

That'll teach me to keep my hands to myself.

21

Austin

> Flexibility: The ability of muscles and joints to move through their full range of motion. In football, flexibility is crucial for injury prevention, improving performance, and enhancing overall athletic ability. (But it's very bad for my dignity... and my ability to win over Dani Marshall.)

Dani joked about my confidence problem—but my ego is seriously going to take a hit in this class. The moment the instructor walks in, I can tell I'm in the wrong place. She's tall and slender, probably in her mid-sixties, and deathly serious about yoga. When she walks in, her eyes immediately find me, assessing. She clearly finds me wanting. And I wonder if it has to do with my performance in games thus far—or the fact that I obviously don't belong here.

I'm guessing the latter. I'm not sure how many yoga instructors are football fans, but I'd assume the crossover is low.

Dani tells me that the class will start out slow so I can get warmed up—but the very first move is one where we raise our hands and then lower them to touch the ground in front of us.

I take a deep breath, raising my hands, and then hinge at the hips while I exhale and ... yeah, my body doesn't do that. Even with my gorilla-long arms, my hands only make it to just below my knees. I glance to my right and Dani's entire palms are on the ground, her legs straight. She's practically folded in half. There's an older gentleman to my left, so I look to him for some camaraderie—but even his hands are at his ankles.

I grunt, trying to get a little closer to my toes, and Dani turns at the sound. A giggle escapes from her and my eyes narrow at her. Her lips are pressed together, attempting—feebly—to hold back her laughter.

"Got a long way to go there, Brady," she teases.

"In more ways than one," I sigh, my hands still hovering a solid foot above my toes.

We're only ten minutes into the class when the instructor zeroes in on me for the first time. We're in a move that sounds like gibberish—utta parvasomething-rather. I can read a defense like it's second nature, anticipate blitzes, and adjust plays on the fly, but all of these instructions somehow are going way over my head—which way should I be pointing my toes? Which hand should be raised, and which should be down? I feel like the only one in the room who has no clue about what's going on.

"Sir?" the teacher interrupts her instruction, a thick German accent punctuating her words. "Sir?" she repeats, and I realize she's looking at me. And now so is the rest of the class. She leaves her yoga position to come all the way to the back of the room, attempting to maneuver me so that I'm in the right position. I'm in a weird squat/lunge hybrid and she grabs my front foot, shifting it so it's facing the front of the mat. Then she takes my arm and pulls it down. I feel like a preschooler being scolded by his teacher. "Hmm. I suppose we'll have to do some modifications for you." She says this as if modifications are an affront to Buddha himself. "I've never had to do modifications for this pose before," she says loudly enough for everyone in the class to hear. A much older woman in the front corner of the room chuckles.

Great.

Once the instructor has sufficiently modified my pose with an armful of yoga blocks and maneuvering, she's back at the front of the room, leading us into another pose. The name of it sounds like it has way too many consonants stacked together with not enough vowels and ends with sananana. Everyone in the class seems to know exactly what she's talking about—I'm the lone person staring at her while trying to mimic her position. It's like I'm one of those meerkats, poking my head up in a vast desert of yogis.

My eyes seek out Dani's, her mirthful brown eyes dancing. I never thought I could win over Dani the Unbreakable by making a total fool of myself in yoga class—but something about this experience has softened her toward me.

At the end of the class, when the instructor has us in corpse pose, where we're essentially just laying down, I tilt my head to Dani's side and whisper, "This is my best pose."

Dani snorts with laughter, quickly clapping a hand over her mouth to hold it in. The instructor shoots us a glare, but it doesn't keep me from adding, "I'm killin' it."

She giggles again, a light and airy sound that fills the corners of my chest. When she lets her hand fall back to the mat beside mine, her fingertips brush against mine, sending sparks all the way up my arm. When the class ends, I find that I don't want to move—and, seemingly, neither does Dani.

Maybe, just maybe, yoga isn't so bad after all.

22

Austin

> Audible: A change in the play called by the quarterback at the line of scrimmage, usually in response to the defensive formation. An effective audible can turn a potentially disastrous play into a successful one.

It wasn't until after I'd invited all of my starting offensive teammates over for dinner that I realized I don't really have enough furniture to accommodate anyone, let alone ten other NFL football players. I pace around my home while doing a quick Google search for home furnishing companies before getting overwhelmed. I'm in uncharted territory with this whole furniture situation.

I could text one of my sisters for help, but my mind keeps circling back to a much more appealing option.

Dani.

She's been filling my mind—and my schedule—as I've found every way conceivable to spend time with her. Every moment of her time has been hard-earned, but always worth it. Last week, when I invited her to lunch with me after practice, she turned me down. But this week, she said yes.

I don't even care that she wouldn't let us go to Five Guys but opted for Fresh Kitchen where I was forced to eat an inhumane amount of vegetables. I happily ate every single one of those broccoli heads, with her sitting across from me.

My mom would be so proud.

And now, I'm addicted.

Not to broccoli, of course. But to Dani Marshall. So I don't even hesitate to pull up her number, texting her like it's the most normal thing in the world.

> I need help. It's kind of bet-related.

I grip the phone, staring hard at it, as if that will make Dani text me back faster. When she doesn't respond right away, I return to pacing around my house. Finally—an entire four minutes later—she responds.

> "Kind of"?

> I'm having the team over for a meal tomorrow but I just realized I don't really have furniture for all these guys.

Immediately, Dani's name lights up my screen and I pick up. Before I can say a single thing, she says, "Why are you throwing a party when you should be studying?"

I can't help but chuckle. Dani is nothing if not focused—perhaps to a fault. "I've done as much studying as one person can do. Besides, I need to win over my teammates. That's part of winning football games too."

When Dani's end is silent, I add, "Would it make you feel better if you quiz me?"

"Fine, but if you fail my quiz, you need to cancel this party."

I laugh. "I'm not doing that. But I'm also not failing your quiz. Trust me, Dani."

"Trust isn't exactly my forte."

"You trust the numbers."

"Exclusively." She sighs, and then says, "Double Reverse Flea Flicker Z-Y Banana Spider Out of the Watermelon Formation?"

"I hand off the ball to Malik, who's gonna take it like he's running up the middle. But then, he's gonna hand it off to Landon coming around on the reverse. Landon will then lateral the ball back to me. As I get the ball back, I'll be looking deep for Ellis running the post route. Meanwhile, Jake is running a banana route to the sideline to draw their coverage away from our deep shot."

Dani doesn't respond to my accurate memorization of the play, only moves on to the next one. "Triple Whammy Power Toss Bootleg Pretzel Twist?"

"I take the snap and fake a hand off to the fullback diving up the middle. Then, I'll pitch the ball to the running back who's sweeping out to the left. As the defense bites on the run, I'll bootleg to the backside, pretending like I'm going for a long run. While this is happening, our tight end will run a crossing route to keep the linebackers occupied."

"Fine," Dani says. "Send me your address."

And I can't help it, I smile.

Dani Marshall never disappoints. Within an hour of me sending her a text, we're in a private showroom at a home furnishing store with a very discreet designer hmming and ahhing over the photos Dani's showing her of my house. They're tossing around words that mean absolutely nothing to me, like 'mid-century modern' and 'distressed wood.' It just kind of sounds like they want to make my house look . . . old? Is that the goal? I shake my head as I inspect a series of funky lamps that don't seem very practical.

As we browse, Dani throws out plays for me, quizzing me. But once she realizes I really do have the playbook memorized for this week, she starts to relax.

And I find that I really like Dani Marshall when she's relaxed. Heck, I really like Dani Marshall when she's wound tighter than Aaron Rodgers' spiral, but seeing her like this—at ease in my presence—makes me like her even more.

"I'm thinking something that's pragmatic for hosting a bunch of giant football players but doesn't scream 'bro,'" Dani says. The designer leads us to some leather couches. I sit in one after another, but they all feel the same.

"Anything stand out to you, Mr. Taylor?" the designer asks.

"They all feel the same to me, but I guess I like this one the best," I say, gesturing to a dark leather couch with some kind of vertical lines in the back of the leather.

The designer nods enthusiastically. "Yes, the Rourke," she says. The couch has a *name*? I manage to not roll my eyes, but barely.

"You can have this delivered today?" Dani asks.

"You can have this exact one."

"Sweet, thanks," I say, thinking we're almost done.

Come to find out, we are *not* almost done. The couch was just the beginning.

Two hours later, I have a couch, matching armchairs and ottomans, a coffee table, several lamps, throw pillows and blankets, some mirrors and other artwork, and for some inexplicable reason, two rugs for the same space. I'm completely baffled by all of these things—and their price tag.

Somewhere out in an alternate universe, there's an Austin Taylor who didn't get picked up by the Bucs. He's a high school teacher coaching varsity football. *That* Austin Taylor is gagging at the price of my new furniture while *this* Austin Taylor hands over my credit card.

"I might need a drink after that," I tell Dani when we leave the store. She laughs, tilting her head back to catch the rays of the setting sun on her face. It's the most casual I've seen Dani, and I just want to soak up this moment.

When I mentioned getting a drink, I thought she'd scoff and wave me off, but instead she says, "I think I have a place in mind." She types something into her phone, pulling up an address. "We've got an hour or two to kill anyway while they set up your furniture. It's better if we're out of their hair."

We climb into my Jeep, listening to George Ezra's "Shotgun" as we drive to the JW Marriott. On the 27th floor is a rooftop bar called Beacon. Dani gets an espresso martini while I order something called Pistoles at Dawn, which is rich and layered with bourbon, Montenegro, and mezcal, with a balance of sweetness, herbal bitterness, smokiness, and warm spice. We get a charcuterie board to share and settle into the outdoor seats that overlook the bay. With the setting sun and the alcohol warming my chest, I realize just how romantic this all feels. I glance out of the corner of my eye, wondering if Dani's thinking it too.

We chat casually as we eat and drink. I tell her about my family and she tells me about growing up as an NFL latchkey kid—fending for herself as she's dragged from team meetings to drafts to pro days. It's no wonder she's as knowledgeable as she is.

We laugh about Coach Clive's funny sayings and she cracks up when I tell her about the rookie hazing I received. She confesses to not getting along with Ethan, with whom she made the infamous bet.

"It's like he has to disagree with me about everything. And he's a jerk about it too."

"I really wish you'd bet him on something we could actually win, so we could take him down."

"I wouldn't make a bet I didn't think was winnable."

I smile at her, appreciating her confidence—even if I don't share it. "You know," I tell her. "I know this Ethan guy is a jerk. But sometimes these types of guys, it's a sign of respect if they argue with you."

"What do you mean?"

"Well, if he thought your ideas were really that dumb, he probably wouldn't waste his breath."

"Hmm," she says, and I think I've convinced her about Ethan as much as she's convinced me about our ability to win this bet.

"Did you play any sports growing up?" I ask her, sensing she could use a subject change.

"I danced," she says as she kicks off her heels and tucks her feet up under her. "Mostly ballet, but some tap and jazz. That's what my stepmom, Heather, did growing up so when she married my dad, that's what I did too." She scrunches her nose adorably and I laugh.

"I'm guessing you didn't love ballet?"

"Football is my first and only love."

"I can relate to that."

She gives me a small smile and we fall into a comfortable silence as we finish off the charcuterie board. I try hard—and mostly fail—to not stare too much at her. But the way she's watching the horizon as she sips her drink, it's intoxicating. The pinks and oranges of the sunset are reflecting off of her skin, making her look like she's glowing. The whole setting is making me wish I were on a date with Dani. And I wonder what she'd say if I just asked her.

But watching her, the relaxed way she's sitting as she enjoys the sunset, I realize that I don't want to mess up our mojo. We've got a good thing going with our partnership. And if I know Dani, she'll put her walls way up if I make a move.

So I don't. At least, not yet.

When we leave Beacon, I convince Dani to let me take off the Freedom panels on my Jeep—which opens up the top of the vehicle. It's basically like a giant sun roof. "We'll take the scenic route," I tell her.

We cruise down Bayshore Blvd, the ocean on one side and multi-million-dollar houses on the other. Dani raises her hands through the open top of the Jeep as we sing along to Macklemore's "No Bad Days." I've been listening to his album, *Ben*, on repeat lately, and this song seems to perfectly encapsulate this moment. The rising moon glitters over the water as the song reverberates through the car, the music itself getting through my skin, the melody echoing in my chest.

I keep glancing over at Dani, her elegant hands catching the wind as she shout-sings, "I'm just doing me, I got no bad days."

I can't help but smile as I watch her, so at ease with herself. Seeing her like this sparks a desire in me to make this happen even more. And, just like that, I've got a new goal: do everything I can to get this version of Dani as much as humanly possible.

23

Dani

Statistically speaking, there's a 28% chance of falling for someone when you start spending time together outside of work. (Note to self: stop hanging out with Austin Taylor outside of work.)

I wake up the next day on cloud nine. I won't say it's because I had a fabulous day with Austin Taylor yesterday.

It's true, but I won't say it.

There is an infinitesimal part of me that feels guilty for not involving Claire in our day yesterday. She would be the perfect person to bring along with us as we decorated Austin's riverside bungalow. It's her thing. Not to mention that she would be Austin's perfect counterpart. I *should* introduce the two of them so they can go and have perfect babies.

Ugh.

I shove those thoughts from my head and convince myself that the joy pumping through my veins is not because I get to see Austin again today as we watch film.

When I get to the AdventHealth Training Center, Austin is already in the film room, waiting for me with coffee.

I could get used to this.

I manage, just barely, to keep a smile off my face while reminding myself that I am a professional and I've worked way too hard to get to where I am only to let a man—an NFL player at that—get in the way. But Austin is making that really hard.

Today, I'm showing him some old footage of Peyton Manning during his 2013 season when he broke the record for the most touchdown passes in one season. "See this," I tell him, highlighting a sequence from his game against the Ravens, where he threw for seven touchdowns. "Manning was nowhere near the fastest guy on the field, but his awareness and decision-making were top-notch."

We watch together, discussing Manning's game until I pause the film, shifting to look at Austin. "This is you, Taylor." I wave the remote at the screen. "All day."

Austin gives a self-deprecating laugh. "You keep comparing me to NFL legends, Dani, and I'm going to get a big head."

"I'd rather you step out onto the field with confidence. Besides, it's true. You've got what it takes—the decision-making, the ability to read the field. The skills you possess are the hardest to teach."

His eyes search mine before he gives a quick nod and I can tell he wants to change the subject—that he still feels like my faith in him is misplaced.

"So, Miss QB Analyst, does that mean that you track all my stats during the game?"

"That's my job."

"What's that involve? You calculate completion percentages, passer rating . . . ?"

"Yeah, that, and your decision-making under pressure, red zone efficiency, rushing stats, all of that. We also have GPS on you so we can track your movement, speed, heart rate, and so on."

Austin leans in, a smile playing on the corners of his mouth. "You can see my heart rate during the game?"

"Well, yeah."

He lowers his head, rubbing the back of his neck as he takes in that information. "That feels oddly . . . intimate," he says, glancing up at me underneath a stray curl that's fallen in his face. My fingers itch to move it out of the way.

"You can take it up with my boss," I say, deflecting.

But in this moment, I'm glad no one has a heart rate monitor on me. Because the data would be conclusive: Austin Taylor officially makes my heart race.

24

Austin

Wine and Dine: a crucial strategy for winning over teammates by hosting an extravagant meal that costs way too much money.

The doorbell rings and the muscles in my shoulders tense. I'm having my offensive teammates over tonight—and yesterday, I thought this was a good idea. Today, however, I'm second guessing myself. How fun is it to hang out with the guy who's responsible for tanking your chances at a Super Bowl win?

But there's nothing to be done about it now. I was going to grill for everyone, but Dani convinced me to hire a personal chef—I mean, who does that? And who has the number of a personal chef on speed dial?

Apparently, Dani Marshall does.

The chef has been here since the early afternoon, cooking up a storm. From the looks of it, there will be about fifteen courses. I cringe when I think about how much money this one dinner is going to cost me.

I take a deep breath and open the door.

Our wide receivers, Jordan Ellis, Mike Donnelly, and Malik Washington, our tight end Jake Foster, and our running backs Landon Mitchell and Isaiah Roberts are standing there, looking a mix of curious and wary.

"Hey, guys," I say, stepping aside to let them in. "Come on in."

"Nice place," Jordan says, though he sounds a bit hesitant as he looks around.

"Thanks," I reply, trying to sound casual. "I, uh, got some help with the decorating."

They spread out, checking out the living room. It's cozy with a big sectional couch, a coffee table, and a flat-screen TV. Dani's touch is everywhere—subtle, stylish decor that I never would have thought of on my own. There are framed prints of vintage football posters on the walls and a few potted plants that add a touch of greenery. And, of course, she insisted on the massive TV and told me to have a game playing when the guys show up. The place feels like home for the first time since I arrived in Tampa three months ago.

The guys start to relax a bit as I hand out drinks. Some of them post up inside on my new couch while others join me on the patio, where the chef set up some appetizers of grilled chicken and vegetable skewers, and a charcuterie and hummus display. The smell of charred meat fills the air, mingling with the crisp evening breeze. My yard backs up to the Hillsborough River, with a cluster of Oak and Cypress trees filling the space, each with Spanish moss hanging from their branches. Occasionally, an alligator will slide past in the water or a family of turtles will bask in the sun on the bank of the river.

Toto, we are *not* in Ohio anymore.

"So, Austin," Malik starts, a mischievous glint in his eye. "How are you handling all the attention from the ladies now that you're the starting QB?"

"Ah, you know, just focused on the game right now." I feel my face heat up, and I try to play it cool. "The attention has been overwhelming. The first time I logged on to my socials after that first game, it was . . . a lot." I rub the back of my neck. "I had hundreds of DMs that were equal parts women coming onto me and dudes telling me how much I suck at the game of football. I haven't been online since."

Jordan claps me on the back, laughing. "Dude, last week when I missed that pass, I got this super angry DM from a guy who said I messed up his $50 prop bet. He told me to cover myself in peanut butter and feed myself to the alligators."

"That feels oddly specific," Landon says with a laugh. "Do alligators even like peanut butter?"

"Is there anything out there that doesn't like peanut butter?" Isaiah says.

"Maybe some alligators are allergic, like humans," Malik says. "You get one to start eating you and he spits you out."

"Dude, under what circumstances am I actually slathering myself in peanut butter and hopping in a lake with alligators?"

"Maybe if you put peanut butter on your hands, you'd catch the ball next time," I say.

The guys crack up, ribbing Jordan, who claps back with, "Whatever you say, Icy Hot."

We laugh, and it feels like for the first time since Nolan Reese got injured, like I'm really part of the team.

When dinner is ready, we spread out between the patio table outside and the dining table inside. I sit outside with Jake and Mike, along with our kicker, Liam Turner, and one of the linemen, Tank. As the night goes on, I chat more with Liam. He's the only one who brought something—a couple six packs of Bootleggers, a local Tampa brewery. I thank him for the beer and we fall into a conversation about the latest craft beer trends and his favorite local breweries. I tell him about Omar and how he's started dabbling with his own microbrewery.

Dani was right, once again. The food is incredible—perfectly cooked steak, guava BBQ salmon, and a veggie hash with sweet potatoes, bacon, corn, and spinach. I hope there are leftovers for later, because I could eat this all week long. Except the guys are throwing down like they've never eaten before and I'm sure there won't be a single ounce of food left when they leave.

After dinner, a few of the guys huddle around the TV and play Madden while the rest of us play poker. Dani convinced me to get a dining table with a top that flips over to reveal a card table on the other side.

As soon as we start playing, I regret it. Most of these guys have been in the NFL for a few years, which means they've lost their sensitivity to the sheer amount of money that they make—and spend. They're throwing out several thousand dollar raises like it's pennies. I fold when I can, but I know I have to play eventually. When I finally get a good hand, I grit my teeth when I match a four thousand dollar raise. It's painful—but I win the hand.

By the time they leave, I feel a sense of accomplishment as I survey the mess the guys left. Beer bottles, dishes, and poker chips are scattered through my dining and living rooms. It'll be a headache to clean up, but it was worth it. I know that winning over my team isn't just about what happens on the field, and tonight was one step in the right direction.

If only we could get a few steps in the right direction on the field too.

25

Austin

> Play Action Pass: A passing play that starts with a fake hand off to the running back to trick the defense into thinking it's a run, thus creating an opportunity for the quarterback to throw the ball to an open receiver.

It's game five at home against the Giants. If Nolan Reese were here, we'd be smashing this team. But we don't have Nolan Reese, we have me.

And I'm getting crushed. Literally, the linebacker that just sacked me might've completely deflated my lungs.

Basically, our current offense highlights all of my weaknesses and utilizes none of my strengths. I take the vast majority of snaps under center—which means I'm squatting directly behind the center, the top of my hand pressed into the sweaty crotch of a three-hundred-pound offensive lineman. It's not my first choice for hand placement—I'd much prefer my fingers high and dry and away from anyone's sweaty butt.

We mostly just run the ball. When we do pass, it's either play action and/or boot legs, which require me to turn my back to the defense and throw on the move. I don't like this for multiple reasons: when I turn my back to the defense, I lose the mental picture of the defense that I had before the snap. I have to recalibrate once I get into position. Secondly, I don't throw as well while running.

I do well when I get to stand in shotgun—which means I'm about five to seven steps behind the line, so that gives me a few extra seconds to look at the defense and make the proper adjustments if needed. I get rid of the ball quickly and I'm fearless in the pocket—I'll step into a throw that I need to make, even if that means I'm about to get creamed by the defense.

Being a good pocket passer is akin to staring down a stampede of raging bulls as they charge at you. Not only do you need to stay calm in the chaos so that you can throw the ball with the accuracy of a sniper, but you have to step toward the charging bull as you throw. Add in the fact that the bulls are getting paid millions of dollars to hit you—and they enjoy it. They *live* for the moment when they get to stare down at your prone body at their feet. They revel in it.

And yet, I can throw the ball. I can find my receivers.

Like a sniper who can slow his heart rate before taking a shot, somehow I can be the eye of the storm and find my receivers, getting the ball to them even as these psychotic bulls are chasing me down. Not many people can do that—and very few people can do it well—but I can.

If only Coach would let me.

The first part of the game was a slog. We had a lot of three and outs—meaning that we didn't get any first downs and had to punt the ball. Coach is still trying to have me play to not lose the game instead of letting me help try to win the game. The team is clearly frustrated, the energy is low and my receivers are getting antsy because they're not getting many opportunities.

I understand why Coach Clive is hesitant to trust my passing game—I threw a pick-six in my very first game after Nolan's injury when I had zero practice. But now I've got a few games in and a fair amount of practice—along with Dani's faith in me thrumming through my veins—and I'm ready to be unleashed.

By halftime, we're losing 3-10. Our only score was a 57-yard field goal—an absolute smash by Liam. With a minute left in the half, we decide to punt on a fourth-and-1 from our 50-yard line. The booing from our fans was audible down on the field. The shame I felt in that moment was almost paralyzing.

When we head inside the locker room during halftime, I can hear all the guys around me grumbling. They want to be unleashed too—but I'm holding them back because Coach is holding me back.

Inside the locker room, Malik throws his helmet against the lockers, the sound reverberating through the room. "We gotta stop playing not to lose," he shouts. "Let's play to win!"

His anger blankets everyone in the room so that the air is thick with negative emotion. Coach Clive catches my eye and nods me over. He runs a massive paw over his sweaty face, his eyes tired as he stares at me. I'm half afraid he's going to bench me—except there's no back up to take my place.

"Alright, Taylor," he says with a sigh. "We've tried it my way. Let's try it your way."

26

Dani

It's scientifically proven that the moment you look away from the game is when your team will score their most impressive touchdown.

I'm going to lose this bet.

I'm in the staff box seats watching the game. My palms are sweating and a trickle of moisture drips down my neck, despite the frigid air conditioning in here.

I really thought we'd win this game—it's one of our best chances at a win—and we're still losing. Coach clearly didn't take into consideration my plea or Austin's progress in practice. I swipe my fingers underneath my eyelids, wiping away the bits of mascara that are pooling there.

Ethan keeps smirking at me, which makes me want to wrap my fingers around his scrawny neck and squeeze. Ugh. I'm going to lose this bet against *Ethan* of all people. I step to the buffet to get away from his obnoxious gaze and load up a plate, even though I'm too queasy to eat right now. I spend an inordinate amount of time picking through platters of deli rounds, fruit, and cheese. I'm so thorough in my distraction that I don't even notice our guys are back onto the field until I hear a roar from the fans.

And from the sound of it, it's a positive roar. I drop my plate on the buffet table and hurry to the window, where I catch Malik Washington doing a touchdown dance in our end zone. Beside me, staff members are high-fiving and clapping.

"We scored?" I ask, eyes wide and incredulous as I look beside me at one of our secretaries, Martha.

She nods, her hair sprayed locks not moving an inch with the movement. "Yes sirree we did."

"Taylor threw a 50-yard pass to Malik," one of the scouts tells me.

Okay, I know I've talked a big game to Austin about my confidence in him—but I was beginning to doubt that Coach would ever let him loose on the field. It's not my most faithful moment when I shriek, "He did what?!"

"Don't tell me you were losing faith in the guy already," Ethan snarks from behind me.

I scoff. "My trust in Austin wasn't diminishing one iota."

He raises his eyebrows, letting them do the talking for his skepticism.

"My belief in the *system* might have slipped momentarily."

"Whatever you say, Dani." He juts his chin out at the field. "One touchdown is a long way from winning six games, though."

"The journey of a thousand miles begins with a single step."

"Is that one of your dad's sayings?"

I roll my eyes. "It's the Chinese philosopher Lao Tzu."

"Whatever, you didn't know about Marlon Brando."

"Marlon Brando's not winning my bet for me." I tap my fingernail on the window. "But Austin Taylor is."

End Zone Report ✓
@endzonereport

Tampa Bay Buccaneers beat Giants 17-10 in an epic come-from-behind win in the 4th quarter.

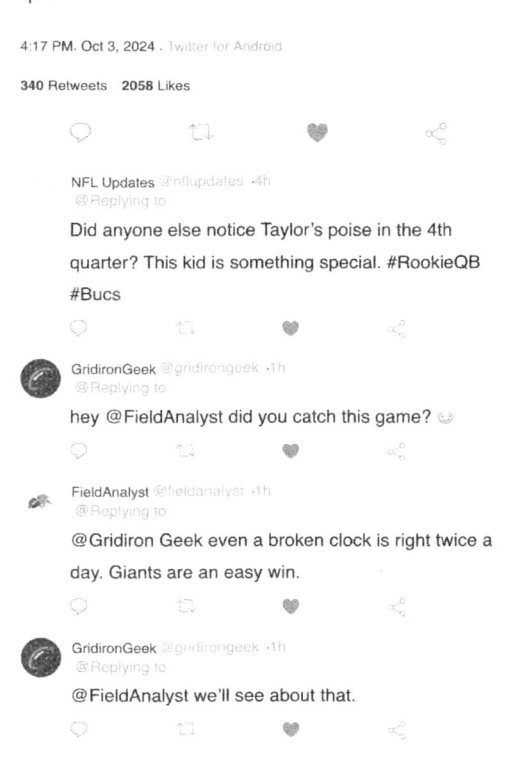

4:17 PM · Oct 3, 2024 · Twitter for Android

340 Retweets 2058 Likes

NFL Updates @nflupdates · 4h
@Replying to

Did anyone else notice Taylor's poise in the 4th quarter? This kid is something special. #RookieQB #Bucs

---

GridironGeek @gridirongeek · 1h
@Replying to

hey @FieldAnalyst did you catch this game? 😏

FieldAnalyst @fieldanalyst · 1h
@Replying to

@Gridiron Geek even a broken clock is right twice a day. Giants are an easy win.

GridironGeek @gridirongeek · 1h
@Replying to

@FieldAnalyst we'll see about that.

27

Austin

> Reverse: A misdirection play where the ball is handed off to a player who then hands it off or pitches it to another player running in the opposite direction, aiming to fool the defense.

We're celebrating our win against the Giants at Rooster and The Till, a Michelin Bib Gourmand restaurant. It's the kind of place that you'd pass on the street and never know it was someplace nice—but once you get inside, the dark and modern vibes make you forget you're in the middle of Seminole Heights. Exposed bulbs hang from the ceiling all around the central bar while a huge portrait of a rooster takes up the wall behind us. The energy in the room is electric, and I'm riding high on the victory. This is the first time I've felt like part of the team, and I can't help but bask in the camaraderie. The table is laden with gourmet dishes, short rib, gnocchi, and plenty of foods I can't even pronounce. The laughter and banter flow as freely as the drinks.

Jordan Ellis leans back in his chair, a satisfied grin on his face. "Man, that touchdown pass was a thing of beauty, Taylor. You keep that up, and we might start calling you the new Brady."

I laugh, shaking my head. "Let's not get ahead of ourselves."

Mike Donnelly raises his glass. "To Taylor, leading us to victory! May there be many more to come."

We all clink glasses, and I can't help but feel a swell of pride. This is what I've worked for, what I've dreamed of. Even the chef comes out and congratulates us on our win.

As the evening winds down, I notice my teammates exchanging sly glances. Malik Washington suddenly stands up, stretching exaggeratedly. "Man, I'm beat. I think I'm gonna call it a night."

One by one, the guys start making their excuses. "Yeah, early film review tomorrow," Landon Mitchell says, stifling a yawn.

"Gotta get home to the wife and kids," Jake Foster adds, patting his stomach.

Liam claps me on the shoulder. "Great night, Taylor. We'll see you tomorrow."

Before I know it, they're all slipping out the door, leaving me sitting there with a stack of plates, glasses, and a sinking feeling in my stomach. I glance around the table, realizing what just happened. It's a classic rookie move—sticking the new guy with the bill.

I wave the waiter over, trying to hide my embarrassment. "I guess I'll be taking care of this," I say, pulling out my credit card. The waiter nods sympathetically, and I can't help but chuckle at the absurdity of it all.

As I sign the receipt, I shake my head. "Welcome to the NFL, Taylor," I mutter to myself.

The bill is hefty, but I try to remind myself that it's all part of the initiation, a rite of passage. Besides, tonight was worth it. We won, we celebrated, and for the first time since coming into the NFL, I feel like I truly belong.

28

Dani

40% of new marriages in the United States involve at least one partner who has been married before and 16% of children live in blended families. (And 100% of me wants to be back in my original, unblended family.)

We're celebrating Uncle Clive's birthday at my dad's house. Tuesdays are the Saturdays of the NFL. Birthday parties, doctors appointments that can't be put off until the spring, even my dad's date night with Heather—all on Tuesdays.

So, here we are, on a Tuesday for a birthday party.

Even though it's the end of September, it's still hotter than the deepest depths of the underworld in Florida, so we're all in our swimsuits by the pool. My cousin, Portia, is lounging beside me in the water. My dad has a zero-entry pool so we've dragged chairs into the shallow part of the water so that our bodies are mostly underwater but our hair isn't at risk of getting wet.

Portia is a confident goddess of a woman—good looking enough to be confused with an NFL cheerleader with her curvy yet toned body. She keeps her hair natural and I'm slightly jealous of her perfect coils that sprout in all directions from her head, each with a life of its own. Her hair is a product, in part, of having a mom who knew how to take care of it—keeping it healthy all through Portia's life with lots of TLC. I catch sight of my stepmom, Heather, standing beside my dad at the grill. She truly did her best with my hair—but that involved a lot of heat and perming, which ultimately led to a lot of damage. My hair was always short or pulled back into a severe bun for ballet, so I switched to braids or extensions when I went to college.

Portia's going to the University of Miami getting her Doctor of Physical Therapy. In the spring, she'll be interning with the Miami Heat and we're discussing what the players might be like.

"It's just really unfair that they're all so good looking," Portia says as she adjusts her lemon-yellow bikini—a perfect contrast against her flawless, dark skin. She's scrolling through the Miami Heat website, looking at the player profiles. "Like, they've got a disproportionate amount of athletic ability, they should be ugly as sin."

I laugh, shaking my head. "Life isn't fair, Portia."

"Clearly," she says, waving a hand in my direction. "Supermodel brainiac over here."

I roll my eyes. "You're beautiful, too, Portia."

"Oh, girl, I know," she says, tossing her hair from one side to the other. "We're obviously here to make everyone else feel bad about themselves."

I cackle. "And to think, you're so humble too."

"Time to eat, girls," my dad calls. We gather around our outdoor table, a massive display of all kinds of grilled meat and veggies spread across the tablecloth. I take my seat between Portia and her mom, Auntie Rox. Growing up, Auntie Rox was what I thought every mom should be like—fun, nurturing, gave great advice, and always had the best snacks at her house. My dad was too busy to have snacks around, and when he married Heather, her idea of snacks were fruit or veggies with dip. Not exactly thrilling to a ten-year-old—not when Portia had Gushers, Doritos, and Dunkaroos lining the shelves of her pantry.

Heather sits down near my dad, and Lucas and Layla wriggle into their seats between them, looking like a perfect picture of domesticity with the four of them. Heather's pretty in an obvious, former-cheerleader type of way with her blonde hair, tanned skin and light blue eyes. I guess I can't fault him for falling for her—but it makes me wonder, is Heather his type? Or was my mom? Because it seems like they both can't be his type, with how different they are.

My dad says a brief prayer, thanking God for the food and for Clive being born, and then we dig in. Roxanne and Clive have two sons, Patrick and Pierre—yep, they love alliteration. Patrick is sitting across from me, polishing off his third drumstick before I've even had a chance to cut up my grilled thigh, but Pierre plays for the Packers, so he's in Wisconsin at the moment.

As it always does, the talk around the table centers around football. We're discussing our epic comeback and the huge pass from Austin to Malik.

"I'm not going to say 'I told you so,'" I say primly to Uncle Clive.

He guffaws good naturedly, but I can feel my dad's eyes on me. "You really believe in this one, don't you?" he asks, his voice low and gruff.

I shrug as casually as I can manage. "His CHOICE scores don't lie, Dad."

"Word is you've got Taylor on some kind of extracurricular training regimen," Clive says, his eyes dancing like he knows he's stirring up trouble for me. Heat flares across my chest and face.

"Just trying to help him succeed, same as everyone else in the organization," I say.

"What kind of regimen are we talking, Danielle?" my dad asks.

"He's been watching film with me in the mornings and I've been helping him with the playbook," I say vaguely, hoping it'll satisfy my dad. Even though that's only a fraction of how much time I've been spending with Austin.

"And apparently yoga," Clive says like the traitorous instigator he is.

My dad's eyebrows raise until they might fall over his bald dome.

"Well, I for one think it's great that you're helping him out, Danielle," Heather says in her Southern drawl. "He's a looker too." She waggles her brows and gives a giggle that is way too immature for her age.

Maybe Heather thinks she's trying to help me—but she's not. I clench my teeth as I face my dad.

"Yoga's proven to enhance range of motion and overall agility," I say. "Taylor needs that. And our training staff doesn't incorporate yoga at all."

"Well if there's something missing in our training regimen, we should remedy that, Clive, so that our analysts don't have to get their hands dirty," my dad says—his words pointed at Clive, but his eyes boring into mine. His intention is clear to me: I should let the coaches and training staff worry about the players and stick to my own job.

The only problem? I'm way too invested in one player to back off now.

29

Dani

> On average, a prominent NFL player in their team's city receives approximately 15-20 requests for autographs and selfies during a single public outing, particularly in popular venues. (And Austin Taylor's average is higher because he's so dang nice, and, as previously noted, easy on the eyes.)

It's Thursday at lunchtime. Austin and I head to Fresh Kitchen while I quiz him on this week's new plays for the game against the Patriots. This has become our routine: watching film in the morning, then I go to work and Austin goes to practice and meetings, we reconvene for lunch and playbook memorization. Some afternoons we go to yoga and occasionally I'll help him cram at night too.

What can I say? It's a wonderful, football (and Austin) filled life.

Everywhere we go, Austin stands out like a prime number in a sequence of even numbers. The guy is hugely tall—ducking through the doorway as we enter the restaurant—and jaw-droppingly handsome. Even if he wasn't a newly famous NFL player, he'd still catch people's eyes no matter where we went. But he *is* famous, so we endure the typical round of people asking for autographs and selfies when we go out.

Austin, being the nicest person alive, obliges every single person. His boyish smile never wavers as he takes picture after picture. We've finally gotten our food and have settled into a table at the back of the restaurant when none other than Claire Beaumont walks in.

And even though she's my very best friend in the world, my heart drops. I don't even want to read into why that is, but I have a feeling it has something to do with the football player sitting across from me, whose knees are brushing against mine under the table as we eat.

I know that Austin Taylor is completely off-limits for me—for many, many reasons, the least of them being that he's a football player and I don't date football players. Plus, my dad's reaction to finding out about my assistance with Austin is burned in my head. Sure, he didn't specifically say something to me—but it's the look on his face and his tone that won't leave me alone.

But he's not off limits for Claire.

Claire, my best friend who dreams of getting married and having tons of babies, would be perfect for Austin. I've known this for weeks now and have withheld him selfishly from my friend. Seeing her in here is like picking at an open wound. I'm a bad friend—I should've immediately set them up the moment I realized they'd be a good pair—and I didn't. Still don't want to, in fact. If Austin could be hidden in any way, shape, or form, I would do it right now.

Instead, I stand and give Claire a hug when she approaches our table. "Have you met Austin Taylor?" I say, even though I know she hasn't met him.

"So nice to meet you, Austin," she says with her adorable smile and her dimples that match Austin's. Their children will have dimples and be so incredibly good-looking that it's really unfair for the rest of the children in the world. "I heard you had a great game on Sunday. Congrats."

"Thanks," Austin says, and I'm sure he's smiling his million-dollar smile at her and she's smiling back—but I can't watch it. I keep my eyes fixed on my sweet potatoes and grilled chicken.

"Let me grab my food and I'll join y'all."

A few minutes later, when I scoot over to let Claire sit beside me, it's physically painful to think about Claire's knees knocking up against Austin's now. I know, I know, it's just *knees*. But that's how it all starts, doesn't it?

It takes everything in me to not completely tune out of our lunch conversation as Austin and Claire get to know each other. I'm worse than a third wheel—I'm the spare tire that's in the trunk that you forget about. After lunch, I go to refill my drink and when I turn back around, Austin and Claire are clearly exchanging phone numbers.

I tell myself I should be happy for my friend. For Austin. But I can't even summon that lie right now.

"So, Austin Taylor." Claire raises one perfectly shaped brow at me when Austin gets swept away by an influx of fans. "How long were you going to keep that secret from me, hm?"

I shrug, feeling a nasty combination of guilt and envy.

"So that's how it's going to be, is it?" Claire titters, her laugh as cute as she is. "I see how it is, Danielle Marshall." She leans against me, whispering, "I'll get more intel out of you soon about the hunky quarterback you've been keeping all to yourself."

My face heats as Claire pokes me in the ribs, making me squirm in more ways than one. If only Claire had a clue how it really is. But I'll never tell her.

The atmosphere in Gillette Stadium is electric, but I notice Austin looks unusually calm as the game begins. From the first snap, everything seems to click. Our offensive line holds firm, giving him the time he needs to find his receivers. Malik Washington is on fire, catching everything thrown his way, and Jordan Ellis breaks free for a spectacular 60-yard touchdown that sets the tone early. The Patriots' defense, known for its complexity, looks like a puzzle Austin is finally able to solve.

Every drive, Austin stays focused, executing Coach Clive's game plan with precision. I can't help but feel a swell of pride as I see the plays I slipped under Coach's door working like a charm. I can't wait to chart Austin's plays for this game—I'm sure his CHOICE scores must be off the charts tonight. By halftime, we have a solid lead, but I'm still fidgeting in my seat in the box as we take the field again.

In the second half, our defense steps up, giving us great field position, and we capitalize on every opportunity. The final whistle blows with the scoreboard reading 34-17 in our favor. Walking off the field, Austin looks elated and relieved. It's not just a win; it's a statement. He's proven to himself, to the team, and maybe even to me that he has what it takes to lead this team to victory. And watching him out there, I can't help but feel we're on the verge of something truly special.

30

Austin

> Screen Pass: A short pass play designed to catch the defense off guard. The quarterback quickly throws the ball to a receiver or running back behind the line of scrimmage, who then follows blockers downfield.

I'm sitting in the GM's office, feeling a mix of anxiety and excitement. The room is spacious, with large windows overlooking the practice field, but it's the presence of Darius Marshall, the man who holds my career in his hands, that makes the room feel a bit smaller. Not to mention this is Dani's dad.

No pressure.

"Austin, you've been making waves," Darius begins, his deep voice steady. "The win against the Patriots really put you on the map. We've got a lot of interest coming your way—sponsorships, advertisements, interview requests. People want to see more of you."

I shift in my seat, the leather creaking under me. "I appreciate that, sir, but I'm not sure I'm ready for all that attention. I mean, I know my time as a starter is . . . temporary."

Darius raises an eyebrow. "Temporary or not, you're in the spotlight now. This is part of the job."

"I get that," I reply, trying to sound confident. "But I want to be genuine with the brands I support. It doesn't feel right to just slap my name on something I don't believe in." I grimace, thinking about the offer I received from *Sports Illustrated*. "And I definitely don't want to do something I'll regret once my football days have passed."

"That's a good attitude to have." He nods, a small smile playing at the corners of his mouth. "You don't have to take all the interview options, but I'd recommend it. The brand deals are up to you. Win a couple more games and you'd probably be able to approach any brand you'd like."

I chuckle nervously. "Well, ever since moving from Ohio, I've been all about wearing shorts. I never want to wear pants again if I can help it. If there's a brand that wants me to wear shorts, I'm in."

Darius bursts into laughter, the sound filling the room. "Shorts, huh? You're a simple man, Austin."

I grin, feeling a bit more at ease. "What can I say? It's hot here."

"I feel you on that one." He shakes his head, still smiling.

He clears his throat, his voice regaining his typical seriousness. "This is your moment, Taylor. Make the most of it—we don't get too many of them in the NFL. And don't worry too much about the future—focus on what you can control now."

"I will, sir."

"That's all for now, Taylor."

"Thank you, sir." I rise, shaking his hand before heading to the door.

"Oh and Austin?"

"Yes, sir?"

"Get yourself an agent."

"I'll look into it," I tell him, though I can't imagine needing an agent for my last six weeks as an NFL starter.

31

Dani

> Despite the glamour and high-profile nature of NFL careers, less than 10% of NFL players receive endorsement deals, and even fewer get the opportunity for major magazine features.

It's a Tuesday evening after family dinner, where Uncle Clive and Aunt Roxanne joined in. My dad and Clive are sitting outside while the twins play on the trampoline. I'd much prefer to join their conversation than sit with Heather and Auntie Rox—who are pouring glasses of wine and sitting on the couch. But Auntie Rox commandeers me before I can make my escape. "Danielle, can you help me with my hair?" she pleads.

Auntie Rox has Sisterlocks, a type of tiny dreadlock with an interlocking technique. She retightens them about every six weeks, but sometimes has a hard time tightening the locks on the back of her head. She's taught Portia and I how to tighten them with a little tool—and sometimes, even Uncle Clive will tighten them during the offseason.

I don't usually opt to sit and talk with Heather if I can help it, but Auntie Rox being here softens the blow. I can only handle so much of her reports of Layla's gymnastic team drama and the other mundane complaints of an uber-rich housewife.

I settle on the couch, Auntie Rox sitting in front of me. She fishes a bag out of her purse, handing me the loc tool, a spray bottle, and a bunch of clips. I section off her hair, finding the parts that need to be retightened, as Heather and Auntie Rox chat. I zone out of their conversation as it revolves around nonfootball topics, focusing instead on Auntie Rox's hair. I spritz her hair, take one loc at a time, loop the end through the tool and then thread it through the base of the loc. It's a soothing process as I loop the hair through, pull, rotate it, then loop it again.

I'm lost in my own thoughts until I hear Austin's name come out of Heather's mouth. My hands pause, the loc tool hovering in the air as I reorient myself into their conversation.

"Darius said *Sports Illustrated* wanted to do one of those shirtless spreads with him," Heather says. My brows shoot up, but I force myself to focus on the task at hand, even though every fiber of my being strains to catch every word Heather says about Austin.

Loop, pull, twist. Loop, pull, twist.

"I believe it," Auntie Rox says, taking a sip of her white wine. "I'm sure everyone wants to know what's under that jersey."

I clench my teeth, feeling oddly possessive of Austin Taylor. I have no right to feel this way, yet a strange, possessive coil tightens in my stomach at the thought of women across the country seeing him shirtless and oiled up.

Heather leans forward and lowers her voice. "Well, he turned them down."

Auntie Rox sits up, tugging her loc out of my hand in the process. "He did *what* now?"

"He told *Sports Illustrated* he wouldn't do a shirtless photo shoot." Heather smiles over her wine glass, knowing full well that she's delivering juicy gossip.

I press my lips together, trying to hold back a laugh. Of course Austin Taylor—the most unassuming NFL player to ever walk the earth—would refuse to take his shirt off for *Sports Illustrated*.

"What was his reasoning?" Auntie Rox asks. And, let me just say, I'm so glad she's here right now—because she's asking all the right questions so I don't have to. It helps me save face. Because I don't need to seem more interested in Austin Taylor than is strictly necessary for my job.

"He said he felt uncomfortable with the idea of his mom being in the grocery checkout with his oiled up, half-naked body right in her face."

At this, I do laugh—and Heather and Auntie Rox with me. "I can't believe he said that to *Sports Illustrated*," I say, breaking my vow of silence.

"Well, he told it to your dad," Heather clarifies. "Who had to then turn around and tell it to *Sports Illustrated*."

"The guy needs an agent," Auntie Rox says. "Darius can't be acting as his go-between with the media."

I shake my head, knowing Austin is *not* going to want an agent. He barely sees himself as a starting NFL player—he still thinks his days as a starter are limited. But I know they're not.

"What did *Sports Illustrated* say?" I ask as nonchalantly as possible. Auntie Rox really needs to step up her question-asking game, because I need to hear this story to its conclusion.

"Apparently they doubled their offer and said he could keep his jersey on."

I bite my lip to hold back my smile as I loop another loc of Auntie Rox's hair.

Good for you, Austin Taylor.

32

Austin

Third-down Conversion: Successfully gaining the necessary yardage on third down to earn a new set of downs, allowing the offense to continue their drive. This is crucial for maintaining possession and advancing down the field.

We're in Cleveland this weekend to play the Browns, so Omar and Caleb come to visit. My family will come for game day, but since Will has his homecoming this weekend, they couldn't come overnight. I'll miss the extended time with them—we'll literally get to see each other in passing after the game—but I'm still grateful for the time with Caleb and Omar.

The night before the game, we go out for dinner at a place called Cordelia and then catch a movie. Since we're not in Tampa, I'm surprised when people come up to me and ask for a picture or an autograph. The look of glee on Caleb's face is as if they asked *him* for an autograph. Omar, however, wears a continual 'I told you so' smirk.

It's nice to be with friends—people I don't have to explain myself to or feel on edge with. Even though I'm making inroads with my teammates, there's nothing quite like kicking it with people you've known since you were a kid.

But as we settle into our theater seats—Caleb with seemingly every concession option possible while Omar sips a Diet Coke and I nurse a bottle of water—it feels like something is missing.

Something, perhaps, Dani-shaped.

The chill in the Cleveland air does nothing to dampen our spirits as we take the field against the Browns. From the first huddle, I can sense the confidence building in my teammates. We're coming off a big win against the Patriots, and I'm determined to keep that momentum going. Having my family and Omar and Caleb in the stands, their voices echoing through the crowd, only fuels my drive.

Our offense clicks right from the start. I connect with Malik Washington on a deep route for an early touchdown, setting the tone for the game. The Browns' defense is tough, but our line holds strong, giving me just enough time to make my reads. Jordan Ellis breaks through for a crucial 30-yard gain, and Mike Donnelly's veteran presence is invaluable, snagging a critical third-down conversion.

By the fourth quarter, we're ahead, but I know we can't let up. With the crowd roaring, I orchestrate a final drive that seals the deal—a perfectly executed play-action pass to our tight end, Jake Foster, for another score. The final whistle blows with us on top, 28-14. Walking off the field, I spot my family and friends, their cheers blending with the roaring Bucs fans. It's a defining moment, a testament to our growing strength and unity as a team. We're building something special, and this win is just another step towards proving it.

33

Dani

> Studies show that around 25% of dog owners report making new friendships and social connections through their pets, and a notable portion of these connections can turn into romantic relationships.

It's a Wednesday afternoon, which means that I'm sitting in Claire's gallery, eating pumpkin scones and sipping mulled apple cider. Curled up in an oversized egg chair, I'm enjoying the way it closes me off from the rest of the world, while Claire gently swings back and forth on the wooden swing hanging from the ceiling. During the spring and summer months, the ropes of the swing are twined with vines and flowers, but with the advent of fall, the flowers were swapped out for orange, yellow, and red leaves.

Claire's favorite Forrest Frank playlist plays overhead as the afternoon sun filters through the gauzy curtains beside us. The warm cider is making me feel sleepy and content. Isabella had an interview today, so she's not here—which means it's approximately 34% more quiet.

My best friend looks like she stepped out of a fall J. Crew catalog. Her blazer is cuffed at the sleeves, revealing a burnt orange top underneath and her tailored jeans are tucked into Stuart Weitzman tall boots. Meanwhile, I'm wearing my typical uniform of a suit and heels—today I'm rocking a cream houndstooth pattern with a navy blouse and Gucci ankle boots.

Claire's in the middle of telling me about her date with a guy she met at the dog park. They took their dogs to a local coffee shop and it sounds like it was going great, until . . .

"Claire, you did not tell him you got a dog to meet men!"

"Well, not in those words, no," she scoffs. "I just said that I thought it would help me—okay, fine, yes, I did say that!" She throws up her hands. "He got super weird after that. Kept checking his phone and fidgeting—guys who are into you do *not* fidget—and then he finally said he had to get going, even though he'd told me he didn't have anything planned the rest of the day."

"I'm sorry, Claire bear. That's rough."

"Do I have 'crazy lady' tattooed on my head or something?" She gestures dramatically across her face, mussing her side bangs in the process so they're sticking out.

"Well . . . " I grimace as I lean forward, smoothing her hair.

"Dani!" She swats my hand away. "You're supposed to make me feel better!"

"You're not doing yourself favors by telling them why you bought Gronk. That's, like, at least fourth-date material."

She groans, hanging her head so that her blonde hair falls in front of her face.

"You didn't say the thing about the pad wings getting stuck to your leg, right?"

"No!" She blows a sharp breath upward, making her bangs fly before she faces me. "I stopped after that one guy."

"Good. That needs to stay locked in a vault. Throw away the key, forget the security code."

"You know what I want to do?" she says, her voice taking on a wistful tone that makes me nervous.

I raise an eyebrow. "What's that?"

"I want to go on *Love is Blind*. They're coming to Tampa, apparently."

"No, Claire, absolutely not—"

"Dani, listen, look—*Love is Blind* is all about falling in love with someone for who they are on the inside. It's amazing. I love seeing all of those couples fall in love."

"Okay," I say, drawing out the word. "But what about the fact that your personal life is splashed across the screen for all of America to see?"

"Seems like a small price to pay for love."

I grunt, trying to sound neutral, but inside I'm thinking: No one is worth that price.

Claire falls silent as she twists herself up in the swing, spinning once, twice, three times, before letting go. When she lands, she looks at me and says, "Tell me about Austin Taylor."

And my heart drops. Because I knew it would come to this—Austin is the most eligible bachelor I know and he's a really good guy. It makes the perfect sense to set him up with my best friend. But the thought of it knots my insides.

I take a deep breath, steeling myself as I say, "He's a really great guy, Claire. I could set you guys up?" The words are painful coming out of me—like someone's trying to pull out my molars while I say it. I'm afraid to look Claire right in the eye, afraid of the hope and desperation I'll see there.

But instead, she laughs. And not a sweet, gentle Southern belle laugh—a full-bellied guffaw. I narrow my eyes at her. Maybe she really has lost it.

"Danielle, I'm not asking about Austin for *me*, I'm asking about him for *you*."

Relief rushes through me, but I still manage to be selfless enough to say, "You're joking, right? You guys would make a perfect couple."

Claire stands up from her swing, swaying softly to the song playing, "Only Be You" by Forrest Frank and Anees. "If Austin Taylor looked at me the way he looks at you, I'd go out with him in a heartbeat, trust me."

I snort. "Austin Taylor doesn't look at me like anything."

Claire picks up a pumpkin scone, doing a little dance step in time to the beat of the song as she takes a bite, humming to herself. "You keep telling yourself that, Dani. But you're too smart to be naive."

I stare down at my lap, brushing away crumbs from my scone. I want her to detail everything she means—how, exactly, does she think Austin looks at me? But I have a feeling that if I let Claire do that, it's a slippery slope toward admitting feelings I'm not ready to confront.

Claire reaches for her phone, turning up the song. "It could only be you," she sings along as she shimmies closer to me. Before I know it, Claire's pulling me up and forcing me to dance as she continues to sing in a very off-pitch voice. "You're so heavenly," she sings as she traces my curves in the air with her hands and I can't help but laugh and slap away her hands.

As the song ends, Claire brings me another scone. "Next time you're with Austin Taylor, just pay attention. See how he looks at you. I promise that you won't be disappointed."

I fold myself back into my egg chair. "Claire, you know I don't date athletes."

"Look, I get that Jared messed you up—"

"He didn't mess me up," I argue, my pride flaring. "He just taught me to have boundaries with players. I *thought* we were dating, until he showed up on the front page of E! with that supermodel the day after he told me he loved me." I shake my head, shame flaming through my body from head to toe as I recall the moment I realized he'd played me. I resolved then and there to never let something like that happen to me again.

"I know that was awful, Danielle. We were young and naive—"

I scoff. "*We?*"

"I had a front row seat to your relationship with a rookie NFL player who was more arrogant than that Terrell Owens guy. I should have said something, done something."

I almost laugh at her reference to T.O.—Claire Beaumont must be the only person on the planet to ever call him 'that Terrell Owens guy.' "The responsibility falls squarely on me."

"You know I'm not good with numbers, but I'd say it's at least 92% Jared's fault that he was two-timing you—and doing it so publicly."

Claire gives me her wide-eyed, innocent look, which gets a small smile out of me—and an eye roll. "Your stats are overblown, as per usual."

She reaches out and takes my hand. Her tone is gentle when she asks, "So, is Austin Taylor anything like Jared?"

The answer comes to me immediately—*no*—but it takes much longer for me to admit it. I fiddle with my pumpkin scone, examining the sugar glaze and how it ripples over the scone. "Not as far as I can tell."

Claire's genteel exterior drops and she smacks my hand. "You can be in denial right now, but not forever, Dani girl. I'll let you pretend this naivety for one more week, and that's it."

I roll my eyes, feigning indifference to what she's saying. But in the back of my mind, all I can think is this: The only thing worse than gaining Austin Taylor's affections would be to lose them like I did Jared's. And that's not a risk I'm willing to take.

34

Dani

> Studies show that approximately 70% of NFL players experience significant fatigue and exhaustion during the season due to the rigorous demands of training, practice, and games. This can affect their performance, concentration, and overall well-being, necessitating adequate rest and recovery measures.

As we gear up to play the Ravens on Sunday night, the tension among the team and staff is palpable. Now that we've won some games, we're greedy for more. So far we've beaten teams that are relatively easy to beat—but this game will show Austin's chops. Or his weaknesses. Though I'm willing to bet—heck, I've *already bet*—that he's got what it takes.

Practice has been grueling and Austin is carrying himself with exhaustion etched into every line in his face.

On Thursday, when we meet up to watch film of the Ravens, Austin starts gently snoring halfway through the game. I glance over at him, his golden-brown eyelashes fanning over his cheeks, his chin tilted forward onto his chest, his breath smooth and even. I don't even think of waking him up—even though I totally should, he needs to see this defense.

Instead, I shift slightly closer to him so that the full length of his arm is pressed up against mine. I blame the frigid temps in this room—Austin is just a warm body, nothing more. A moment later, when his head lolls to the side so that it rests against my shoulder, I bite my lip to hold back a smile.

I sigh into him as he continues to sleep, leaning against me. I keep telling myself I'll let him doze for five more minutes and then I'll wake him up to finish watching the game. But it's almost an hour later when Austin finally wakes. I quickly move away from him so he doesn't realize how close I was.

"You missed the whole second half, Taylor," I say in a stern voice.

He yawns, wiping his face with his hands, groaning into his palms. "I didn't even realize I'd fallen asleep."

He has a crease down the side of his face where it was pressed on my shoulder—I have the insane urge to run a fingertip down the line, tracing his cheek to his jaw.

Time to get out of here, Dani girl.

I stand up and chuck my notebook into Austin's lap. "I took good notes for you," I tell him as I hastily gather my things.

"Don't you need these?" He holds up my notebook, but I'm already darting from the room.

"Nope, it's all yours," I call to him over my shoulder as I leave the room. "See you tomorrow!"

I pretend I don't even hear him when he asks me about going to lunch.

Because I really enjoyed snuggling with Austin Taylor—and I really need distance from him right now so I don't lose my sanity.

I get a call on Friday night from Austin.

"I don't think I can do it, Dani," he says, his voice heavy with defeat. "The new plays are all mixed up in my head."

"Hey, hey, it's alright, Austin. I'll come over and we can run through the plays until you've got them down."

"I've been going over them all evening and my eyes are going to bleed if I look at them again." We're both silent for a moment until Austin says, "What if you're wrong about me, Dani?"

The question is so vulnerable that it threatens to split me in half. "I'm not wrong, Austin."

"How do you know?"

I lick my lips, finding my voice. "Look, it's all about how you connect the dots, right? You can connect them in one way: you never won a bowl game in college, you threw a horrendous pick-six in your first NFL game—"

Austin scoffs. "Really helping here."

"But I'm connecting different dots in the same matrix: your decision making, your stats with the squad you were given. Same matrix, but I'm choosing to connect the dots in a different way. A better way, one might argue."

"What if I'm connecting the dots correctly and you're not?"

"All the dots are real—both your dots and mine are technically accurate. But it's a choice how we connect them. We each decide which dots are most important. And why not choose the positive ones, instead of the negative?"

"Hm," Austin says, and I'm not sure I've convinced him.

I press my lips together, feeling like I'm in unchartered territory right now. I know how to do the hard work, the rote memorization, the pushing past boundaries. And Austin's done all of that to prepare for this game. But what are you supposed to do when your brain, or your body, can't handle that anymore? I don't even know. I wish I could just call Austin's family to come here—I know how much they mean to him and how much they could help him right now. But they're all in the middle of nowheresville, Ohio. And he's stuck with boring ole me. "How about we do something . . . fun?"

Austin laughs almost caustically. "Fun? What's that?"

Compassion fills my chest. This sweet, easygoing man is stressed out of his mind. Surely I can think of *something* fun for him to do. "Look, I know exactly what we can do. Just take some deep breaths and I'll be there in fifteen."

Okay, I totally lied. I don't know exactly what to do. The minute I got off the phone with Austin, I googled "fun things to do in Tampa." When that didn't offer any life-changing ideas—mostly daytime activities like the beach or Busch Gardens, or nightlife options that neither of us are up for—I literally ask ChatGPT:

You're an NFL player who needs to do something to de-stress before a big game but you don't want to do anything that will potentially injure you and doesn't revolve around alcohol. You live in Tampa and it's nighttime. Give me ten options.

I scroll through the ideas—a nighttime walk at the Riverwalk, dinner at Seasons 52, an evening yoga class, a spa night, a guided meditation. Something tells me Austin wouldn't appreciate a yoga session and I want to avoid going out in a public place like a restaurant where he might be bombarded by fans with well-meaning advice for winning the game on Sunday.

A few of the last options include an evening swim and float therapy. I glance out my condo window at the pool below. I *never* use the pool. In large part because I'm too busy, but also because it's such a hassle if I get my hair wet. My braids take *so* long to dry and the chlorine is so terrible for my natural hair. But as I watch the sun setting over the Hillsborough River, the orange and pinks reflecting on the pool and the river, I know what we should do.

I text Austin:

> Bring your swimsuit. Be there soon.

I'm not sure why I thought it would be a good idea to go swimming with Austin Taylor. For starters, he's shirtless. So I now have a truly unnecessary image of this absolutely perfect specimen of a man stuck in my head for all time. Second, *I'm* in a bathing suit. No explanation needed.

I wonder if it's not too late to fly his family out so they can de-stress him without me.

Argh.

Other than that, the night is perfect. Breezy and just warm enough to warrant a swim. The sun has set and the stars are out in their full glory on this moonless night.

"Have you ever done a float?" I ask Austin as we wade into the pool.

"Done a float? Like in a parade? Or have I ever floated in a pool?"

"No, like a float where you go to one of those spas and get in a water tank with lots of Epsom salts and it's like sensory deprivation. You float there and relax." The water ripples around us as we shuffle around the shallow end, both seemingly unsure how to be in a pool alone with each other. It's as if I've never been in a pool before—what do I do with my hands? I flutter them nervously through the water.

"Dani, do I look like someone who has done sensory deprivation at a spa?" Austin tilts his head down at me, raising his brows and I can't help but laugh.

"No, definitely not." I really can't picture Austin Taylor seeking out a float therapy spa—much less paying for something like that. "But I thought we'd do something kind of similar, here."

"You want me to float in your pool?" The skepticism is clear in his voice.

"Yes, but I'll help you."

"I, uh, appreciate the offer, but I don't think I need help floating in the water."

I roll my eyes. "It's about the experience. I'll guide you through a meditation while you float."

"Ah. Okay." He shifts awkwardly from foot to foot before saying, "So, should I just . . . float?"

I suddenly feel very vulnerable for offering this idea. What if it's a total bust? What if he thinks I'm an idiot for suggesting it? "Um, yeah. Just get on your back and relax."

Austin dunks under the water, running his fingers through his hair before coming up and shifting so that he's on his back. I go to his head, placing my fingertips at the base of his skull, giving him support as he floats. His arms and legs go out into a star shape. It takes a moment, but eventually Austin is floating with minimal movement on his part—only an occasional flip of his hands to keep him at the top of the water. His legs fall down, relaxed, while his upper body bobs in the water. I keep my eyes fixed on the bridge of Austin's nose so that I'm not tempted to count his abdominal muscles.

I'm just *really* into counting, that's all. But abs should be off-limits. Right?

"Take a deep breath," I say, keeping my voice soft like my yoga instructor does. "In through your nose, out through your mouth." Austin's eyes catch on mine before fluttering close. I breathe easier without his gaze on me. Then, I talk him through a short meditation—a mash-up from a zillion yoga classes I've taken. Even though he's completely silent, I can tell that Austin is in tune with everything I'm saying. His head gets heavier in my hands as he relaxes, his breathing in time with my instructions.

I wrap up the meditation with, "Take one more deep breath. Hold it for five, four, three, two, one . . . release it. When you're ready, open your eyes."

Slowly, Austin's eyes open and find mine. Holy calculus, the man looks heavenly even when he's upside down. How is that possible?

Even though the meditation is over, neither of us move. Austin floats in my hands, his eyes fixed on mine. It's like we're in our own little bubble. Nothing exists outside of this. Tiny pinpricks of electricity run from my fingertips up and down my arms, lighting my whole body on fire.

I want to blame this on the meditation—it was a spiritual, transcendental experience, *obviously*. But the logical part of my brain is telling me that this is purely Austin and me. Some kind of physics magic they never taught me at MIT. Maybe I missed that class on quantum entanglement, where particles remain connected no matter the distance between them. That's how it feels—like we're entangled, our very atoms resonating in perfect harmony, creating a frequency that only we can hear. My heart beats to this rhythm, each pulse sending waves of warmth and light through my veins.

Until a huge splash overwhelms us, laughter echoing through the night as several intoxicated guys rush the pool. The spell is broken—along with my formerly dry hair—and I find that I'm slightly relieved. Because I can't afford to get entangled with Austin Taylor.

35

Austin

> Strip Sack: When a defensive player tackles the quarterback and simultaneously forces a fumble by stripping the ball from the quarterback's grasp.

An hour later, I'm still recovering from Dani's DIY float therapy—I'm convinced she's got some kind of voodoo magic in her fingertips. Somehow I feel both completely relaxed and also like I can sense every nerve ending in my whole body.

Is this a Florida thing I just don't know about? Voodoo float therapy in condominium pools?

But no, I know this is just a Dani Marshall thing. The more I get to know her, the more entranced I am.

If only she felt the same way.

Once we towel off, we drip dry on the lounge chairs by the pool. She asks me about my family, how they're doing, if they're planning a trip here, and so on. I'll admit it's nice to take a break from thinking about football and Dani must sense that's what I need. Because I know if there's one topic Dani can talk endlessly about, it's football. But she hasn't brought it up, not once. Which is almost as miraculous as the feel of her hands on me.

We go up to her condo to get changed and order food. Dani sprays something in her hair that smells like a tropical island and it's driving me wild. The scent will be burned into my memory for all of eternity—I'll see her face every time I smell something with lime or coconut.

When I step out of the bathroom, I swear that Dani's looking at my phone—at least, the case of the phone she's holding looks suspiciously like mine. But when I step around her and take a seat on her couch, my phone is exactly where I left it, the screen face down on the coffee table. It's not that I mind—I don't have anything to hide—but I don't really know why Dani would be looking at my phone. If she was.

I watch her as she innocently types on her phone, and I begin to believe I got it wrong. We order CAVA bowls and watch Gordon Ramsey yelling at chefs.

"Is this triggering?" Dani asks me while Ramsey dresses down a chef for making undercooked chicken. "You don't have, like, PTSD from coaches yelling at you your whole life?"

I chuckle, shaking my head. "Ramsey's way nicer than any coach I've ever had."

"Oh, c'mon, Clive is a big teddy bear." Dani takes a bite of her Blondie—the girl has no shame in downing treats while chiding *me* about abstaining.

"A big teddy bear that I do *not* want to cross."

"Hah, fair enough."

For the first time all week, I'm able to really relax. I haven't thought about football or plays in hours. And sitting here, with Dani curled up on the couch watching a show—it just feels like home.

Like I could get used to this.

We're out on the practice field, the brisk morning air sharp with the promise of a tough game ahead. The Ravens are known for their ferocious defense, and Coach Clive has us running through every play like our lives depend on it. This isn't a full-contact practice, just a walk-through, but the tension floats in the air like the thick Florida humidity.

I stand behind the center, calling out the snap count, my eyes scanning the defense our coaches have set up to mimic Baltimore's notorious line. Malik lines up wide, his gaze intense and focused. Jordan is in the backfield, ready to spring into action. The linemen crouch, muscles coiled, every one of them knowing the stakes.

As I take the snap, I go through my progressions, imagining the Ravens' defenders breathing down my neck. The ball feels smooth and familiar in my hands, but the pressure is relentless. I fake a hand off to Jordan, watching as the linebackers bite on the play-action. Malik cuts sharply on his route and I fire the ball to him. He catches it cleanly, turning upfield with the grace of a panther.

Coach Clive calls us back to the huddle, his voice booming with instructions. "Stay sharp, focus on your reads. The Ravens' defense is no joke. They'll punish you for any mistake." His words hang in the air, a reminder of what's at stake.

We run through the play again, and then again, each time smoother than the last. My body still aches from the pounding it took in the last game, but there's no time to dwell on it. Every rep counts, every moment is an opportunity to get better.

I catch Dani watching from the sidelines, her ever-present notebook in hand. Seeing her all bundled up—it's cold for Florida, but it's not *that* cold—makes me smile despite the intensity of the practice. She gives me a nod, a silent encouragement that fuels my determination.

I push my body in practice until I think I can't push it anymore—and then I dig in and push it some more. The endorphin high that comes from realizing I can do more than I thought is invigorating in a way that nothing else is.

Until I see Dani's smile, and that takes the cake. I don't know what, exactly, is being released in my brain when she gives me a hard-earned smile, but it's like all of the dopamine, endorphins, and every other feel-good chemical is throwing a rager in my brain.

When practice ends, I head back to the locker room, the adrenaline still coursing through me. This is our time to prove we can hang with the best, and I'm ready for the challenge. And I know that Dani's elusive smile will be propelling me every yard.

I'm back home after practice when there's a knock at my door. After last night's much-needed break, I'm back to being elbow deep in our playbook. I push the iPad away, rubbing my eyes as I glance down at my phone. I haven't ordered anything, so I really don't know who or what could be at my door. Maybe a stray

Amazon delivery? I'm about to leave it be and just continue studying, but when the knock comes again, I lumber to the door.

"Surprise!" My mom's voice greets me as soon as I open the door. Both of my parents, my brother, and sister are standing at the door, holding a sign that says "Taylor-Made For Victory!" With my number emblazoned on it. My sister shimmies the sign as she stands behind my parents, cheering.

I hug them tightly, in shock that they're here. "What are you all doing here?" I ask, my voice a mix of surprise and pure joy.

"We wanted to surprise you before your big game," my dad says, clapping me on the back. "And maybe take your mind off football for a bit."

"Well, you definitely succeeded in the surprise part," I say with a grin. "Come on in."

After settling them in, we decide to keep things low-key and enjoy a relaxing day together. First up, we head to Hyde Park Village, a charming open-air shopping area with boutique stores and cozy cafes. We wander through the shops, my sister dragging us into every store that catches her eye. My mom finds a pour-your-own candle shop, and we spend some time testing the scents. Mom and Olivia leave with a candle blend of lemon zest, bergamot, cypress, and vanilla bean.

For dinner, we grab a bite at Bartaco, where we try out every taco combination on the menu. We sit outside, laughing and catching up, the familiar taste of home grounding me.

After we eat, we take a leisurely stroll along the Tampa Riverwalk. The weather is perfect, with a gentle breeze coming off the water. We stop to watch rowers glide by on the water and take in the views of the city. My parents hold hands, walking a few steps ahead, while my sister and brother joke about my upcoming game.

As the evening turns to night, we make our way back to my place, where we settle in for a movie night while I sneak in some more studying. We pick a family favorite, and my sister makes popcorn while my mom brews some herbal tea. As the movie plays, I find myself feeling incredibly grateful for this time with my family. Their support and presence mean the world to me, especially with the pressure of the upcoming game.

As the credits roll, I look around at their faces, lit by the soft glow of the TV. "Thanks for coming, guys. This was exactly what I needed."

My mom smiles and squeezes my hand. "We'll always be here for you, Austin. No matter what."

With my family by my side, I feel ready to take on whatever challenges lie ahead. Tomorrow's game against the Ravens might be tough, but tonight, I'm just grateful for the love and support that surrounds me.

36

Dani

> According to studies, athletes' performance can be significantly influenced by social support from family and friends. In fact, athletes with strong family support networks have shown a 20% improvement in performance metrics during critical games and competitions.

I made the mistake of checking on Austin's family before the game started. It's really a tactical error—the fastest way to get my heart involved in a decision that should have been purely about optimizing Austin's performance for today's game. He needed his family cheering for him in his corner. It's not sappy or sentimental. It's pure logic.

But seeing his whole family decked out in Bucs' gear and waving a sign with Austin's number on it, my heart squeezes. I don't know them and I already love these people.

And, as a rule, I don't really like people. Especially strangers.

But Austin's family don't feel like strangers, they feel like an extension of Austin himself. When I introduce myself, Austin's mom wraps me up in a warm hug and . . . I let her. My arms even move of their own accord around her ample waist, squeezing back. Her vanilla scent feels homey and nice. Like a mom should smell. Austin's dad shakes my hand, but then seems to change his mind and gives me an awkward hug-pat with his other hand.

"Dani, why don't you sit with us?" Austin's sister, Olivia, asks. "Emily couldn't come, so there's an extra seat here."

"Oh, um, I usually sit in the box so I can chart the plays."

Mrs. Taylor frowns at me. "Can't you do that here? Aren't these better seats?"

To be fair, we *are* front and center. When I asked Austin's mom what she'd prefer—box seats with the staff and other family members or tickets close to the action, she hadn't hesitated when she'd told me she wanted to see the sweat coming off her son's face. Strange, but true.

"Mom, this is her job. She's working today, let the lady work," Olivia hisses to her mom.

"I do need to work," I tell them. They all stare at me expectantly, seemingly waiting for me to tell them when I'll see them next. "But I'll come down and find you after the game."

"Alright, but if you don't find us, we'll find you," Mrs. Taylor says, which earns her an elbow from Olivia along with a muttered, "*Mom.*"

"I'll be back, Mrs. Taylor," I assure her.

"Call me Patty," she says, reaching out her hand and giving me an affectionate squeeze on my arm.

"Thanks, Patty."

She smiles at this and I'm suddenly nervous I made the wrong decision by bringing Austin's family here. Because now that I've seen his family, I'm not sure I can keep my own affections for Austin in check.

37

Austin

> Turnover: A turnover in football occurs when a team loses possession of the ball to the opposing team, either through a fumble or an interception. This is a critical error as it immediately halts the team's offensive drive and gives the opposing team an opportunity to score. Turnovers are often momentum shifting plays that can significantly impact the outcome of a game.

Seeing Dani with my family in the stands while I warm up is, in a word, thrilling. For a moment, I let myself imagine a world where Dani is sitting there because she's mine and not just betting on me.

Don't get me wrong, I'm glad Dani's willing to bet on me. She may truly be the only one. But the more time I spend with her, the more of her I want.

I wave up at them and my family responds with wild screams and waves. But I'm looking at Dani, waiting for her subdued wave. When she finally moves her long, elegant fingers in my direction, I smile.

It's not much, but I'll take what I can get with Dani Marshall. For now.

The roar of the crowd is deafening as we step back onto the field for our game against the Ravens. I can feel the tension in the air, each breath heavy with anticipation. The Ravens are living up to their reputation. Every play feels like a battle, every yard hard-fought and won.

Our running backs, Landon and Isaiah, are doing their best to break through the line, but the Ravens' defense is a wall. Our offensive linemen are holding their own, giving me just enough time to find my receivers. I drop back, scanning the field. Malik's cutting across the middle, and I fire the ball to him, a quick, sharp pass. He catches it, taking a hard hit but holding on. We gain a crucial first down.

As the game grinds on, we take a few hard hits. Jake Foster pulls down a high pass, taking a linebacker with him as he lands. Mike Donnelly runs a perfect route, shaking off his defender for a 20-yard gain. But it's Jordan Ellis who makes the play of the game. With less than two minutes left, I fake a hand off to Isaiah and spot Jordan streaking down the sideline. I launch the ball, praying he gets there. Jordan leaps, catching the ball just before stepping out of bounds. It's a spectacular catch, and it puts us in scoring position.

With the clock ticking down, we're on the Ravens' 10-yard line. The stadium is electric, the noise vibrating in my bones.

I call for the snap, and Landon takes the handoff, smashing through the line for a 5-yard gain.

Second down.

I glance at Coach Clive on the sideline, who gives me a nod. It's up to me now.

We line up again, the tension palpable with only twenty seconds left on the clock. I take the snap, faking a handoff to Isaiah before rolling out to the right. The Ravens' defense is closing in, but I spot Jake Foster in the end zone. I plant my feet and throw, a perfect spiral cutting through the air. Jake catches it, and the crowd erupts.

Touchdown.

The scoreboard lights up, and we've done it. The final whistle blows, and we've beaten the Ravens. Relief pours through me in waves—this is the game no one said we could win.

We did it. We actually did it.

The guys mob me, cheering and jumping on me. I catch sight of my family on the sidelines, waving their sign. I'm so glad they were here to witness this victory—it feels all the more sweet because of that.

We shake hands with the other team and Lamar Jackson claps me on the back and says, "Great game, Taylor. It's impressive to see a rookie handle the field like that. Keep it up, man."

I open my mouth to respond—but no words come to me. *Lamar Jackson* just spoke to me. And not only that, he complimented my game play.

He's already moved on to talking with some of the other players, but I call out, "Thanks, man!" like the dork that I am.

As we head to the locker room, the exhaustion hits me, but it's mingled with pure elation. Tonight, we were scrappy, we were tough, and we came out on top.

This is what football is all about.

After our win, Dani tells us that she made a reservation for us at Bern's Steak House—one of the nicest restaurants in Tampa.

"You're coming, right, Dani?" Olivia—ever the wingwoman—asks Dani.

"Oh no, it's just for you guys. Family time."

"Nonsense, Danielle," my mom says, scolding Dani in her sweet way. "You're joining us, and I won't hear otherwise."

Dani chuckles nervously, glancing between my mom and me. "You should come," I say, as casually as I can muster.

"Okay, sure," she says, fidgeting with her hair. "Sure," she repeats, seemingly uncertain about what to say. "I'll meet you all there."

When Dani shows up to Bern's, she looks like the dancer that she is—floating on air, her hair piled on top of her head, showcasing her long, elegant neck. She's wearing an outfit that Olivia calls a jumpsuit—which sounds like something a paratrooper would wear, and not the sexy woman standing in front of me. Dani's legs look like they're a million miles long, unfortunately covered up by the pants of her jumpsuit.

Bern's is one of those places where you don't know if it's pretentious in a very real sense or an ironic one. We're led to a private room, all wood paneled and cluttered with portraits, where the waiter takes his job very seriously.

It's a long, lingering meal. We dissect the game over expertly cooked steak, mashed potatoes, and some kind of fancy broccoli. Everything is tender and flavorful and I'm terrified to see what it will all cost. After what seems like a million courses, we're led upstairs to the dessert room.

"I can't tell if it's nice or rude that they made us get up out of our seats to eat dessert," Olivia jokes as we settle around a new table. The dessert room has dim lighting, with semi-enclosed tables that feel like we're in our own little bubble.

"I'll take one of everything," Will says when our new waitress appears. She chuckles politely before her eyes land on me and there's instant recognition. This is a bizarre experience for me still—and despite all of Dani's belief in me and the wins behind me, every time someone asks for a selfie or autograph, imposter syndrome rears up within me.

The waitress—Kaitlyn—takes our orders, laughing and flirting when she can. I don't know if I'm reading into anything, but Dani's tone with her is curt and almost dismissive. Then again, Dani's not exactly rainbows and sunshine—though she's been very warm with my family thus far.

When Kaitlyn leaves, Dani's staring down at the table, fidgeting with her napkin. I reach under the table and nudge her foot with mine. "Hey," I say, "What'd you order?" Even though I know exactly what she ordered, I just want an excuse to get her eyes on me.

"The espresso mousse cake," she tells me, her own coffee-brown eyes gazing steadily at me. Her walls are up and all I want to do is break them down. I leave my foot pressed against hers. She doesn't move away.

"Thanks for coming with us," I tell her.

"You should be thanking her for more than that, sweetheart," my mom cuts in from the far side of the table. Of course my mom is in the middle of our conversation. "We wouldn't be here without her."

I tilt my head at Dani. "Really?" Her eyes immediately return to the table, rearranging cutlery. "Tell me more, Mom."

"Danielle called us on Friday night and said she'd like to arrange a trip for us. Worked everything out for us from flights to the rental car. Apparently that's a typical surprise for the rookie players."

"Is that so?"

Dani presses her lips together, giving a half-hearted, "Mmh-mm."

"Dude, being in the NFL is lit," Will says from across the table.

"Well, how about making your grades lit, hmm?" my dad says. Will groans, rolling his eyes.

My parents start politely chiding Will about his grades and I turn my attention back to Dani.

"So, what other rookie have you done this for this season?" I raise my brows and I can feel the nerves coming off of her in waves.

"Oh, um, I don't know. I don't arrange all of them. Just . . . this one."

"I see." I lean forward, putting the heat on her. "And how'd you get my mom's number?"

She waves a hand, trying to sound casual, but her voice comes out in a squeak. "It's in your paperwork."

"Oh, right. My 'paperwork,'" I say with a smirk, knowing full well I didn't put my mom's number in any "paperwork."

I can't help but laugh. Because Dani Marshall may have her walls up—but they're coming down. Slowly but surely. I press my foot against hers again and say in sincerity, "Thank you, Dani. This was really special."

She gazes up at me through her eyelashes. "You're welcome, Austin."

After dessert, we're waiting for our cars at the valet. Dani's car pulls up and she hugs my family members one by one, saying goodbye. I stand by, waiting for my hug. I've never hugged Dani Marshall before—and even though I'm not quite sure I want this to be the first time, with my family present—I'll take whatever I can get when it comes to Dani. But when she finally reaches me, instead of her arms going around me, she thrusts out a hand.

For a handshake.

My brows raise and I let her hand linger between us for a long moment before I take it. She's about to shake my hand and move on when, at the last second, I tug her into me, wrapping my other hand around her back for a hug. Albeit an awkward one, with our hands caught between us.

I lean my head down to her ear and whisper, "Thank you for bringing my family here. Though you have some explaining to do about how you got my mom's number."

Dani steps back, a smile tugging at her lips. "I told you, I'm good with numbers."

I laugh, shaking my head as she walks toward her car, turning to wave to my family once more.

"Austin," Olivia hisses at me. "This is the part where you walk her to her car and kiss her, you idiot."

"Or at the very least ask her on a proper date," my mom says.

"You could tip the valet for her," my dad adds.

I turn to my family, hands splayed toward them. "Does anyone else have an opinion on what I should do?"

"You definitely shouldn't let her get away," Will says with a shrug.

I scoff, pivoting my gaze to where Dani's getting into her car. And before I can stop myself, I'm jogging to her car. By the time I reach her, she's already inside with the door closed. She rolls her window down and gazes up at me. I lean my arms into the window, lowering my head so it's only inches from hers.

"Olivia says I should kiss you," I blurt. I thought she'd laugh at this, but instead she stares at me, wide-eyed. "But I think I'll take my mom's advice instead."

"What's that?"

"Can I take you out, Dani Marshall?"

She bites her lip.

"No family members, just me and you. We could go fancy or chill, whatever you want." *I don't care what we do, as long as I'm with you*, I want to add, but I don't.

"Austin . . . " Dani stares straight ahead, her hands gripping the steering wheel as she considers what she's going to say to me.

My heart is beating so hard in my chest that I'm sure Dani could see it if she glanced at me. I shift my weight, trying to maintain a casual air even though I'm practically screaming in my head: *say yes, say yes, say yes.*

"We're just friends," she says finally, though the look in her eyes when she eventually looks back at me tells me that she views me as more than that. "We can only ever be friends."

And with that, Dani pats me on the arm. I step back and she drives away.

Just like that.

38

Dani

Studies show that getting your hair done can reduce stress levels by up to 60%. (And, it's 100% effective in avoiding a certain NFL quarterback.)

Austin Taylor asked me out.

Which means two things: I'm epically failing at keeping my distance from him. And, Claire was right. He likes me.

Or, at least, he *did* like me. Before I patted his arm like he was a toddler and told him we're just friends—even when everything in me was screaming to just say yes.

So I responded like any reasonable person would: I'm dodging him like a QB evading a blitzing linebacker.

And one of the best ways I can think of avoiding Austin Taylor is by getting my hair done. I have such a love/hate relationship with going to Tetee's Salon. On the one hand, I love getting a reset on my hair and it's nice to talk to people who don't have anything to do with football. On the other hand, I always feel anxious taking time away from work—*a lot* of time. As in, four to six hours in the middle of a work day.

Two nights ago, I re-watched our game against the Ravens while unbraiding and deep conditioning my hair. This morning, I got up extra early to tackle my emails before heading to the salon. I've tried charting games while sitting in Tetee's salon chair before—but Tetee doesn't stop talking long enough for me to pay attention to any plays.

Since Tetee's is in Ybor City, I stop by La Segunda Bakery for breakfast sandwiches and cafe con leches for Tetee, her mom—Bisi—and me. The rich, buttery aroma of freshly baked Cuban bread mingles with the savory scent of sizzling bacon and the creamy, sharp notes of melted cheese, making my mouth water. As I take a deep breath, the faint, smoky fragrance of ham wafts up, adding to the symphony of scents filling my car during my ride to the salon.

The familiar chime of the doorbell rings as I step into the braiding salon. The air is thick with the sweet scent of shea butter and the hum of chatter and laughter.

"Dani! My favorite client!" Tetee calls out from her station, a wide grin spreading across her face. I'm sure she says that to all of her clients, but I still come to expect it—and appreciate it. Her hands are deftly weaving intricate patterns into a young girl's hair, but she gestures for me to take a seat on one of the overstuffed chairs at the front next to the girl's mom.

"I brought you breakfast," I say to Tetee, holding up the brown paper bag and tray of drinks. Bisi walks out from the back and snatches up the bag.

"I know you brought something for me," she says with a wink. She sits in the chair across from me as we eat our breakfast sandwiches—greasy and dripping into the paper on our laps.

I think of Austin and how he'd give me a hard time for forcing him to eat a balanced breakfast while I eat something that actually tastes good. I remind myself that I'm here at the salon to forget about Austin—not entertain thoughts of his stupidly handsome face.

"You look tired, Dani," Bisi says.

"What every girl wants to hear."

She leans in, whispering, "A boy keeping you up at night?"

I almost groan. If only she knew. "You know me, Bisi. No time for that," I say, forcing a smile that feels more like a mask.

There's a television on the far wall of the salon, which alternates between cheesy romantic comedies and CNN. When Bisi has control of the remote, it's a rom-com. When Tetee's in charge, it's CNN. This morning, it's on CNN so we watch a few minutes of weather news while polishing off our sandwiches.

Tetee finishes up with her client and waves me over to her chair. Bisi brings out the hair extensions, a slight chemical smell following her. She has my regular color along with some red that Tetee will weave into my braids. The perfect shade of Buccaneer red.

"Go eat your sandwich," Bisi instructs her daughter. "I'll get her started."

Tetee shrugs and takes her sandwich to the back room. Bisi puts a crooked finger to her lips, shushing me as she riffles through her daughter's station. When she produces the remote control, she raises her hands in a silent cheer before changing the channel on the TV. She tucks the remote in between her ample bust and begins sectioning off my hair, putting pieces into clips, her fingers moving with practiced ease.

When Tetee comes back in, she immediately chides her mom for changing the channel. "Dani doesn't want to watch this! It kills off brain cells," she huffs. "Like marshmallow fluff for your brain."

"Dani has plenty of brain cells to spare," Bisi says, looking at me to defend my brain cells. I hold up my hands, unwilling to get in the middle of this battle. If it were up to me, we'd be watching the Chargers vs. Saints game, but nobody asked, so here we are.

When they start braiding, Tetee and Bisi take opposite sides of my head, starting at the front and working their way back as they weave the extensions into my hair. I'm always surprised at Bisi's gnarled fingers and the speed with which they can still braid. I watch her through the mirror, mesmerized.

Tetee catches me up on how her children are doing—one daughter in law school, the other practicing medicine, and a son still in high school. Both daughters are unmarried and focused on their careers, just like Tetee trained them. She recounts her son's latest escapades, bemoaning his focus on soccer instead of school. The syllables in her words rise and fall like each sentence is a song, each word harmonizing with the next.

I close my eyes, the familiar rhythm and gentle tug of their hands lulling me into a place where I eventually tell them about everything I'm going through—from signing Austin to Nolan getting injured the same week that Drake got sent to rehab, then Austin taking the starting QB position and the bet I made with Ethan.

I don't know how these women manage to do this every time—but as their skilled hands work, my walls come down, and I spill my guts, finding solace in their understanding eyes.

As soon as I'm done detailing our Bern's outing, Bisi comes to Austin's defense with the gusto of a Nigerian grandma, her voice rising in passionate conviction. "Ah, Dani, you see, a man like Austin is rare. He takes you to Berns, that's a man who knows how to treat a lady! You should not be so quick to dismiss him."

I open my mouth to tell her that I was the one to make the reservations for Bern's, but Tetee's already saying, "You don't need a man, Dani. Keep focusing on your career, you're making something of yourself. Love can wait."

Normally, I'd be buoyed by Tetee's words. But today, they fall short and I'm left wondering if she's right after all.

"Career is important," Bisi agrees, her tone serious as she dips the end of my braid into boiling hot water to seal the braid. The steam rises, and I watch in fascination as the synthetic hair transforms, becoming flexible and smooth, almost like it's coming to life. "But love is what makes life sweet. Don't be like me, waiting too long."

Though I try not to let her words affect me, they do. These past few weeks with Austin have felt sweeter, though perhaps that's just because it's nice to have him as a friend. I realize that they're both looking at me expectantly, so I say, "I promise, if there's ever any news, you two will be the first to know." Though I'm quite certain there will never be any news between Austin Taylor and me. I'm sure he'll move right along to whatever supermodel bats her eyelashes at him first.

Tetee exchanges a knowing glance with Bisi. "We'll hold you to that," she says gravely.

The conversation shifts to lighter topics—weekend plans, the latest salon gossip, and upcoming events. With each dip of my braids in the boiling water, my hair feels more secure and vibrant, adding to the intricate pattern forming on my scalp. The subtle scent of the Kanekalon hair mingles with the fragrance of the hair products, creating an oddly comforting aroma that fills the room. I wasn't exactly sure how the style would look on me, with the red woven into the braids, but I love it. It's not too overpowering—Tetee kept the red pieces thin and interspersed with the rest of the hair, just like I asked her to. A little bit of team spirit, without looking gaudy.

With every braid, I feel a little more like myself, a little more centered. Even though I'm usually resistant to spending so much time here, I'm always glad I came. The salon is a haven, a place where I'm surrounded by these strong, vibrant women who care about me beyond the statistics and plays that dominate my life. They remind me of the importance of balance, of taking time to nurture not just my career, but my heart as well.

When Tetee finishes, I look at my reflection and smile. The braids are perfect, as always. I'll probably have a headache tomorrow from the tight braids, but beauty is pain, isn't it? "Thanks, Tetee. I feel like a new woman."

"Anytime, Dani," Tetee says, giving my shoulder a reassuring squeeze. "Remember, you're making something of yourself. You don't need anyone holding you back."

Bisi, standing nearby, gives me a knowing look. "But also remember, Dani, life is more than work. Make room for love."

As I leave the salon, I feel a renewed sense of possibility. Maybe the time is coming to let a little more than football into my life. Maybe it's time to see if there's something—or someone—out there worth making room for. But for now, my heart and mind are tangled up in Austin, and I'm not quite ready to unravel those knots.

39

Austin

> Draw Play: A running play disguised as a pass. The quarterback drops back as if to pass, then hands the ball to a running back who takes advantage of the defense's pass rush to gain yards.

In the days after our dinner at Berns, Dani Marshall goes back to being elusive. She begs off watching film with me for three days straight and I'm beginning to think I've royally screwed things up with us. She's come up with an excuse each day—a doctor's appointment, extra work, getting her hair done ... but who has a doctor's appointment at six a.m. on a Monday? We've gone from watching film together five days a week, having lunch together most days, a bi-weekly yoga session, and plenty of playbook memorization together to zero interaction.

I still haven't seen her by Wednesday after practice. We've showered and are heading to physical therapy. The guys are discussing the new physical therapist, Allie, and are doing what naturally happens when there's an overabundance of testosterone. They're dissecting her.

"She's fit," Malik says, waxing poetic about some of Allie's standout physical traits.

"I'm more of a face guy," Jordan says. This leads to them debating whether Allie's face is nice enough for someone who's a "face guy."

Landon turns to me. "What about you? Face guy or body guy?"

I'll be honest, I don't know why I have to decide between the two, but I'm not about to share that with these guys. My mind inadvertently flits to Dani, with her exquisite face and her body, which is utter perfection. But she's so much more than that. "I'm more of a mind guy," I say with a cheeky grin, thinking of Dani's brilliance.

Landon rolls his eyes, like he knows I'm not being honest. Jordan seems confused. Malik, on the other hand, lets out a loud, "Brrrooooooo," and smacks me on the shoulder. "Austin's got those spicy vibes."

I shrug off his hand. "Nah, man."

Landon, who sighs like he's managing a bunch of toddlers, says, "Austin's trying to pretend like he's above this conversation by saying that he likes smart girls."

Malik isn't buying it though. He waggles his brows at me and taps his forehead. "I see you, man. I see you."

When we head into the PT room, Allie is assigned to me and the guys keep making faces at me like we're in middle school. As we work together, I can acknowledge that Allie is cute—she's petite, blonde, and has nice eyes—but there's no attraction there. At least not on my part.

After our session focusing on mobility and strengthening exercises, Allie walks with me out to the hallway, giving me some tips on my shoulder stability and core strength. But as we walk,

I get the sense there's more here than her just wanting to give me some extra help. She uses any and every excuse to lean into me, touch my arm, and laugh wildly at anything I say that's remotely funny. She's a cute girl, I should find this charming or endearing, but I totally don't.

I stop at the doors to the parking lot—mostly because I don't want to keep talking in the hot sun, and because I'm afraid Allie might climb into my car with me if given half a chance. She's continuing to talk about stretches and my eyes begin to roam the hallway, looking for someone to interrupt this conversation.

That is, of course, when Dani Marshall rounds the corner.

The flash of envy that sparks in her eyes when she sees me talking with Allie is all I need to keep hope alive. I give Dani a casual nod—as if she hasn't been blowing me off all week—and return my gaze to Allie. I lean forward, nodding and smiling as if what she's saying is the most engaging thing I've ever heard. I feel Dani's eyes burning into us and it's insanely satisfying.

Once Dani's walked past us, I tell Allie I've got to get going. She gives me a sad smile and I get out of there before she can talk to me any more about stretches I'm never going to do. Unless it's with Dani, then I'll do them.

By the time I get home, I've got a text message waiting for me:

Dani

Film tomorrow?

The next morning, when Dani's late for watching film, I think she's blowing me off again. I pick up my phone to order myself some food—I scrambled here and skipped breakfast—when I notice another text from her:

> **I can't watch film. I've got a migraine.**

I stare at the message for too long, wondering if she's still in avoidance mode or if she really does have a migraine. I text back:

> **Can I bring you something?**

Three dots appear on the screen, so I know she's typing back. They appear and disappear several times before finally she says:

> **Caffeine.**

I'm surprised that Dani actually texted me back, and that she's taking me up on my offer to help. She must really be struggling.

> **Pick your poison, I'll be there soon.**

I don't know what someone with a migraine might want—other than caffeine, apparently—so I Google it. Twenty minutes later, I'm coming out of CVS with a headache ice pack, some essential oils, Gin-Gins, and over-the-counter pain meds. Dani texted me her caffeine requirements, so I pick that up as well and head to her house.

She texted me the code to get into her condo building and left her front door open for me, so when I arrive, I step inside. Her condo is dark, cool, and very quiet.

"Dani?"

Her voice comes out weak and thready, "In here."

I head to her bedroom, pausing in her doorway. Blackout curtains keep her room dark, but I can still make out her form in her bed. She's propped up in bed with some kind of silk wrap on her head and an eye mask over her eyes. But she must sense that I'm here because she says, "Hey."

I take that as my cue to enter. "I've got your Coke," I whisper. She shifts her mask up, her eyes fluttering up at me in a way that makes my chest tight. She sits up, reaching for the cup.

"Thank you," she says in a low voice. "I don't have any in my house. It'll only make my migraine worse if I skip my morning caffeine."

I kneel beside her bed, my head level with hers. "No need to explain," I tell her, though I'm grateful for the explanation, since it helps me understand what she needs. "I would've bought you a pony if you told me that's what you wanted to help you feel better."

I might be seeing what I want to see, but I swear the corners of her mouth pull up slightly. "I'm more of a dog person," she says. And I know that she's whispering because she has a migraine, but there's something about her low, husky voice that's driving me wild. It's actually probably a good thing that she's got a migraine—or else I might make decisions that aren't the smartest right now.

"Have you eaten?" I ask.

"Mm-mm," she says as she takes a sip of Coke. "I'm just feeling nauseous."

"I got some Gin-Gins." I pull the bag of ginger chews out of the CVS bag and hand them to her. "What if I made you some toast or something light for your stomach?"

"Okay," she says, and the way she says it, I can tell she's uncomfortable with me taking care of her. And for some reason, it makes me want to take care of her all the more. But I don't want to smother her, so I leave her in peace while I make toast and put the ice pack in the freezer. I notice she has a similar contraption already in the freezer, so I take it out to thaw a bit while I make her toast.

I spend the next few minutes making sure Dani eats before getting her medicine and setting up the aromatherapy next to her bed. When she's finished her Coke, she pulls the headache ice pack that I brought her from the freezer down over her eyes and sinks lower into her bed.

While I'm tidying up, she lets out a tiny groan—and I know immediately that she didn't mean to, she wouldn't let on how much she's struggling if she could help it at all.

"Would it help if I rubbed your head?"

"Can you apply pressure, but don't rub?"

"Show me what you mean," I tell her, lifting her hand to my head. She peeks from under her ice pack, finding my head with her other hand. Her fingers press into my scalp and then lift, find another spot, press down and then lift.

"Like that," she whispers and I almost want to cup her hands with mine, to keep them on me. Instead, I put my hands on her head, pressing down in just the way she showed me.

"How's that?"

She gives a little moan in response and I take it to mean I'm doing it right. I press on her head for several minutes, kneeling beside her bed in silence. I watch her face, every flinch of her mouth, every exhale. I study her lips, the way they part when she wants to say something then . . . doesn't.

Finally, Dani says the thing she's wanted to say: "So, that new physical therapist is cute." Her tone is casual, but I can feel the tension in her body.

"She sure is." I smile at her, even though she can't see it. I want to laugh because I know exactly what game she's playing: Dani Marshall wants to have her cake and eat it too. And I wonder if I'm one step closer to breaking down her walls.

I could kiss her right now.

Her eyes are closed, covered by the ice pack. She wouldn't even know it until my lips were on hers.

I don't—I absolutely won't kiss Dani Marshall unless she truly wants me to—but I could.

And something tells me she'd let me.

"I thought you were avoiding me, when I saw your text," I tell her, because I need to distract myself from thoughts of kissing her.

"I *was* avoiding you. I was avoiding you so hard it made my head explode." She pinches the bridge of her nose between her thumb and forefinger.

"It's not nice to avoid your friends," I tease.

She's silent for a moment before she says, "Is that what we are, Austin?" Her voice is so soft, I can barely hear it. "Friends?"

When I don't answer right away, she lifts the edge of her ice pack, squinting at me from underneath her curly lashes. I smile as I stand up, needing to leave for practice.

"For now," I tell her.

End Zone Report ✓
@endzonereport

The Bucs continue their win streak, defeating the Chargers at home 27-19.

10:17 PM · Oct 20, 2024 · Twitter for Android

265 Retweets 4876 Likes

GridironGeek @gridirongeek · 1h
@Replying to

@FieldAnalyst this is becoming a pattern . . .

FieldAnalyst @fieldanalyst · 1h
@Replying to

@GridironGeek you need to meet my co-worker. Both of you are Austin Taylor groupies. If he farted, you'd say it smelled like roses. It's nauseating.

GridironGeek @gridirongeek · 1h
@Replying to

@FieldAnalyst sounds like we would get along.

FieldAnalyst @fieldanalyst · 1h
@Replying to

@GridironGeek for all intensive purposes, my coworker is like your twin! 😉

40

Dani

Despite the clear statistical advantage of going for it on 4th and short, many NFL teams remain conservative. In the 2020 season, only 28.4% of 4th and short situations saw teams go for it, preferring to punt or attempt a field goal instead.

The conference room buzzes with low conversations as the coaching staff and analysts settle in for the weekly meeting. Coach Clive stands at the front, his hands resting on the large table covered with playbooks and game notes.

"Alright, let's get started," Coach Clive begins, his voice commanding the room's attention. "We need to go over our performance against the Chargers and see what adjustments we can make moving forward."

Everyone's pretty pumped about our performance, so the comments are largely positive until Ethan cuts in with his analysis. "I've been looking at our fourth down situations, and statistically, we should be going for it more often. We are punting too much in those situations and it's hurting our win probability."

Coach Clive raises an eyebrow. "And you're basing this on what, exactly?"

Ethan pulls up the stats on his computer, turning it around so the coaches can see. "This is data from our last five games. On fourth and short, we've converted 67% of the time. Every time we punt when we should go for it, we give up about 1.2 expected points. In simple terms, most of the time it's much more beneficial to go for it than to punt, which is an automatic loss of possession."

The room is silent for a moment as the coaches exchange skeptical glances. "Ethan, you know as well as I do that statistics don't always account for the real-life pressure on the field," Coach Martinez, the defensive coach, interjects.

"But they do account for the potential gain," I speak up, my voice firm. "The numbers show that we have a higher chance of maintaining possession, scoring and therefore winning if we are willing to follow the data and buck convention."

Coach Clive leans back in his chair, contemplating. "Sounds risky."

"Calculated risks offer proportionate rewards," Ethan insists. "If we don't take these chances, we're limiting our own potential. We may have won this game, but we will lose more in the long run. Look, the Ravens game showed we can compete, but we need to push our boundaries to maximize our potential."

Martinez continues to defend his position, saying, "When we choose to punt in those fourth down situations, it's because the momentum isn't on our side."

"We don't need momentum on our side when the stats are on our side," I say.

"The problem with momentum," Ethan says, "is that you can't quantify it, whereas—"

"I been a coach for thirty-five years," cuts in our assistant coach, Gary Hershon. "And you better believe I can quantify momentum."

"Look, at the end of the day, we trust our defense and sometimes you have to play the field position game," Martinez says.

"To win games we have to score more points than the other team," Ethan says, his voice dripping with disdain. "Defense does not win games."

"*Our* defense wins games since our franchise quarterback broke his leg," Martinez charges back at Ethan.

Beside me, Ethan scoffs. I can tell he gives up the argument when he leans back in his chair, crossing his arms over his chest.

I'm about to open my mouth to respond to Martinez myself when Coach Clive gives a polite nod and says, "We'll consider it. But for now, let's move on to the rest of the game analysis."

The meeting continues, but Ethan and I exchange a glance. After the meeting wraps up, we linger behind as the rest of the staff files out. Ethan groans, pinching the bridge of his nose. "Dude," he says to me.

"I know."

"That was brutal. It's like these boomers don't understand basic probabilities at all."

"Gotta get our punter out there," I say in a mock-voice to sound like Martinez. "Or else we won't win this game."

Ethan cackles. "Hey, that's a pretty good impression."

I smile. "Thanks."

"Thanks for backing me up."

"I stand with the numbers," I tease. This is the first time Ethan and I have bonded over our positions with the coaches. It's refreshing to not be at each other's throats.

"I just couldn't even argue with them anymore when they started talking about defense winning games," he says with a snort. I think about what Austin said about guys like Ethan—that he'll argue if he respects you. It was clear when he gave up arguing with Martinez because our defensive coordinator was being illogical. Ethan's never done that with me, and now I'm wondering if Austin was right and it is a sign of respect.

"Well, the numbers are right. And I got your back the next time it comes up." And then, I do the strangest thing I've ever done: I reach my hand out to fist bump Ethan Driver. We knock fists like this is no big deal and go about the rest of our work day.

But it feels like a small miracle.

41

Austin

> In 2019 alone, the NFL and its teams contributed over $500 million to various community initiatives and charitable causes, including health and wellness, education, and youth football programs.

On Tuesday after the Chargers game, we have a PR event for the grand opening of the ViaTech Center for Equine Assisted Therapy. Before the season began, all of the players chose non-profits we wanted to support. Since my cousin is a wheelchair user after a car accident, I was drawn to the equine-assisted therapy center that offered specialized therapy for wheelchair users. Apparently, the organization started in Ft. Lauderdale and is now expanding to Tampa. I'm supposed to come, take some pictures and sign some autographs.

But we're also flying to London on Friday for our game against the Rams and we've added new plays to combat the Rams' formidable pass rush. The plays have Dani Marshall written all over them—a way of combining my strengths as a passer with Coach Clive's love for play action. But there's so many variations on each play, it's difficult to keep them straight.

Even though I need to spend my afternoon with my nose in the playbook, I want to honor my commitment to ViaTech. But it doesn't stop me from trying to kill two birds with one stone. "Hey," I say when Dani picks up. "I gotta go to this PR opp. It's almost an hour away. Any chance you're free to come with me and quiz me on the plays?"

Dani agrees quicker than I thought she would—and I wonder if I've officially taken a few bricks off of Dani Marshall's impenetrable wall.

I drive while Dani quizzes me—chiding me when I don't know a play and giving me a quick nod with a small smile when I get it right. It might be the most effective training method out there—I'm beginning to live to see this girl smile.

When we arrive, I spend some time taking pictures and talking to the media. Then there's a presentation in one of the arenas. A man named Luke, wearing a cowboy hat, sits in the center of the ring in a wheelchair. He introduces himself as the lead therapist for ViaTech and then presents one of the owners, Anya, who's atop a large black horse.

Luke begins to tell Anya's story. She was once a Grand Prix show jumper who had a tragic accident that resulted in her being paralyzed from the neck down from an incomplete spinal cord injury. She was bedbound, depressed, and had given up on life. When her sister found a way to get her back in the saddle—using specialized equipment and assistance from her now-husband, Alex—it changed Anya's life. After that first ride, Anya was able to regain motion in her fingers. Over the course of months, with a lot of therapy, Anya's mobility increased until she had the ability to use her shoulders and arms.

"Of course," Luke says. "Not all of us are as lucky as Anya. But it's not a coincidence that Anya regained movement in her arms after riding. Horses are remarkable healers." He goes on to recount various ways that horses benefit their riders, particularly from a therapeutic perspective. "And the benefits aren't just physical—it's emotional as well. Horses are excellent at helping humans regulate their emotions."

At this point, Anya and her mount are standing beside Luke, who puts his hand on the horse's chest. "Horse's hearts are much larger than ours, and they offer what's called heart rate variability coherence, which is a fancy word to say that when you're around a horse, your heart rate starts to sync up with theirs. This has a calming effect for us, and you don't even need to ride to experience this, simply being around the horse will help."

Together, Luke and Anya go through a brief version of what a therapy session might look like while on horseback. After they're done, the visitors are invited to join Luke and Anya and the other volunteers and therapists in the barn to groom the horses for an on-the-ground therapy example.

I'm really trying hard to focus on the presentation, but I keep glancing over at Dani, tracing her lips with my eyes. My mind flits back to last week when she had a migraine and I was so close to her, inches away from pressing my lips against hers. I wonder—not for the first time—what she would do if I did kiss her. Just like that, my mind is whirring away as I picture a lonely corner of this barn where I could kiss her senseless.

If only she'd let me.

42

Dani

A study published in the Journal of Alternative and Complementary Medicine found that 80% of participants experienced improved balance, muscle strength, and motor skills after participating in therapeutic riding sessions. Additionally, 75% reported enhanced emotional regulation and reduced symptoms of anxiety and depression.

I'm standing next to a massive horse, rubbing him down with a round brush that's apparently called a curry comb. It's a cooler day today—for Florida—and I can feel the warmth coming off the horse. And, to be honest, I don't know if I want to run away from this huge, scary horse or if I want to lean into his warmth.

Which is exactly how I feel about Austin Taylor.

I glance over at him as he chats with the owner and therapist, Anya and Luke. Austin is one of those people who seems to get along with everyone—when I'm with him, I feel like his smile and the glimmer in his gorgeous eyes are just for me. But watching him with other people, I see that he's like that with everyone. So at ease with the world, so able to open up and let people into his orbit.

It makes me feel foolish for thinking I'm something special to him. Sure, he asked me out, but what does that really mean? He's Austin Taylor—he could have literally any girl in the world right now.

Eventually, Austin leads Anya and Luke over to me, both of them wheeling through the barn aisles in their wheelchairs. Luke's in a manual chair but Anya's looks like a futuristic contraption with a gazillion buttons.

Austin introduces me to them and Luke says, "You're Darius Marshall's daughter, right?"

I nod, surprised. Unless Austin told Luke who I am, very few people know that detail about me.

"My dad went to UF at the same time as your dad. He always raves about those being the glory days of Gator football. He's always kept tabs on your dad since then."

"Ah, yes. I've heard too much about those *glory days*," I say, using air quotes. "Are you a Gator fan too?"

Luke takes a utility knife off of his belt, flipping the knife out and turning the handle toward me so he's handing me the knife. "Cut me open," he says. "I'll bleed orange and blue."

Beside him, Anya rolls her eyes, grabbing the knife handle from him. "You'll have to excuse Mr. Craig," she says dryly. "He has a taste for theatrics."

"You love it though," Luke says, flirtation coating his words.

"I endure it," Anya says with a completely straight face. "For the sake of your six pack." She shrugs at me when she sees my eyebrows raise at her comment. "It's quite phenomenal," she says matter-of-factly. "Don't just take my word for it, he'll be happy to show you. It's half the reason he has it in the first place."

Luke shakes his head, grinning. "She's always trying to get me to take my shirt off," he says, waggling his brows. "But I keep telling her it's *unprofessional*."

Anya's facade slips as she laughs, slapping Luke's chest. It's then that I notice the huge diamond ring glinting on her hand. Luke captures her hand, kissing it. I glance over at Austin, unsure if we should back away and give these two some space—but Austin's watching them with warmth.

To be fair, they *are* adorable. I just don't know what to do with these kinds of displays of affection. "You guys have built something really fantastic here," I say when it looks like Luke is inches away from pulling Anya into his lap. "I appreciated your story. You've gone through a lot."

"Everyone needs healing," Anya says, putting her professional face back on. "Some of us, our need for it is a little more obvious. And, honestly, because of that it's easier in some ways to get help. It's those of us with the hidden hurts that need the extra help. And horses can do that for us." She gives me a look, her blue eyes boring into me like she can see every wound within.

I'm grateful when a staffer interrupts Luke and Austin, pulling them in the opposite direction. Anya grabs a brush and starts running it over the horse's coat. The horse, whom she introduces to me as Harry, has a golden-brown coat with a white mane and tail. I follow Anya's lead and brush the top of the horse while she brushes the horse at wheelchair height.

"So, Miss Marshall, what wounds of yours need healing today?"

I balk, and she must sense it because she laughs. "You don't have to tell me," she says. "Tell him." She waves a hand at the horse and with that, rolls away. I watch her for a moment, wondering how she could know that I have wounds—but then, maybe when you've gone through what she's gone through, you can see more than the average person.

I pivot back to Harry and place a hesitant hand on his cheek, warmth spreading into my palm. Do I really need healing? I wonder.

I feel fine.

Lies. A small voice within me says.

Okay, so I'm not *great*—but I'm perfectly content with my life and the way things are.

Laughter catches my attention and my eyes find Austin. I envy his easy way, how relaxed and at home he is in his own skin. He's not afraid of life—seemingly content if he's off the bench or on it. How does a person get like that?

The answer comes to me unbidden and painful: love. A person gets to be like that because they've been loved so deeply, so fully, that they're infinitely at home in themselves.

And as much as my dad has loved me in my life, I've been missing the love of my mom for over a decade. At the minimum, I'm down 50% of my allotted love from my parents. And, if I'm being honest with myself, I feel like Heather and the twins have stolen some of my other 50% allotment.

It's a difficult admission—it smacks of bitterness—but it feels good to acknowledge it.

I press my forehead into the crook of the horse's neck and head—absorbing his warmth, and also whatever intangible healing power he has. I was skeptical before, when Anya and Luke were talking. But being here, processing these hurts and feelings, I'm becoming a believer. There's something magic here as I let the tears flow—mourning my mother's death in a way I haven't as an adult. Acknowledging the resentment I've felt toward my dad for remarrying and starting a new family where I felt like I didn't fit in.

But right here, right now, in this moment, I feel like I can let go of that for the first time in a long time.

43

Austin

> Queen of the Night: A rare type of cactus flower that blooms exclusively at night and only once a year. The blossoms are large, fragrant, and spectacular, but they typically last only for a single night, making the event a special and fleeting experience.

On the way home from ViaTech, Dani is quiet as she stares out the window while I drive. She seems pensive, thoughtful. I want to burrow into her mind, to understand what makes her tick—but Dani strikes me as the kind of person that needs to be coaxed into opening up. Slowly, gently. Like a rare flower blooming in the dead of night.

We drive for about twenty minutes without a word between us, until Dani says, "I think I've been mad at my dad for getting remarried." She's staring out the window, and her voice is so small that it almost seems like she's talking to herself. I really don't know what the best move is here, if I should ask her questions or keep silent to give her space to keep talking.

After a beat of silence, I say, "Tell me more."

And, surprisingly, she does. She tells me about the early days after her mom's death, when she and her dad were like ghosts, barely present in their lives. The pain of waking up morning after morning to realize her mom was still gone. Adjusting to life with one parent instead of two—and a parent with a high-stress, demanding job at that. Getting dragged from meeting to meeting during after-school hours and finding that she liked the front office work of football. When we stop at a red light, I notice her fingers trembling slightly as she speaks, her gaze unfocused, as if she's looking at something far beyond the window.

"I felt like I was finally getting used to our rhythm when he married Heather and it changed again," she says, fiddling with one of her braid cuffs. I've noticed she switches them out regularly. Today, her cuffs are silver and she has a few cuffs on one braid, stacked at various intervals. "All of a sudden I was a daughter again, but to a mom who wasn't mine—and wasn't anything like my mom."

At this, I reach out and gently take her hand as Alex Warren's "Carry You Home" plays on the radio. The warmth of her skin surprises me, grounding me in this moment. It's a tentative connection, fragile yet strong, like a lifeline in the midst of her emotional storm. I hold my breath as I twine my fingers through hers—at first, I think she won't let me. But she squeezes my fingers, her other hand going to her mouth, and I sense that she's holding back tears.

The rest of the drive, I hold Dani's hand, letting her talk when she needs to, and sitting in silence when she has nothing left to say.

44

Dani

> Studies have shown that making deals with handsome quarterbacks can lead to heart problems such as rapid heart rate, skipping heart beats, and, in some extreme cases, falling in love.

This week, we're prepping for a game in London against the Los Angeles Rams. We have a slight advantage over the Rams in this setting because coming from Tampa, there's only a five-hour time difference for us in London versus an eight-hour time change for them. And at this stage, we're looking to use any advantage we can find.

We're on our way to yoga on Thursday when I tell Austin, "If we win this game, you know what that means, don't you?"

"That we won your bet and you get to keep your car?" Austin runs his hands over the dashboard as he speaks.

"Well, yes, that," I say. "But it also means that your win percentage will be 66.67%, that's the top third of the league. Not bad for a lowly UDFA who was third on the depth chart."

We're stopped at a stoplight on Kennedy Blvd and I feel Austin's eyes on me, making me think back to my conversation with Claire.

"I love how much you love your numbers," Austin says with a cheeky grin, his words—and eyes—making me uncomfortably hot. "Alright, what will we do if we win the London game? I think we'll have to celebrate."

"Sure," I say noncommittally.

"Dani." Austin levels his gaze at me. "If we win, you owe me a celebration. One where I can eat whatever I want."

I laugh, rolling my eyes. "Fine, fine. If you win, we'll celebrate."

"If *we* win, we celebrate."

I swallow, pressing on the gas as the light turns green. I might regret this later, but I say, "Deal."

45

Austin

Research from the Journal of Sports Science & Medicine shows that NFL teams experiencing a time zone change of three hours or more can see a noticeable impact on player performance and recovery time. Specifically, teams facing a five-hour time change, like the Buccaneers, have a 15% higher win rate compared to those with an eight-hour time change, such as the Rams.

The air in London is crisp and cool as we step onto the field at Tottenham Hotspur Stadium. The crowd, a mix of Bucs and Rams fans and Londoners just looking for a good game, buzzes in anticipation, electrifying the atmosphere. The Rams are tough; their defense is fierce.

This is going to be a battle.

From the first snap, it's clear that the Rams came to play. Their defense is relentless, and we scrabble for every yard. I drop back, scanning the field. Jordan Ellis is covered, but Mike Donnelly breaks free on a slant route. I sling the ball at him, and he catches it. Their defense tackles him but he holds on to the ball. We move the chains with a critical first down.

Our offensive line, led by Mosi and Tank, is holding strong, giving me just enough time to make my reads. But the Rams' defense just keeps coming. Isaiah takes a hand off and breaks through the line, before he's quickly brought down. Landon manages to push through for a few more yards, but it's tough going.

We're down by a touchdown—13-20—as we head into the fourth quarter. The pressure is mounting, and I can feel the weight of the game on my shoulders. I take a deep breath, Dani's smile coming to mind unbidden—I want nothing more than to celebrate this win with her. And it's that thought that's propelling me forward even though the jet lag and wear and tear on my body is threatening to drag me down.

With the clock ticking down, we're on the Rams' 20-yard line. I call for the snap and drop back, looking for an opening. Malik is running a deep post route, and I see a glimmer of daylight. I let the ball fly, slicing it through the air. Malik leaps, snatching the ball from between two defenders and pulling it into his chest.

Touchdown.

The stadium erupts, but we're not finished yet. We nail the extra point to tie the game, and now the Rams have possession. Our sideline is electric—everyone's on their feet, shouting at the top of their lungs as our defense takes the field. The Rams systematically work their way down the field, making it almost to the 50-yard line with ninety seconds on the clock. It's second and short when Matthew Stafford drops back, scanning for an open man. One of our defensive ends bursts through the Rams' line, coming from Stafford's blind side, he hits him in the back.

The ball pops loose on impact and there's a mad scramble for it, with players from both teams piling on top of each other.

Mosi and Tank are beside me, nudging me as we wait to see who has possession.

The ref pulls players off and then his voice echoes through the stadium, "The ball was fumbled. Recovered by Tampa Bay. First down, Buccaneers!"

The crowd goes nuts and I almost drop my helmet as Mosi and Tank jostle me in celebration. But we can't celebrate for long—we're back on the field.

I snap my helmet on. Just over a minute to go.

This is our shot.

I huddle up with the guys, their faces set with determination. "Let's finish this," I say, and they nod, ready for battle.

We line up, and I take the snap, dropping back. Jake Foster runs a perfect seam route, and I hit him in stride. He barrels down the field, breaking tackles and pushing us into field goal range. The clock is ticking, and I signal for a spike to stop the clock.

With only seconds left, our kicker steps up and sends the ball sailing through the uprights. The final whistle blows, and we've done it.

The guys swarm me, clapping me on the back and cheering. This win was a team effort, and we pulled it off together.

As we head to the locker room, the exhaustion hits me, but it's mingled with pure elation. Tonight, we proved that we can compete with the best, and we came out on top. This is what football is all about. And I can't wait to celebrate with Dani and the team tonight.

As soon as I'm out of the shower, I call Dani. I want to catch her before she can escape to the hotel and not come out.

"We won your bet," I tell her, not able to keep the grin off my face.

"*You* won my bet," she says. "I knew you would."

Her belief in me is expansive—as if the entire galaxy swirls inside of me. I can do anything with Dani Marshall's faith in me. It makes me really happy that I have something planned tonight that may come close to measuring up to all that Dani deserves. Thanks, in large part, to Claire Beaumont and her influence. I got her number at Fresh Kitchen a few weeks ago, hoping that she'd be an ally in breaking down Dani's walls—and she's coming through in epic ways.

"We're celebrating tonight," I tell her. I don't ask, because I can't risk Dani saying no. Besides, Dani needs this just as surely as I need her belief in me.

"Oh, um." Dani's clearly scrambling for an excuse to get out of this, to put her walls as high as they'll go. But I thought of everything, and she's celebrating with us no matter what. "I'm thrilled, really, that we won. But, y'know, jet lag." She gives the fakest yawn I've ever heard.

"Dani," I growl.

"I don't have anything to wear," she sighs, moving on to her next excuse.

"Don't worry about that." I can't help the mischievous grin that takes over my face. "Just be down in the lobby by eight."

Before she can come up with another excuse, I hang up and text Claire, initiating the first part of my plan.

46

Dani

> Research from London suggests that a woman's likelihood of weak knees increases by 84% when she's given thoughtful gifts, taken to a fancy dinner, and twirled around the dance floor.

The Austin Taylor who didn't know how to (comfortably) spend any of his money a few weeks prior has suddenly been found. The man has planned an exquisite—and expensive—evening out like he's done this a thousand times before.

When I get back to the hotel, I rifle through my suitcase for something—anything—that would be appropriate for a night out with Austin when there's a knock on the door. A posh-looking woman greets me with a rack of clothes. "Dani Marshall?" she asks. It takes me a moment to register her words. She looks like a Burberry model—tall and slender, clothed in various shades of cream and tan, her clothes hanging off her as if they were custom-made.

"Yes?" I finally reply.

"These are for you," she says, gesturing at the rolling rack of clothes beside her. When I don't move, she blinks at me. "Can I come in?" she asks slowly, as if I might be hard of hearing.

"Oh, uh, sure."

Inside my room, the woman dissects me with her eyes and then grabs three outfits off the rack, splaying them out on my bed. "Now that I see you, I think these would be best."

I flip through the outfits—all pricey designer pieces that have Claire Beaumont written all over them. And they're all dresses. "No pants? Rompers? Jumpsuits?" My voice has an edge of hysteria to it as I shuffle through the outfits for a third time, searching for something I'd be comfortable wearing. I don't do dresses. Never wear skirts.

"I was instructed specifically to only do dresses."

"Of course you were."

Claire freaking Beaumont has officially been demoted from best friend to frenemy.

The stylist must sense my anxiety because she says, "Why don't you try these on and see how you feel?"

I grab the three dresses she put out and head into the bathroom. The first one is a black number that is way too short for my long legs, but the next one—a Bucs-red midi dress that hugs my curves while still covering all of them—is a winner. It has one sleeve, with a cut out around the shoulder. The material wraps around my neck but leaves the top part of my back exposed. It's way sexier than anything I'd ever wear in real life—but it feels like *me*.

I sigh, running my hands down my waist as I turn in the mirror.

I *suppose* I'll let Claire back into BFF territory.

The stylist gives a squeal as I come out of the bathroom. "That's the one! Absolute perfection." She waves a finger, signaling for me to turn in a circle. I oblige, and she whistles long and low. "Here, shoes," she says, handing me a pair of strappy silver heels that sparkle in the light.

"Oh, and there's this." She hands me a jewelry pouch, which I take hesitantly. I caved on the dress thing, but I'm *really* not a jewelry person. But when I reach inside, there's a folded note that says: *I know you're not big on jewelry, but thought you'd like these. – Austin*

A familiar fluttering fills my chest, a sensation that's become more frequent the longer I know Austin Taylor. Because how many men in my life make note of the fact that I don't wear jewelry? And yet, Austin has. I empty the contents of the bag into my palm and find silver braid cuffs. A few of them have tiny football charms dangling from them.

It's not just the fact that the silver perfectly matches my outfit—it matches *me*. "He thought of everything, didn't he?" I say to no one in particular. But the stylist, who's gathering the rest of the outfits, says, "He's a keeper."

I'm inclined to agree, even though I don't know practically what that would look like for us.

After the stylist leaves, I spend extra time on my hair and makeup. More than I would have in any other situation. She left me with a liquid liner in a silver color that matches the shoes, and it takes me a solid twenty minutes to get the winged look right. But the end result is, well, amazing.

I don't often feel beautiful in a feminine way—I'll never be cute and sweet like Claire—but this look makes me feel powerful *and* feminine. Like I could own a boardroom, while also dancing a tango through the streets of Argentina.

For my hair, I do a half-up/half-down style where I wrap one of my braids around the base of the updo, leaving a few strands free around my face. I place the football braid cuffs strategically around my hair, with one dangling on a strand near my ear.

I snap a quick picture and send it to Claire. She sends back a series of GIFs in response: a cartoon wolf with his eyes coming out of his head and his tongue lolling out of his mouth, Leslie Knope doing a silly dance, and a penguin getting hit in the chest with Cupid's arrow and then falling back onto a bed of hearts.

Claire

> **Austin's going to fall in love with you.**

My heart twists at her words. Do I *want* Austin to fall in love with me? The thought thrills and terrifies me in equal measure. Before I can allow myself to answer that question, I tuck my phone into my purse and head downstairs.

I'm feeling like a million bucks, until it's time to leave the elevator and enter the lobby. I know on the other side of the elevator door, Austin Taylor—and probably the rest of the football team—will be waiting for me. I wonder if it'll change their perception of me to see me like this. I don't want the team to see me as a piece of meat—or even as a *woman*—because I want them to see me as an equal. A fellow professional with her head in the game.

My breath catches in my throat as the doors open and I step hesitantly into the lobby. Standing in the center of the raucous group of players is none other than Austin Taylor in a dapper gray suit. Malik Washington is behind him, stringing several silver iced out chains around Austin's neck. The guys are egging him on as Jordan records the moment. Austin's being a good sport about it, but his cheeks are pinking in a way that makes me think he's not all that comfortable with being the centerpiece of the next Kirk Cousins-esque viral TikTok.

Then it happens: as I approach the group of players, who are jostling each other and laughing together, they go silent. Heads swivel to me, taking me in, in the worst way possible. My coat hangs over my arm and I clutch it like a lifeline. I feel greedy eyes devouring me and I want to shrivel into myself.

Until Austin looks at me.

His steady hazel eyes capture me, staying fixed on mine. I walk toward him on wobbling legs, tuning out the rest of the team and their gazes. It seems to take an eternity for me to make my way to Austin and yet his eyes don't slide down my body, not once, and it gives me the confidence to keep going. Once I reach his side, the breath I'd been holding releases.

Austin leans down and says quietly, "You are stunning. Sorry the guys can't keep the drool off their chins."

I give him a small smile, grateful that he's somewhat aware of how I feel. Before I can say anything, he gently runs his fingers down one of my braids, stopping at the football braid cuff. "I see you got my gift."

I can't find my words, can't find my breath—all I can think about is how I want Austin *closer*. But then I remember that the team is all around us and I manage to splutter, "They're perfect. Thank you." I raise a hand, running a tentative finger over one of the chains at his neck. "Nice ice," I tease.

"I only bring it out on special occasions," he says with a wink. "Shall we?" He gestures toward the front doors and our rowdy group heads outside.

An Escalade limousine picks us up from the hotel. The guys who are with us—mostly offensive starters—are decked out in flashy suits. Even wearing Malik's jewelry, Austin's look is quite subdued compared to the rest of the guys.

We dine in a private room at Aqua Shard, a sleek restaurant on the 31st floor of The Shard with stunning views overlooking the Thames and all of London. The guys are goofing off, champagne is flowing, and Austin's eyes keep finding mine across the table. Apparently, Malik felt under-dressed without all of his jewelry, so he takes it back from Austin—which I think was a relief to Austin.

"Hey Dani," Malik shouts from across the table. "You gonna wear my jersey when we go to the Super Bowl?"

I roll my eyes as the guys start fighting over whose jersey I'm going to wear. Austin is noticeably silent, watching me. "I don't wear jerseys," I call out above the chaos. "I'm a professional analyst and I dress like a professional. I don't wear jerseys," I repeat for good measure.

The guys go back to being, well, *guys*. But Austin's eyes gleam at me from across the table. "So, is that a general guideline that you don't wear jerseys, or is it a rule?"

"It's a rule," I say, with as much force as I can possibly summon with Austin looking at me like that—making me want to break all of my rules. An image of me in his jersey, his number seven emblazoned over me like a brand, pops into my head.

The corner of his lips tilt into a smirk that I feel all the way down to my toes. "We'll see about that," he says, pouring gasoline on the flames that are spreading through me.

47

Dani

> Studies show that food tastes 75% better when shared with Austin Taylor—especially if accompanied by a side of flirtation.

After dinner, we head to Annabel's. Not one for nightlife, a quick Google search tells me that Annabel's is one of the most exclusive clubs *in the world*. Intimidation wracks me as we walk in. The facade of the establishment is decorated to look like a hot air balloon with the door made to look like the basket of the balloon.

Inside, there are several different lounge areas—wood paneled and classy with a touch of the eclectic and fantastical. The servers are dressed whimsically, some with top hats and tailcoats, others with vintage pilot outfits. I see one server with a massive pair of wings—not the cheap kind you might get from the dollar store, but a set that could've come off the set of *Lucifer* with real feathers.

Most of the guys head to the club downstairs to dance. I get a drink called the Sky High Spritz with Prosecco, Elderflower liqueur, and blue curaçao. A violet flower sits as a garnish, delicate and pretty atop the drink. Despite there being so many people here, and so many people in our party, I'm aware of Austin's presence at all times. I can tell that he's at the back of the lounge, shrouded in darkness with a couple other players. But I know he's there just as surely as I know where my left pinky is.

I dally at the bar, unsure where to go—everything in me is screaming to go be with Austin, but there's still a part of my logical brain that won't let my feet move. I take a few sips of my drink, fizzy and sweet. Maybe the alcohol will give me the liquid courage I need to go be with Austin—or maybe I shouldn't be drinking and should just leave. That would certainly be safer.

The back of my neck tingles just before a hand presses to my back. The hand isn't on my lower back—it's chastely set on the center of my back—and yet it still feels like a wildfire is spreading across my skin. I know without turning that it's Austin.

"We're heading downstairs," his voice is in my ear, his breath tickling my skin as he speaks. "Want to come?"

I turn to him, my heart beating erratically in my chest as I register his proximity. His suit-clad shoulder presses against my bare one, his hand lingering on my back. I try—and fail—not to shiver. "Oh, um, I'm not really into dancing."

Austin raises his eyebrows. "The *ballerina* isn't into dancing?"

I roll my eyes, but the action has lost its power because I feel so drunk on Austin's closeness. "It's not the same."

"I know," he says. "I have a theory about it, though."

"What's that?"

"You might like it more if . . ."

"If, what?"

He shrugs, takes another sip of his drink, keeping me waiting.

"Austin, if *what*?"

"If you let loose," he says, a playful glint in his eyes, "with me."

I swallow, my throat suddenly dry at the prospect of "letting loose" with Austin Taylor. It's all I want, and yet, it's also the most dangerous thing I can think of. What are the statistical odds of me falling for Austin if I let loose with him? My brain can't even compute it.

Not a good sign.

When I don't respond, Austin backs away, and my heart drops because I think he's leaving without me. Until I feel his hand in mine, pulling me with him. "C'mon, Dani. Tonight is about celebrating our win. Celebrate with me."

I take a shuddering breath and then let Austin pull me to the dance floor downstairs. Statistics be darned.

We dance until my legs shake from exhaustion and Austin is coated in sweat. The longer we dance, the more I shed the data analyst version of myself—and I just have fun. Perhaps it's because I'm in a new city, a whole different country, but I feel less driven by my professional goals and more driven by the need to be close to Austin Taylor. It's irresponsible, really, but I can't stop myself.

"Wanna get out of here?" Austin whisper-shouts in my ear, his hand on my waist as he leans in. Despite the heat from the dance floor, I shiver at his words. A minute ago, I didn't want to go anywhere—but now that Austin is offering, all I can think of is getting out of here with him. Whatever that means.

"Sure," I say casually, though my insides feel anything but casual. My stomach feels like a tangled quadratic equation with too many unknowns, all jumbled and impossible to solve. What it should be computing is the fact that Austin is dangerous—we work together, I'm insanely attracted to him, and whatever this crazy magnetism is between us, it's making me oddly illogical. And yet it's like there's someone else inside of me, pressing random buttons—I'll call it my Claire Brain—so that I follow Austin out of Annabel's.

The cool London air wraps around us and I take a deep lungful, hoping the extra oxygen will help me make good decisions while I'm with Austin.

"You hungry?" he asks.

"Starving," I say. "The food at The Shard was amazing, but the portions . . ." I shrug, trailing off.

"My thoughts exactly." He smiles at me in a way that sends a bolt of lightning from my head straight to my toes that have gone numb from dancing. "I think," he says, tilting his head toward me as we walk along the sidewalk, "we've earned some calorie-laden, positively unhealthful, fried, greasy foods. Since, y'know, we won that bet."

"And by 'we,' what you really mean is 'you.'"

"Well, I did win you that bet."

"You did."

"Ohh, look at this." His hand wraps gently around my wrist, tugging me toward a restaurant called MeatLiquor. We get greasy burgers and fries, and Austin eats a whole basket of Buffalo wings and two sides of mac and cheese. "It's good to know these Londoners are capable of making food that actually tastes good," Austin says with a mouthful of burger.

"All they're truly missing is a Waffle House."

"Don't remind me," Austin groans. "I haven't had Waffle House in forever."

"It's been five weeks."

"Like I said: forever."

I laugh, shaking my head. "It's really unfair that you can eat all of that and look like that." I wave a hand at him—he's shed his coat and his slightly damp button-down shirt clings to his muscles in all the right ways. It really is unfair.

He leans across the table, his eyes dancing. "I could say the same to you." His tone is flirtatious and I almost don't know what to do with this version of Austin. "It's not fair to be that beautiful, Dani. You couldn't have left some beauty for the other girls?"

"Other girls, like Allie?"

A smile tugs at the edge of his lips. "Allie who?" His eyes linger on mine—I know he knows exactly who Allie is, but his rhetorical question is pointed. And I'm left wondering just how pointed. I desperately want to read into this, for it to mean he can't think of any girl other than me. But that would be preposterous. Because this is Austin Freaking Taylor we're talking about. And I'm, well, *me*.

And yet... Austin is flirting with me. I'm as confident of this as I am about the Central Limit Theorem. Which is to say, I'm pretty freaking confident.

I let the smile that I've been holding back finally take over—spreading deliciously across me as Austin's own smile descends on me like a charm. And we're left grinning at each other across a table full of the greasiest food in all of London, the heat and tension between us growing as we pack on the calories.

When we leave MeatLiquor, Austin takes my hand—Claire Brain tells me this is thrilling—and leads me to a waiting chauffeured car. We drive around London, soaking up the nighttime sights as we listen to music, at times singing at the top of our lungs and at other times simply sitting beside each other.

We pass Big Ben, standing tall over the Houses of Parliament. The London Eye is lit up in various colors, shining brightly in the night. I barely catch the sights out of my window—Trafalgar Square, Piccadilly Circus, even Buckingham Palace—because all I notice is Austin Taylor, still holding my hand.

When we get back to the hotel, Austin walks me to my room. This feels like a moment scripted by Will Smith in *Hitch*. If I had a set of house keys in my hand, I'd be rattling them around in my hand. Instead, all I have is the plastic hotel key card, which I pivot around my fingers without opening my door.

Everything within me is screaming to him: *This is your cue to kiss me*.

Austin leans against the wall, crowding me deliciously into the doorway. His hand finds my waist, scorching me through my dress.

All sanity and logic has fled my brain. All I can think of are these two eloquent words: *Kiss me. Kiss me. Kiss me.* Like some kind of avid fan chant gone awry in the best way possible.

Just as Austin gets close enough for me to feel his breath on my lips, the door beside mine bursts open. Austin springs away from me as I turn toward my door, slapping the key card ineffectually against the handle. My hands are shaking, my breath is coming in weird spurts like I'm having a panic attack.

"Bro!" Malik's horrible, horrible voice bursts out. "We've been waiting for you, where you—Oh, hey Dani." Malik looks drunkenly from me to Austin then back to me. "You guys—"

"I was just making sure Dani got back safely to her hotel room. Didn't want any of you guys thinking of anything—"

Malik smiles a knowing grin. "Uh-huh. Sure. Safely to your room, Dani Banani Fanani. Let me watch and make sure nothing happens to you—"

Austin grabs Malik's shoulders, spins him around and shoves him back into his room. All I want is for Austin to just hurry up and kiss me—but I'm certain that the moment he kisses me, the rest of the guys in Malik's room will bear witness. And I can't have that.

"Goodnight Austin." I spare a glance over my shoulder as I enter my room, Austin's hazel eyes following me, though he stays safely on the other side of the door.

48

Dani

> Over 46 million turkeys are consumed in the United States on Thanksgiving Day alone. This accounts for nearly 20% of the total number of turkeys eaten each year in the United States.

When we get back from London, things continue on as usual—with Austin and I watching film and eating lunch together and going to yoga. Neither of us has brought up the fact that we won the bet and therefore don't really need to keep working together like this. I try to write it off like I'm just being helpful until the rest of the season—when in reality, I couldn't leave Austin alone if I wanted to. We're stuck to each other like two variables in an inseparable equation, linked by the same underlying formula.

I'm not complaining. In fact, I keep thinking—fantasizing more like—about that almost-kiss in London. Wondering what his lips would feel like on mine. What it would feel like to have those massive quarterback hands pull me against him.

I rationalize it in every way I can—I can still kiss him and not *date* him, right? Friends can kiss each other, in a totally experimental kind of way... If I just kiss him once, I'll get it out of my system and we can move on to being strictly professional.

It's a bunch of hogwash, but it keeps me from going insane.

From what I can tell, Austin isn't much better off. As we go through our regular schedule together, it's as if we're both finding every opportunity to touch each other—a lingering hand on my back as we walk into lunch, an unnecessary assist in a yoga pose that Austin already knows how to do, our knees brushing together as we watch film. It's thrilling torture and I'm eating it up with a big spoon.

We start meeting up extra early to watch film so that we can work on writing plays together afterward. At first, it feels like a justification for spending more time with each other. But it turns out that writing plays with Austin is better than writing plays alone. Our strengths complement each other—as if we're pieces of a puzzle that fit perfectly together.

This week is Thanksgiving. It's not a typical holiday for anyone in the NFL, since there are games on Thanksgiving day and all weekend long. No one who works for the team is flying home to see family. Except the Beaumonts, who are on their island in the Caribbean—and yes, I said *their island*. The Beaumonts originally built their fortune around luxury real estate, including developing private islands for their billionaire buddies.

It's a tough life, really.

We do a small celebration as a family on Tuesday with Uncle Clive and his family. Portia comes up from Miami and stays with me for a couple days before she has to head back home. We eat jerk turkey, rice and peas, and top it all off with a Jamaican rum cake—not your typical American Thanksgiving cuisine, but for our family it's perfect. We do another celebration with the team where we eat the traditional turkey, mashed potatoes, and various casseroles.

Portia and I watch cheesy holiday movies—at her insistence—while we do deep conditioning masks on our hair and Korean sheet masks on our faces. I tell her about London, but she's nowhere near as enthusiastic as Claire.

"Look, I'll be the first to say Austin Taylor is scrumptious—but, Dani, you gotta think about all that you've worked for here. Like, what happens when someone gets footage of you partying it up with these NFL players? How will that look for your professional image?" I watch her lips moving, the movement pulling at the sheet mask so that it bunches around her mouth. Her words make me feel foolish—like I've somehow confused yards per carry with completion percentage.

"I'm all for you falling in love, but there's a reason you set that line for yourself of not dating athletes. You're protecting yourself emotionally but also professionally."

I agree with everything Portia's saying—I've said the exact same things to myself over these past weeks with Austin.

So why am I suddenly internally fighting against everything she's saying?

49

Austin

> Since 1920, the NFL has played games on Thanksgiving Day almost every year, with over 100 million viewers tuning in for the holiday matchups.

In the days after London, while I should be gearing up for my last game before Drake comes back from rehab, my mind is instead filled with all things Dani Marshall. I'm sad when her family Thanksgiving celebration takes her away from me on Tuesday and then when her cousin joins us for yoga the next day. I freely admit that I want her all to myself.

But the mounting pressure of this last game is also getting to me. With all of the wins under my belt, I know there's a chance Coach will choose me to start, even once Drake is cleared to play. And now that I have hope . . . well, hope is a dangerous thing, isn't it? A few months ago, I would have been fine to ride the bench and watch Drake play. But now, Dani's faith in me is like the most glorious poison spreading through my veins, infecting me with the desire to play. To win.

On Thanksgiving Day, I sit at my dining table in Tampa, staring at my laptop screen. The familiar faces of my family fill the screen, gathered around the dinner table back home in Ohio. My mom's bustling in the background, making sure everything's perfect, while Dad carves the turkey. Emily's making funny faces, trying to cheer me up.

"Happy Thanksgiving, guys!" I say, forcing cheerfulness into my voice despite the homesickness gnawing at me.

"Happy Thanksgiving, Austin!" they reply in unison, their voices overlapping in a warm chorus that makes me feel a bit closer to home.

Mom steps into view, wiping her hands on a towel. "How's everything going there, honey? Are you eating well?"

I hold up my plate, showing the takeout spread. "Yeah, not quite your cooking, but it'll do. Got turkey, mashed potatoes, and stuffing."

Dad chuckles. "Looks like you're making do. How's the game prep?"

"It's going well. Coach has us on a tight schedule, but it's all good. Just wish I could be there with you."

"We miss you," Mom says softly. "But we're proud of you. We're with you in spirit."

We chat about family news, and I listen to Olivia's school stories and Dad's neighborhood gossip. As they gather for the Thanksgiving prayer, I bow my head, feeling a sense of unity despite the miles. When it's over, I look up and smile.

"Hey, any progress with Dani? You kissed her yet?" Livvy teases.

I scoff, shaking my head, but I can't hold back a smile. My younger sister takes this to mean I *have* kissed Dani—so she begins singing, "You love her, you want to marry her, you want to—"

"That's enough, Olivia," my mom interrupts. "Your brother will inform us of his private life when he's ready." My mom turns back to the screen, eyebrows raised as if to ask, *Are you ready yet?*

"Uh, there's no news on the relationship front, guys. Just focused on football." It's more or less true. Although with how distracted I've been with thoughts of Dani this week, it's less true.

We chat for a few more minutes until I beg off to study.

"We love you, Austin," Mom says, and the rest of my family echoes her.

"Love you too," I reply, waving at them before closing the laptop. The room feels a bit emptier, but my heart is full. This Thanksgiving might be different, but I wouldn't change it for the world.

50

Dani

On average, NFL teams convert on third down only 38% of the time, making the Rams' 55% conversion rate against us significantly higher than the league average.

The atmosphere in the coaching and analyst meeting is jovial as we gather to review the game against the Rams in London. We've won six games in a row with our third-string quarterback—I know I bet on Austin, but it's still a modern-day miracle that he pulled it off. The room buzzes with the subtle hum of laptops and the shuffling of papers. Coach Clive stands at the front, waiting for everyone to drift in, his huge frame making the room feel a bit smaller.

"Seems like I owe you a public apology about Taylor," Ethan says, leaning in. For some reason, he smells like a Happy Meal and I have to press my lips together to keep from laughing.

"We could start with an apology right now," I say with a raised brow.

Ethan shrugs, a smile on his face. "We'll stick to the public one."

I roll my eyes but the dynamic between us feels much different than it normally does—this is light and fun, not tense and competitive. Ethan pulls out his phone and we schedule a time for me to come on his podcast—which feels just as surreal as the dynamic between Ethan and me.

"Alright, let's get into it," Coach Clive claps his hands to get our attention. I hide a smile behind my knuckles because I'm going to be on *The Fantasy Playbook*. It's a dream come true and I want to shout it to the whole room. Instead, I focus my attention on Coach Clive as he says, "We're here to dissect what went right and what went wrong against the Rams. Dani, why don't you start us off?"

I nod, adjusting my notes. "Overall, we saw some strong performances. Austin Taylor's passing accuracy was solid, he had a completion percentage of 67% and had no turnover-worthy throws. However, our red zone efficiency needs work. We were two for five inside the twenty, which isn't going to cut it."

We discuss Austin's stats for a few minutes and then Coach gestures to Ethan. "Ethan, your thoughts?"

Ethan clears his throat. "I want to highlight some defensive stats. Specifically, our third-down conversion rate allowed. We let the Rams convert on 55% of their third downs that were third and six or longer, which is well above the league average. For all intensive purposes," Ethan says, misspeaking the phrase, "we need to tighten up our coverage and improve our pass rush in these situations."

I glance up at Ethan and a shiver of recognition goes through me. *For all intensive purposes*. That's exactly the misspoken phrase that @FieldAnalyst used a few weeks ago. Could Ethan be @FieldAnalyst?

I pull my phone out, tucking it discreetly under the table to pull up some of our interactions. I scroll through his comment about his co-worker being obsessed with Austin Taylor. I press my lips together to keep from laughing. If Ethan is @FieldAnalyst, he was talking about *me*.

I gaze at Ethan again. He's wearing one of a million Bucs shirts he owns—I'm beginning to think the guy *only* owns Bucs shirts—and today his beard is a bit scraggly. He looks like he stayed up too late playing video games—or scrolling through Twitter.

Before I can overthink it, I type out a message to @FieldAnalyst:

> @GridironGeek
> I'm sure you saw the Bucs vs. Rams game. Another win for Austin Taylor.

Then, I watch Ethan's phone, which is perched beside his computer, with its screen up. I hold my breath for one heartbeat, two.

Ethan's phone lights up.

I can't see the message, but I can see that the notification is from Twitter.

Oh. My. Gosh. Ethan *is* @FieldAnalyst. Which means Ethan and I have been friends for a while now—well, as far as you can call a faceless social media person your friend. I shake my head.

I put my phone away, tuning back into the meeting, where we're going over Mark's notes. Ethan is going to die when he realizes who I am. I tuck the information away to use when the time is right.

51

Dani

Research shows that 87% of people feel confident when proposing, but studies have yet to prove that anyone can ever be 1000% sure about anything.

It's a Wednesday afternoon so I'm at Claire's gallery, even though where I really want to be is with Austin.

Not that I'd ever admit that to anyone—even myself.

But, here I am, gliding back and forth on a rocking chair while Claire decorates the gallery for Christmas. Oh, and Elliot Adler is here, discussing his impending engagement to Isabella.

No biggie.

I'm enjoying one of Claire's peppermint mocha cake pops while Claire does the heavy lifting—both in the decorating department, and with proposal ideas. Since Elliot and Isabella's relationship is so heavily founded in pranks—yes, you read that right—Elliot and Claire are trying to come up with prank proposal ideas. And, yes, it's as dumb as it sounds.

"Oh! I know!" Claire's face lights up as she raises white twinkle lights above her head. "Why don't we get Isabella to interview Austin! And we can set up this whole thing where, like, he flirts with her and Elliot pops out of nowhere and defends her honor—"

I scoff, accidentally inhaling pieces of peppermint in the process. So now I'm choking to death, and my last thoughts are going to be of Austin flirting with one of my best friends. Not fun. Even if it's fake.

Elliot pounds on my back while casually replying, "You think Austin Taylor would do that?"

Claire, seemingly unaware that I'm about to *die* here, practically shouts with glee, "Austin Taylor would do *anything* for Dani. He kind of, like, loves her."

Now I'm certain my throat is closing up and I'll never taste oxygen again, though I'm not sure if it's from the peppermint cake pop or from the fact that Claire is broadcasting this information—which cannot possibly be correct, by the way—to Elliot Adler.

"Dude, that's awesome," Adler says as I continue to cough incessantly.

I wave my hands in the air, trying to simultaneously tell them that I still haven't dislodged this peppermint piece while also communicating that this is a terrible proposal idea. Claire glances over at me, frowning when she realizes I'm *still coughing*. "Are you okay? Do you need some water or something?"

Finally, Elliot wacks me hard enough in the back to dislodge the cake pop piece and I clear my throat. "You guys," I wheeze. "That is a horrible, awful, no-good idea."

"I'm a thousand percent sure Austin Taylor will help you with whatever you could ask for."

I hold back a groan—now I *know* Claire's baiting me, because she knows how much I hate it when people use statistics inaccurately. "Claire, if I've told you once, I've told you a thousand times. You can't be *a thousand percent sure*," I gently mock her tone, "of something that is immeasurable—"

"Like Austin's love for you?"

I shake my head, not even deigning to respond. "It's not that Austin *won't* help, it's just that it's not a good idea."

"Do you . . . have a better one?" Elliot asks, his blue eyes staring hopefully at me.

"Just straight-up propose to her. You've pranked her enough, just let this be about your love. Let your love speak for itself, without the pranks."

Claire stares at me like I just told her that her dog Gronk fell in love and is having puppies. There's practically heart emojis coming out of her eyeballs. "Don't look at me like that," I tell her, waving a hand at her overly sentimental face.

"But-but . . . *Daniella*," she whispers, her hands clasped over her chest, the Christmas lights twined between her fingers. "That was so *lovely*." She walks up to me, hugging me tightly, and then places a hand on my forehead, the Christmas lights thumping my face in the process. "Are you feeling okay? You're not feverish." She drops her voice to an even lower whisper. "Did something happen with Austin I need to know about?" She waggles her eyebrows, shimmying with the gesture.

I take her hand and pull it away from my forehead. "No," I say with an eye roll. "I'm just being pragmatic like always."

"That didn't sound pragmatic to me," she says. "Did that sound pragmatic to you?" She turns to Elliot.

Elliot sticks his hands in his pockets and shrugs, as if he doesn't want to get caught in the middle of whatever *this* is. "It actually seemed like the perfect blend of pragmatism and, well, love."

"Hmm," Claire hums under her breath. "That's perfect."

I scoff again—thankfully, no cake pop in my mouth this time—and wave off my best friend, who's still looking at me with heart eye emojis as we plan out Elliot's proposal.

It's Friday evening, the night that Elliot will propose to Isabella. It turns out, we did use Austin Taylor—just not the way that Claire had in mind. Elliot colluded with Isabella's boss at the *Tampa Bay Times* and Austin to get Isabella to an interview with Austin tonight. Except, when she shows up for the interview, it won't be Austin there, but Elliot.

He chose the Oxford Exchange as the proposal spot—the restaurant where Elliot and Isabella had the first interview that brought them back together. Elliot paid to rent the space tonight and we decked it out with flowers, twinkle lights, and photos of the two of them. Austin insisted on joining us. "I didn't want to lie to her," he says. "So at least I really am here." But I'm beginning to think his presence is less about lying to Isabella and more about, well, *me*.

It's not that I think Austin 'like, loves' me, as Claire said. But I can't deny what's happening between us—and what's been happening since the day I met him. I won't put a label on it, but it feels like we're magnets, circling each other, getting closer and closer—and I don't know if we're the type of magnets that will connect and never separate . . . or if we'll eventually repel each other and it'll be a disaster.

I'm trying not to think too much about it.

But seeing this display of love and adoration of Elliot to Isabella, it's sparking something inside of me that has been dormant for so long. Something I forgot I had.

A heart.

We, of course, allow Elliot to propose to Isabella in private. But then we gather with their friends and family in the Oxford Exchange, eating and toasting their love. Normally, this is the kind of event that would have me checking my watch, my thoughts drifting off to stats and games and plays. But tonight, my thoughts—and my eyes—are drifting to Austin Taylor. No matter where he is in the room, I sense him. Our eyes keep finding each other and he keeps offering me little smiles across the room.

Eventually, once the excitement of having an NFL player in our midst wears off and Isabella's family leaves him alone, he finds his way back to me.

"I like your friends," Austin says, leaning his shoulder into mine.

"I do too." I can't help but smile as I watch Isabella, her arm wrapped around Elliot's waist, her eyes shining up at him with such affection it almost makes me uncomfortable. And Claire beside them, with all the hope of a kid on Christmas morning. Just looking at her makes my heart squeeze because I want her to be happy—I want her to have what Elliot and Isabella have.

I glance up at Austin, his hazel eyes gazing at me in a way that makes me think of how Elliot and Isa look at each other. It makes me wonder, could we have that too?

Austin

> Ball Security: Refers to the measures taken by players to maintain possession of the ball and prevent turnovers. This is crucial, especially in adverse weather conditions like rain, where the ball becomes slippery and harder to control. Proper ball security techniques include holding the ball close to the body, using both hands when possible, and being aware of defenders trying to strip the ball away.

The rain is coming down in sheets as we step onto the field at Raymond James Stadium. The ground is slick, and I can feel the weight of the mud clinging to my cleats with every step. This game against the Saints is crucial—it's my last chance to prove I deserve the starting QB spot before Drake comes back from rehab.

The first half is a grind. The Saints' defense is relentless, and the ball feels like a slippery bar of soap in my hands. I manage to connect with Jordan Ellis for a solid gain, and Landon fights his way through the muck for a few hard-earned yards. But every time we get momentum, the rain seems to come down harder, blurring my vision and making every throw a gamble.

The crowd's energy is electric despite the weather, their cheers mingling with the sound of raindrops pelting the field. I can hear Coach Clive's voice booming from the sidelines, urging us to keep pushing. But the pressure is getting to me. My throws are off, and I can't seem to find my rhythm. We rely heavily on our run game, but the Saints D is locking us down.

By halftime, we're down by a touchdown. In the locker room, the tension is palpable. The normally jovial Coach Clive is uncharacteristically quiet, his face set in a grim line. I glance around at my teammates, their expressions mirroring my own anxiety. This is it. This is my chance to show I can lead this team.

I attempt to give a rousing speech to get everyone's spirits up, but my own are down and the words come out as disingenuous. My thoughts begin to slip into pessimism: Nolan would be better at this. Probably even Drake, despite all his shortcomings, would be able to energize the team.

The second half starts, and the rain shows no signs of letting up. We fight our way down the field, inch by agonizing inch. Malik Washington makes a spectacular catch, slipping past the defense for a touchdown.

For a moment, hope flares in my chest, dangerous and unchecked. Maybe, just maybe, I *do* deserve to be here.

But the Saints answer back with a touchdown of their own, and the scoreboard feels like a mocking reminder of the uphill battle we're facing.

Every rain drop that pelts my face feels like a reminder that I don't belong here. That all of those commentators were right—me winning all those games before this, it was just a fluke.

I know my mindset sucks right now, but I don't know how to change it. I try to think of Dani, up in the staff box, and her faith in me. But someone else's faith in you can only take you so far if you don't believe in yourself.

With two minutes left on the clock, we're down by three points. The field is a quagmire, and every step is a struggle. I take the snap, scanning the field for an opening. Jake Foster breaks free, and I let the ball fly, praying it doesn't slip through his fingers. He catches it, and we're within striking distance of a field goal attempt. If we can just get close enough for Turner to kick, we'll tie up the game.

We attempt to run the ball a few times, but don't make it far. The rain is pounding harder now, a relentless drumbeat in my ears. It's third down and six yards to gain. I call for the snap, the ball slipping through my hands like it's covered in oil. I manage to recover, scrambling to my right as the Saints' defense closes in. I see Jordan just past the first down line and throw with everything I've got.

The ball spirals through the air, but it's too high. Jordan leaps, fingertips brushing the leather, but he can't hold on. Behind him, a defender snatches it out of the air. He starts to run toward his end zone, but Jake Foster tackles as the clock runs out and the final whistle blows.

We've lost.

I stand there, the rain mixing with sweat and stinging my eyes. The weight of the loss settles on my shoulders, heavy and suffocating.

The crowd's cheers have turned to a dull roar of disappointment. My teammates clap me on the back, their encouragement hollow in the face of our defeat.

Back in the locker room, the atmosphere is somber. Coach Clive gives a short, clipped speech about keeping our heads up and learning from our mistakes. But all I can think about is the mud, the rain, and the missed opportunities. This was my last shot, and I blew it.

Because I was never supposed to be here.

As I sit at my locker, the noise around me fades, and all I can hear is the pounding of my heart, still echoing the rhythm of the rain.

53

Dani

> On average, a starting NFL quarterback participates in 34 press conferences per regular season, including both pregame and postgame obligations. This number can increase with playoff appearances, special events, or if they make it to the Super Bowl, where the media demands rise significantly.

When the time runs out on the clock, I'm still in denial. Surely there was an error of some sort and they'll put ten more seconds on the clock, replay the down. We'll find a way to win.

But no, the game is over. We lost.

I watch Austin take off his helmet, running a hand through his wet hair before he jogs to the other sideline to shake hands with Derek Carr, the quarterback for the Saints. My heart sinks as my mind races with the consequences of this game—will Austin lose his starting position to Drake when he comes back next week?

Before anyone can say anything to me—*looking at you, Ethan*—I escape to the bathroom where I attempt to collect my emotions. But the thought that's echoing in my brain is that I need to get to Austin. I know he's going to be devastated, maybe even confused, and definitely doubting himself. And I want—no, I *need*—to be there for him.

I wash my hands, splashing my face with cold water to try to keep the hot tears from coming, and then I head downstairs to wait outside the locker room for Austin so I can try to intercept him before he goes to the press conference, where he'll assuredly heap all the blame on himself. And that's not good for optics—he needs to maintain confidence in himself so that everyone else will too.

Downstairs, I position myself so that I can watch the guys leaving the locker room but they won't see me unless they turn around. As I watch player after player walk down the hall, I worry that I've missed Austin. It seems like everyone else has left. The hallway is empty, not a soul in sight. I grab my phone, texting Austin a quick message.

> Me
> Where are you?

A moment later, his solitary figure emerges from the locker room. His hair is still wet from the shower, dripping on his shoulders. It looks like he's carrying the weight of the whole team on his shoulders.

"Austin," I call out and he immediately turns. When his eyes find mine, the look that I find there is like I'm the healing balm to his hurting soul. Without another word, we walk toward each other, and I wrap my arms around his neck as his go to my waist, tugging me against him. His face burrows in my neck and my hands go to his wet hair.

Our hug, which started out as a means of comfort, quickly turns to something else entirely. I'm suddenly very aware of every point we're touching. I'm pressed against his chest, feeling each inhale and exhale. His heart beats steadily against my own rib cage. I breathe in his clean scent, finally taking a deep breath into his skin—something I've wanted to do since I first met him. He smells like amber with a hint of cloves, a Tide pod scent clinging to his clean shirt.

Austin leans back and I almost groan at the miniscule separation between us. "When the game ended," Austin says, his forehead against mine, "you were the only one I wanted to see."

"I only wanted to see you too." *These days, I only ever want to see you*, I want to add.

"Guess I'm not Tom Brady," he adds with a mirthless laugh.

I move my hands to either side of his face, tilting back so I can look him in the eyes. "Forget Tom Brady. You're better than that. You're Austin freaking Taylor."

He exhales loudly, shaking his head. "I told you your faith would be misplaced."

"Never."

Austin looks down at me for a long moment, his golden-green eyes swirling with so much emotion that I'm sure are reflected in my own gaze. His ragged breath fans out over my skin, intoxicating and heady.

At the same moment, I stand on tiptoe as Austin leans his head down. Like a wave crashing to shore, his lips meet mine in the most satisfying moment of my life. My fingers tangle in his wet hair. His massive quarterback hands roam down my waist, sweeping across my back, clutching my hips to him.

I am breathless yet he's giving me life. I am swept away by the current that is Austin Taylor, and yet he's anchoring me in place. I've never experienced anything like this before—and I never want this with anyone else other than Austin Taylor.

I tell him everything I think about him with this one kiss—that I believe in him no matter what. That he could ride the bench for the rest of his career and I'd still have the utmost faith in him. Not because of his football skills—but because of who he is as a man.

Austin pulls back, just a fraction, his forehead resting against mine. "I've been wanting to do that for a long time," he says with a laugh before he kisses me again.

Me too, I want to admit, but I'm too caught up in Austin's kiss.

Our kiss slowly evolves from one person trying to comfort and heal another to something much, much more. Austin tilts my head back to deepen our kiss, and when that's not enough, he bends down, grabbing my thighs to lift me up. I wrap my legs around his waist and I've never felt so dainty in my life as he holds me against him like I weigh nothing.

We kiss for what feels like eternity but could only be a few moments, until we're both breathless. My lips are swollen and tingling. And I am ridiculously happy.

I reluctantly climb down from Austin and he groans before letting me go. "Someone could see us," I whisper.

"So? Let them," he says, leaning down to brush another kiss against my lips.

"That would have very different ramifications for me than for you."

He shrugs as he takes my hand, tangling our fingers together. "What do we need to do? Fill out some paperwork with HR?"

I scoff. "It's not that simple, Austin."

"Why not?"

I roll my eyes. Men. They're always trying to oversimplify things that are meant to be complicated. "Don't you have a press conference to get to?"

He presses one hand on the wall behind my head, bending down toward me as he says, "Nah, I've got better things to do."

I laugh, shoving him away, before thinking better of it. "Wait, Austin," I grab his arm and tug him back to me.

"Greedy for more?" he says with a grin. He playfully backs me against the wall, kissing my neck.

"No."

"Really?"

"I mean, yes, but—"

He goes back to kissing my neck and I have to push him away again as he moans in protest.

"The press conference," I say.

"What press conference?"

"Austin. *Your job.*"

"There is currently only one job I care about right now," he says as he inches closer to me. I hold up a scolding finger. He sighs and takes a step back. "Fine. Press conference."

"I just want you to remember something," I say as I place a hand on his chest, feeling his heart beat on my palm. "You are a better quarterback than Drake Blythe. Objectively. You are accurate, consistent, and way more hardworking. One loss doesn't change that. Whatever you say in there," I point down the hallway, where the press conference is. "Remember that."

Austin sobers, nodding to me. He takes a deep breath, gathering himself as he prepares to go to the press conference. Before he walks away, he turns to me once more and says, "I'll try to remember that, but really, I think the only thing I'll be able to think of is this." He runs his thumb across my bottom lip before kissing me once and turning quickly away toward his press conference, leaving me speechless. Because I'm pretty sure his lips will be the only thing on my mind as well.

54

Austin

> On average, a kiss burns about 2-3 calories per minute. (FYI: we burned a lot more than 3 calories.)

I'm not sure what I said at the press conference—but I'm fairly certain that, despite the devastating loss, I had a ridiculous smile plastered on my face the entire time.

Because I finally kissed Dani Marshall.

And even with the buildup in my head, it was still better than I ever could have expected. I anticipated Dani's kiss to be as hard-earned as her affections have been—but with that one kiss, she opened up to me in ways I never could have imagined.

I've hoped to win Dani over, but actually succeeding in doing that is a triumph unlike anything I've experienced in my life. She's a challenge—a puzzle to solve, a knot to unfurl—and with that one kiss, I have confirmation that she's mine. My challenge, my puzzle, my knot.

My Dani.

And it's her words that are echoing in my ears as I answer reporters' questions about a quarterback controversy. "I'm going to let my stats speak for themselves," I say more than once.

And when it's all over, I don't even think about going home. I head straight to Dani Marshall's.

I don't want to be anywhere but right here. It doesn't matter that my body is aching with a spectacular array of bruises. I should be in an ice bath right now, but instead I'm sitting on Dani's balcony, her legs flung over my lap and her scent wrapped around me. We ordered tacos from Green Lemon and, instead of recapping every second of the game like we normally do as we eat, we're recounting when we first met.

I'm eating up every second of Dani telling me about what she thought when she first saw me.

"The whole flight I was just thinking 'I hope Austin Taylor isn't a tool,' and then I saw you and I was like, 'Oh crap I'm in trouble.' I totally should've stuck around to discuss the contract more with you—got you to sign it right then and there, but I just didn't trust myself to keep my hands to myself."

I twine my fingers through hers, lifting her delicate wrist to my lips, softly kissing her there. "Feel free to not keep your hands to yourself."

She laughs, shaking her head, and the sound fills me up.

Dani is the air I breathe, the life in my blood, the very beating of my heart.

"You know the Chargers called me after you left," I confess to her.

"They did?"

I nod as I trace her long fingers with mine. "They offered me a little more too. Same position, third string, but it wasn't the minimum."

Dani's jaw drops. "Why didn't you take that offer?"

"It wasn't even an option for me," I tell her, my eyes lingering on hers. "The moment I saw you, I just knew that I'd do whatever you asked me to do."

Dani's blinking up at me, speechless. Until she finally snaps out of it and smacks me on the chest. "Austin, you're an idiot. What if I was a complete jerk?"

I laugh, pulling her all the way onto my lap, wrapping her up in my arms. "I was willing to take that risk," I say, tracing the column of her neck with the tip of my nose. "Besides, you did turn out to be a jerk."

She rears back, wide-eyed.

"Torturing me with yoga and healthy foods all the while looking so delicious yet completely untouchable."

She tilts my face so it's level with hers. "I'm glad you didn't sign with the Chargers," she says, pressing gentle lips on mine.

"Me too."

"It was a dumb move," she says. "But I guess you're my dummy now."

"You guess?" I lean away.

"Well, I don't know, are you?"

"How could you not know?" I cup her face in my hands, her almond-shaped eyes gazing up at me, genuinely curious about what I'm going to say. "I'm yours, Dani Marshall. I haven't even thought of another woman since I saw you back in April. It's only you."

She kisses me again, pouring her emotions into that kiss—saying what her words can't—or maybe won't—say yet.

"Seriously, though," I tell her. "Whatever we need to do to make this official or above board, I'll do it. I don't really know what the protocol is with players and staff but, let's make this official."

Dani sighs, and I feel her fingers tighten where they're clasped behind my neck. "Yeah," she says, noncommittally.

"Is that like 'yeah, let's get on that tomorrow' or is that like a 'yeah, Austin, sure thing, buddy'?"

She laughs, but the sound rings hollow. "I just need to ... talk to my dad. First."

"Right. That makes sense. You think he's going to be unhappy?"

She glances off the balcony, into the dark night. "I honestly don't know, but I'm kind of terrified."

To be honest, I'm kind of terrified for her, but I don't say that. Darius Marshall is one scary dude. And that's coming from a guy who gets tackled weekly by three-hundred-pound NFL players.

"Whatever happens, we'll face it together, okay?" I tug lightly on one of her braids.

She nods, and again, I get the sense that she's not one hundred percent committing—and it makes me fearful that I put all of my cards on the table too early. "Want to watch a show?" she offers, standing up and taking my hand.

"I already told you, Dani Marshall," I say, following her inside, "I can't say no to you."

TMZ ✓
@tmzofficial

Bucs' QB, Austin Taylor, seen getting cozy with staffer Dani Marshall after the Bucs game last night.

9:24 AM Dec 2, 2024 · Twitter for iOS

1k Retweets 25382 Likes

BucsFanCentral @bucsfancentral ·2h
@Replying to

Wonder how the Bucs' management feels about this... 😬 #ConflictOfInterest #NFL

LaylaLove @yagirlLayla ·1h
@Replying to

He could have any girl in the world and he chooses her??

Franky Frank @footballfanatic99 ·1h
@Replying to

Looks like the Bucs' QB is scoring off the field too! 😉 #NFLDrama #BucsNation

---

FieldAnalyst @fieldanalyst ·1h
@Replying to

Why is this news? Can't people just live their own lives anymore? Geeze.

55

Dani

In 2023, it was estimated that over 3.6 billion people worldwide used social media, with the average user spending 2 hours and 31 minutes on social media platforms daily. This massive user base means that a single post, photo, or tweet can spread like wildfire, often reaching millions within hours. I learned the hard way that the rapid dissemination of information can turn private moments into public spectacles almost instantly.

I never got a chance to tell my dad about Austin.

Because the daily news cycle does it for me.

The morning after my kiss with Austin, I do what I always do: pull up Twitter and check what my fellow football junkies are saying about the game yesterday.

Except it seems like no one is talking about the game—they're talking about me and Austin. I scroll through my feed, horrified, as picture after picture of Austin and me fills the screen. Austin kissing me in the hallway outside the locker room. A shot of me twined around him. Photos of us on my balcony, me in his lap. Another of me leading him inside my house through the balcony door.

I feel exposed. Violated. And, most of all, ashamed.

Because the comments that are flooding the feed are things like, "Why is he dating her when he could have anyone else?" and "Oh look, another bimbo sleeping her way to the top of an organization."

I should stop scrolling and put my phone away—but it's like trying to tear your eyes away from a car wreck on the other side of I-75. Except this time, the car wreck is *my* life.

When I've mined Twitter for every opinion on my escapades with Austin, I turn to other media sites. I'm everywhere—E!, TMZ, Yahoo Sports, and even Bleacher Report and ESPN—climbing Austin Taylor like he's a tree.

Mortification doesn't begin to quite cover what I'm experiencing.

It's as if I'm having an out-of-body experience—perhaps I've died and my spirit is hovering over my body, watching this nightmare unfold.

It's not even seven a.m. and I already have emails from *People*, *Us Weekly,* and *Sports Illustrated*—along with a slew of other lesser-known sites—with requests for comments. Not to mention the countless phone calls, texts, and voicemails from unknown numbers.

I don't know what to do, so I do the only thing I can think of: I run.

56

Austin

> Media Frenzy: A media frenzy occurs when a news story or event receives an overwhelming amount of coverage from various media outlets. This often leads to sensationalized reporting, widespread public attention, and, in many cases, a significant impact on the individuals involved. Media frenzies are fueled by the public's interest and the media's desire to generate high ratings or engagement.

I show up to watch film with Dani the next morning feeling like I'm walking on a cloud. Sure, my body is battered to shreds from the game yesterday and I'm definitely looking forward to my massage and PT later this morning, but with the memory of Dani's kiss so fresh in my mind, I feel like I could take on any defensive lineman in the whole NFL—heck, throw them all at me, no problem.

I picked up Dani's favorite cafe con leche from Corona's, a cafe near my house, which means I'm a few minutes late. I'm surprised when I find the film room empty and dark.

Dani's never late.

I sit, eating my omelet from Corona's while I text Dani.

> **Me**
> Hey, late sauce. Your cafe con leche is getting cold.

By the time I finish my breakfast, I still haven't heard from her so I decide to call. When it goes straight to voicemail, I wonder if maybe she forgot to plug her phone in and it died or maybe her alarm never went off and she slept in?

It doesn't sound quite like Dani Marshall, but stranger things have happened.

That's when I start to scroll through my phone. Ever since my pick-six became a meme, I keep away from my phone as much as possible. I try not to check it first thing in the morning and typically keep it on silent until after practice. I've deleted my social media apps and, as a rule, don't go on news sites. Especially sports news. So I've missed all of the texts, phone calls, and news bits that have come through during the night.

It's a text from Livvy that reveals exactly what's happened. It's a picture of me and Dani from TMZ: a dark and grainy photo of me lifting Dani up, her legs wrapped around me, arms around my neck. We're kissing.

Quite enthusiastically.

> **Olivia**
> Looks like you finally kissed her! Yay!!
>
> But just FYI, you guys are EVERYWHERE right now. 🫢 🫣
>
> Also, some people aren't being very nice about Dani.

I groan, rubbing my face with my hands. I know immediately that Dani didn't sleep in—she obviously got the news before me and is . . . what? Hiding? Avoiding me? In trouble with paparazzi? The unknown causes a ripple of anxiety to run through me. I glance down at my phone and look at the time. I've got an hour before I have to be back for PT.

I've got to get to Dani's.

57

Dani

A study done in Tampa, Florida shows that when push comes to shove, I'll run.

The moment I step out of the condo building to go for a run, there are reporters in my face.

"Is Austin Taylor up there, Miss Marshall?"

"Can you confirm that you and Austin Taylor are in a relationship?"

"Did Austin Taylor get you a job with the Bucs?"

I understand now why there are so many photos of celebrities with their hand in front of their face. That's exactly what I'm doing right now, trying to block the photos and the questions that are being shot at me like bullets. The reporters follow me down the sidewalk, like they're going to come on my run with me. My heart rate skyrockets. I feel panicked, antsy. Like my insides are trying to jump out of my skin.

I don't know where to go to get away from these people and I can't find my words.

How does anyone deal with this?

I pivot away from the sidewalk and hurry to my car. One of the reporters follows me around to the driver's side and I almost run him over in my haste to get away.

58

Austin

> Hail Mary: A desperate, long pass play typically used at the end of the half or game when the team needs a big gain or touchdown. The quarterback throws the ball deep into a crowd of receivers and defenders, hoping for a miracle catch.

When I get to Dani's, there are several reporters posted up outside the entrance to her condominium building. I'm wearing a hat and sunglasses, but this does nothing to keep them from noticing me. My height alone makes me conspicuous.

"Mr. Taylor! Can you confirm your relationship status with Miss Marshall?"

"Did you spend the night, Austin?"

"Will Drake Blythe take your spot as starter now that he's back from rehab?"

I ignore their questions, keeping my head down as I punch in the code to get through the door of the building. Once inside, I make sure the door closes all the way so none of them get in. Good grief, these people are persistent. It certainly takes a special kind of person to want to be this kind of reporter.

I take the elevator to Dani's condo, holding the now-cold cafe con leche I got her. I knock, but there's no response. I try calling her again and it goes straight to voicemail once again. I call Claire, thinking that maybe she knows where Dani is and if she's okay, but her phone goes to voicemail.

What is wrong with these girls and why does no one want to pick up their phone?

I sigh, leaning against Dani's door. If I didn't have to be at PT in twenty minutes, I'd post up here until she gets back. I wish I had something to write with, to leave her a note. Instead, I leave the coffee and send her a text:

> Me
>
> I'm sorry about the news cycle. We'll get through this. Just letting you know I stopped by. Cafe con leche's by your door. I'll be back after our team meeting.

The text falls pathetically short of what should be said in this circumstance—but I can't think of what else to say. I just want to hold her, to reassure her that no matter what the news cycle is saying, I adore her and I'm in this.

I just hope she is too.

59

Dani

Nearly 59% of US adults believe that being in the public eye often results in negative media attention.

I drive to Claire's without realizing where I'm heading until I'm almost there. Her family lives on Davis Island in a multi-million-dollar mansion that overlooks the bay. Unlike me, Claire opted to live at home when she returned to Tampa after college. For one, her parents' mansion is big enough where she could not see anyone else for a week if she didn't want to. And also, her dad didn't remarry and start a whole new family she wants to avoid. So there's that.

I swipe my gate card—gifted to me by Mr. Beaumont himself when I got my driver's license and drove here almost every day—and pull through the gate to their cobblestone driveway. There's a hint of a sea breeze as I practically run up the steps to their house, grateful that it's reporter free right now.

The allure of the Beaumont's house—which has been featured in Architectural Digest and Southern Living—has long since faded and I don't even pay attention to the vaulted ceilings and chandeliers when their housekeeper, Delora, lets me in. I find Claire still in bed—her gallery doesn't open till ten and she's not exactly a morning person. I flop onto the bed next to her, sinking into the pillow top mattress, feeling very much like an anxiety-ridden teenager instead of a grown woman.

Claire stirs, peeking at me from beneath a silk eye mask. "Oh. I thought you were Gronk," she says, and I don't even have it within me to be offended.

"Have you seen the news?"

Claire scrambles up, checking her phone. I lay in silence, an arm slung over my eyes, as I wait for her reactions. First, the squeal—"He kissed you!"—then, the realization of what's happening—"Oh, no . . ."—and, finally, the outrage.

"I can't believe someone followed you to your house and photographed you guys! That's got to be illegal. Let's get Daddy, he'll fix this—"

"Claire," I grab her arm before she stomps off to find Mr. Beaumont—the owner of the Bucs. The thought of seeing Mr. Beaumont's disappointment in me is almost as bad as the idea of my dad's disappointment. Every time I imagine my dad seeing these photos, pure terror grips me. First of all, because he's my dad and it's just embarrassing. But secondly, he's my *boss*. How can he view me as a professional when I'm photographed like this with one of his players? I shudder at the thought. "I'm pretty sure it's not illegal."

"I'm going to check anyway." She bites her lower lip, worrying it between her teeth as she types furiously into her phone. "Look, ChatGPT says that if there was an expectation of privacy, which I mean, c'mon, it was your private balcony—"

"Claire, he's basically a celebrity. I think the expectation of privacy is unrealistic."

"Can I at least talk to my dad about this?"

I turn over in the bed, groaning into Claire's pillow. Beside me, Claire sighs and begins to run her fingers through my braids, straightening them down my back. I tilt my head toward her and say, "I don't want to cause more trouble than I already have."

"Dani, these reporters are the ones causing trouble—not you."

"I've worked way too hard to get where I am to have a man destroy all of that."

"Let's be clear about one thing, Danielle Marshall: a *man* is not destroying your hard work."

I sit up, pulling a throw pillow into my lap, twisting the edges with my fingers. "Did you read what people are saying?" I can't even look at Claire when I ask the question. The heat and shame whirling within me is just too much.

"Why does it matter what people are saying about you if they don't even know you?" Claire asks—her tone gentle, but her words ruffle me.

60

Austin

End Around: A trick play where a wide receiver or another offensive player takes the ball from the quarterback and runs around the end of the offensive line, hoping to catch the defense off guard.

I try to ignore the comments and teasing from my teammates during PT and our afternoon meetings about the photos with Dani. I'm simply going through the motions, like I'm on autopilot, waiting to hear from Dani. My mind whirls through a hundred different scenarios, imagining her getting stuck somewhere with the paparazzi hounding her, to her deciding I'm not worth the effort. Both thoughts are terrifying, haunting me through the day.

Dani's text comes through after our offensive meeting:

Dani

> I'm sorry, Austin. I just need some space to figure this out.

I throw the phone into my locker, frustration and sadness rippling through me. I sit on the bench with a huff, running my hands through my hair.

I feel insanely stuck. I know Dani—if I press her, she'll only run farther. I need to respect her space, while somehow convincing her to give us a chance.

I just wish I knew how to do that.

61

Dani

A survey by Women in Sports and Events (WISE) found that 56% of women in sports media and operations have faced gender discrimination at work, with many reporting that their professional capabilities were often questioned due to their gender.

I arm myself in my typical black suit for work, hoping the familiar routine will steady my nerves. Conservative black heels, hair in a bun—the kind of outfit that says 'I belong here,' even if my mind is still spinning. I hold my head high as I enter my office space. Heads swivel toward me, watching me without acknowledging me. Everyone except for Ethan, who gives a small wave from his office.

Ethan's casual reaction surprises me—I expected him, of all people, to smirk or gloat. But he doesn't. For the first time since I became a media story, I actually consider going on Ethan's podcast. I'm supposed to record with him on Thursday. I just don't know if I have the energy—or courage—to show up.

I take a seat in my cubicle, setting my notebook beside my computer and opening my email. The morning passes uneventfully until it's time for our meeting with the coaching staff. I make sure I'm early to the meeting—I'm not interested in drawing any attention to myself by making an entrance once everyone's already there. But as I'm walking up to the conference room, I overhear two staffers talking.

"This is why we don't hire women to work in these roles," a voice says, and I'm fairly certain it's coming from one of our scouts. "It's inevitable that they get entangled with the players."

I pause just outside the doorway, my heart hammering in my chest.

"I expected more from Dani," the other male voice says. "But I supposed she's as susceptible to the allure of an athlete as any other woman . . ."

I back up, almost twisting my ankle on my heels as I rush down the hall. Tears threaten to overwhelm me as I hurry toward the bathroom. I turn down another hallway, running straight into Uncle Clive. My bag with my laptop and notebook goes flying, landing in a heap on the other side of the hallway.

"Whoa," he says, steadying me with his meaty hands. "Dani girl, what's up?"

Uncle Clive searches my face before grabbing my bag—holding it like a caveman would, with the straps in a chokehold—and then ushering me into his office. When he holds out his tray of candy, I actually take a handful. He raises a brow as I go for a second handful. "Bad day, huh?"

"You have no idea."

He chuckles softly. "I might."

I sniff, collecting myself. "I just overheard some gossip about me that I wish I hadn't heard."

Coach Clive sighs, taking a fistful of M&Ms and channeling them into his mouth. For a few moments, we crunch in silence on the peanut M&Ms until he says, "People are always going to say something. The higher up you go, the more freely people think they can talk. Pretty soon, it won't be behind your back either."

I nod, knowing he's right—people talk about my dad's decisions as GM of the Bucs all the time. Freely criticizing him, and at times calling him awful names. It's part of the role.

"When I first started coaching, I'd hear it all the time: he's not tough enough, not disciplined enough. He's a defensive coordinator, not head coach material, and so on." He stares down at the candies in the bowl, picking out a few. "My first year of coaching, I had an assistant coach go behind my back to the GM with a list of offenses I'd made. Luckily the rest of the coaching staff stuck up for me." He shrugs, like he's still trying to release himself from that situation. "Here's the thing Dani girl: you can't control what people say about you. You can only control your response. So, what's your response going to be? Are you going to let yourself be victimized or are you going to stand up and fight?"

"I don't even know what that means, Uncle Clive."

"It means that instead of cowering and overthinking and hemming and hawing every time someone looks at you wrong, you take their words and you let it propel you. Show them they're wrong. Learn from them. And more importantly: don't let their voices be the loudest ones in your ears." He leans forward on his desk, his eyes softening as he gazes at me. "The people who know you best, who love you most, those are the voices you gotta listen to."

I sigh as I give him another nod to let him know I hear him and appreciate what he's saying. I don't know how to process it all in this moment, but I am grateful for this talk. "Thanks, Uncle Clive."

He reaches out a hand and I place mine in his huge paw. His calloused hand is warm as he grips my hand. "For what it's worth, Dani girl, you looked pretty happy in those photos."

I pull my hand out of his and stand up, shouldering my bag. "Uh-uh, not talking about that with you," I say as I flee his office, the sound of his laughter following me down the hallway.

His words swirl all kinds of emotions within me—he's right, I need to fight. But what that looks like practically is a little confusing for me. Sure, I can continue to fight to be seen as a professional in my analyst position—Lord knows I already have to fight tooth and nail for that. Talking with Uncle Clive, I'm resolved to show up on Thursday to the podcast with Ethan. I'll prove to the world that I'm a professional, first and foremost. That's worth fighting for, worth showing up for.

But the real question is: should I be fighting for my relationship with Austin?

Because as much as being with him felt like the highest high, it also came crashing down hard. So hard that I don't know if I have the strength—or the heart—to try again.

62

Dani

Research indicates that over 40 million Americans listen to podcasts weekly, with sports podcasts being one of the most popular genres.

I agreed to do the podcast on the condition that Ethan wouldn't mention the photos of me with Austin. I show up on Thursday to his home in Carrollwood, where his office hosts a makeshift recording area. Ethan told me that he typically invites guests to record with him via Zoom, but since I'm local, we might as well record where the sound quality will be best.

I sit in a chair that looks like it belongs to a hardcore gamer and adjust the microphone in front of me so that it's at the right height. "Ready?" Ethan asks, and I give him a thumbs up.

"Welcome back to *The Fantasy Playbook*," Ethan begins, his voice smooth and confident. "Today we have a special guest, Dani Marshall, a fellow data analyst for the Bucs who specializes in quarterback analyses. Welcome, Dani."

"Thanks for having me, Ethan."

He opens his mouth to say one more thing, then closes it. Then opens it again as he says, "Look, I told Dani I wouldn't say anything about the photos of her with Austin Taylor—"

My stomach twists at his words, and I'm afraid I'm going to throw up if he says one more word.

"And I won't remark on the details, but I feel like I need to say this to the people out there who are disparaging Dani Marshall: Dani is the most brilliant analyst I've ever met. Not only does she have incredible recall for every football statistic imaginable, but she's also an insightful surveyor of the game and her knowledge is outmatched, especially considering her age. I mean, seriously, guys, Dani's recall is insane. Like, listen to this: Dani, what was Tom Brady's passer rating in the 2007 season?"

I clear my throat, leaning into the mic as I say, "Uh, he had a passer rating of 117.2 with 50 touchdowns and 4,806 passing yards."

"And what about the total rushing yards by the Giants in their 2008 Super Bowl season?" Ethan asks, and then leans into the mic again, chuckling. "She didn't know I was going to ask her these questions, by the way. I promise she's not Googling them right now."

"I love being put on the spot," I say dryly. "The Giants rushed for a little over 2,500 yards in 2008."

"Impressive." Ethan claps. "I could do this all day, but let's get down to it. Dani, let's dive right in—why did you advocate for drafting Austin Taylor when everyone, including me, thought it was a mistake?"

I lean forward, feeling slightly more at ease after getting quizzed. "Well, Ethan, it all comes down to a metric I developed called CHOICE, which stands for Calculated Heuristic Optimization in Critical Environments. Essentially, it evaluates quarterbacks on their decision-making skills. Not just stats, but how they react under pressure, their ability to read defenses, and make quick, smart decisions."

"Can you give us an example of how this works?"

"Sure," I say, warming up. "Austin scored incredibly high on CHOICE. During his college career, he consistently made optimal decisions even in high-pressure situations. While his physical metrics weren't top-tier, his mental game was off the charts. He knew when to take risks and when to play it safe, which is crucial for a quarterback."

"So, you're saying it's not just about the raw stats?" he says, sarcasm clear in his voice.

"I know, imagine that," I say, laughing with him. "CHOICE looks beyond traditional stats to capture a QB's situational awareness and adaptability. For instance, Austin's ability to process information quickly and make the right call under pressure gave him a CHOICE score of 92 out of 100, which was higher than many first-round picks. Drake Blythe, on the other hand, scored relatively low on his CHOICE scores, despite his flashy game play."

"You've definitely given us something to think about. How has Austin performed compared to your expectations?"

"He's met them in many ways," I say, feeling like the question is oddly personal—even though Ethan's intention isn't. "His decision-making on the field has been a game changer. He's shown that even if you don't have the best physical stats, you can excel by making smart choices consistently. And he's put in the work to keep improving on the other metrics."

"Well, Dani, I have to admit, your CHOICE metric has proven itself and I was wrong about Austin Taylor. I hope you'll forgive me."

"All is forgiven, Ethan. Thanks for having me on the show."

We talk for a few more minutes about the Bucs' stats and overall performance this season then wrap up the segment and I head back home. It feels good to have won the bet and to finally be on Ethan's podcast. But it feels somehow lacking because the first person I want to call when I get back in the car is Austin Taylor.

But I don't touch my phone.

63

Austin

Loneliness: The sensation of your heart ripping out of your chest, over and over again, when the woman you've fallen for isn't around.

Coach Clive calls me into his office on Friday morning before practice. "I'll shoot straight with you, Taylor."

"I appreciate that, sir."

"You've done great. Far beyond expectations." He sighs heavily. "But we're going to give Drake Blythe a chance to show us what he's got."

Dani's voice inside of me screams to defend myself, to show Coach how much I want this. Instead, I say, "I understand, sir." Even though I don't understand—I've proven to everyone on this team that I am here to work hard and play hard. I'm committed, unlike Drake, who could barely make it through two weeks in the NFL without getting suspended. Not to mention that my win/loss ratio makes me one of the top QBs this season.

"The good news is that you'll be one of the best backups in the league," he says. "And you could probably negotiate your contract in a couple years."

I suppose this is good news—if he'd said this to me when I first got picked up, I would've been stoked.

But that was before I met Dani Marshall.

And it's her faith in me that's changed everything. And even though I should probably be happy about what Coach is saying, his good news tastes like sand in my mouth.

Since Dani asked me for space, I find myself chasing her memory. Watching film at six a.m. in the film room.

No Dani.

Fresh Kitchen for lunch.

No Dani.

I even attempt to do some yoga on my own, watching YouTube videos while making a fool of myself in my living room.

No Dani.

And despite being surrounded by my teammates and coaches day after day, I've never felt more alone in my life.

64

Dani

No amount of statistics can prepare you for the moment when the rug gets pulled from under you.

On Friday morning after Ethan's podcast episode airs, I'm called to the assistant general manager's office. I don't know much about Joel Steinman, except that my dad hired him specifically for the business side of things—he's not a football guy, he's a businessman. I'm not sure I've ever seen him at a game. Not that I'm looking for him—he's always given off those 'too good for you' vibes.

When his secretary lets me into his office, Joel is in the middle of typing something on his computer. He doesn't look up when I walk in. His beady, bespectacled eyes are darting back and forth on whatever urgent email he's transcribing as I stand, waiting.

Finally, he glances up at me as if he just noticed I was there. "Miss Marshall," he says curtly. "No need to sit, I'll be quick."

He spreads his hands across his mahogany desk, shifting papers aimlessly. "Look, with all of this drama in the media about you and the quarterback—" I wonder if Joel even knows Austin's name or if he's just a number on a spreadsheet to him. "I thought it would be best if you took some time off. Two weeks paid leave."

His words hit me like a blow—sure, I've heard the whispers from other staffers about me and Austin. But to hear the assistant GM so concerned about it, I honestly don't know how I'm supposed to respond. Can he fire me? I wonder if my dad knows that we're having this meeting. But I also know that I can't go running to Daddy every time something goes wrong in my career.

"I see," I say, though the injustice of it all burns like bile in my throat.

"And Miss Marshall?"

"Yes?"

"No more appearances in the media, no more comments on players—whether inside the Bucs organization or outside of it. Even on little podcasts."

"But Ethan—"

"Ethan Driver has an agreement with the Bucs organization that's detailed in his contract. He came to us with that podcast of his already in place and our legal department bent over backwards to accommodate him because he was so highly sought after. His contract includes very specific terms as far as confidentiality. Terms that you do not have in your contract." His words drip with disdain, making it abundantly clear Ethan's value over my own.

I nod, fighting tears as Joel seemingly dismisses me, turning back to his computer. I pivot on my heel, rushing from the room.

A wave of emotions—anger, sadness, frustration and self-loathing—threatens to overtake me. I stumble to the bathroom, forcing air in and out of my lungs when all I want to do is scream. I feel stupid for allowing myself to get involved with Austin in the first place, when I knew it could be bad for my career. And now that we've been splashed over the tabloids, it's far worse than I ever could've imagined. How could I be so irresponsible?

Joel's words keep replaying in my mind—the unmasked disgust with which he communicated. It slices through me like a poisoned knife, hollowing me out and infecting me with bitterness and rage.

Where is my dad in all of this? Why haven't I heard from him? Part of me wants to storm into his office and demand that he explain why he allowed Joel to do this. But a bigger part of me wants to run away, to stuff my head in the sand and try to forget that this ever happened.

I'm driving aimlessly down Bayshore Blvd. I'm not sure how I got here, I just left the Bucs HQ and started driving. Of course I would come to Bayshore and be reminded of the time that Austin and I took the scenic route, singing along to Macklemore at the top of our lungs.

It's crazy how much has changed in just a few short weeks.

My dad is calling me. I really, really don't want to pick up his calls—and, if he were just my dad, I wouldn't. But he also happens to be my boss.

"Hey, Dad."

"Danielle." His tone is all business as his voice reverberates through my car speakers. "I just heard that Joel put you on leave."

"He did." I keep my voice neutral—I can't risk anyone, even my dad, accusing me of being *emotional*.

"Look, I wish he would've talked to me first, but I don't disagree with him."

Well, that hurts. "Okay."

"It'll be good to get some distance from this media frenzy. Why don't you go stay with Claire for a bit? Or maybe head to Miami to visit Portia?"

"Yeah, okay."

"I'm saying this to you as your boss, not as your father."

I grip the steering wheel with both fists, just wanting this call to be over already. "I hear you."

"But," he says, his voice softening. "When you're ready to talk to me about this as your dad, I'm here."

"I'm not sure I'll ever want to talk with you about it, Dad," I say honestly.

"That's fair. But I *want* to talk with you about it. Again, not as your boss, but as your dad."

I swallow, pushing down the nausea that's building in my throat. I do *not* want to talk with my dad about the pictures of me *making out* with Austin Taylor that are all over the media.

"I'll let you know," I tell him. We say our goodbyes and it takes everything within me not to chuck my phone out the window and into the Bay.

End Zone Report ✓
@endzonereport

Drake Blythe was seen at practice for the Buccaneers on Friday where he took more reps than Austin Taylor. Do we have a QB controversy on our hands??

11:46 AM · Dec 6, 2024 · Twitter for Android

105 Retweets 2034 Likes

FieldAnalyst @fieldanalyst · 1h
@Replying to

Obviously. @GridironGeek where you at? 👀👀

65

Austin

Flea Flicker: A trick play that begins with a hand off to the running back, who then laterals the ball back to the quarterback, setting up a deep pass to a wide receiver.

The word I keep hearing about Drake's first game against the Panthers: *buckwild*. He completed 27 of 34 passes for 350 yards and threw 4 touchdowns without a single interception. Add to that an impressive 95 rushing yards and you've got yourself a starting QB.

Much better than my NFL debut.

Last week, we split reps in practice but today, I've only taken about ten percent of the snaps. I've clearly been demoted to backup.

However, for last week's win, Drake was sober.

This week, he is not.

It's ten a.m. on a Wednesday and I can smell the alcohol coming off of him in waves. He's throwing sloppy passes, seemingly unaware of the defense, and scoffing every time Coach gives him feedback.

We're set to play the Chiefs this week—now is *not* the time to get sloppy.

After practice, I can see Coach Clive attempting to have a heart-to-heart with Drake—I can't hear what he's saying, but everything about his body language tells me he's reprimanding Drake. Yet when Drake turns to cross the field, heading back to the locker room, he's got a smirk on his face.

"Hope you had fun while it lasted, bud," he says to me, slapping my back as he passes me. I grit my teeth, biting back my words. Drake spins around, walking backward as he calls out, "But, hey, at least you got the girl!"

I clench my fists, knowing he's goading me because he got a dressing down from Coach. But his words hit me like a blow to the gut from a linebacker—because I *had* the girl, if only for a moment, but somehow I lost that too.

66

Dani

> On average, around 20-30% of NFL teams will make a quarterback change during the regular season.

It's too difficult to be on leave from work but still be at home, so I head to Miami to stay with Portia for a while. I go through the motions of doing all the Miami tourist things that Portia wants me to do with her—we fry at the beach, take pictures in Wynwood and Vizcaya, go shopping, and eat in restaurants all along South Beach.

It should be fun. It should make me forget about Austin Taylor and the drama with my job. But everything we do, in the back of my mind, I'm just wishing Austin were here too.

When we take a yoga class at a gym in Brickell, I'm near tears as we flow through our first vinyasa. Even though I know Austin isn't here, it's like my heart is still searching for him. Still waiting for him to show up.

But I have to remind myself that I ran away.

I ran away because being in a relationship with him put my career in jeopardy.

I ran away because kissing him put me on the front page of the daily news cycle.

I ran away because my privacy was violated and people I don't know now know personal details about my life—and I don't know if I can live that way; if anyone is worth that loss of dignity.

But even though all of these things are true, my heart still aches for Austin.

For the most part, we watch what Portia wants to watch. I even agree to stay off of my social media accounts and news sites while I'm with her. The exception to the rule? When it's game time.

We huddle around Portia's TV in her tiny Miami apartment and watch the Bucs take the field.

But it's not Austin's number lining up in shotgun—it's Drake Blythe's. Because, apparently, while I was on leave and taking a break from the news cycle, I missed the fact that they'd pulled Austin and put Drake in the starting QB position.

The realization sends ripples of horror and panic through me. Did they bench Austin because of me? Because of the drama that I started by kissing him and having it splashed all over the news?

But no, they wouldn't do that.

So why in the world is Drake playing instead of Austin? Austin proved himself game after game after game.

I can't even sit still while we watch the game. Instead, I pace around Portia's apartment, chewing on my fingernails and tugging on my braids. At some point, my internal dialogue must escape because Portia interrupts my pacing by saying, "You really like this Austin guy, huh?"

I stare at her, unsure why she's even asking me this. She takes my silence to mean that I do, in fact, really like this guy. Though the ripping sensation in my heart that's been there since I last saw Austin hints to far more than 'really liking' him. I flop down on the couch beside her, continuing to watch as Drake runs around on the field like a maniac. He may not make great decisions, but the guy *is* fast. And it's winning them this game.

"I just wish you wouldn't have gotten caught, you know?" She says this like I was trying to get in the media. "Couldn't you guys just have, I don't know, made out *inside* somewhere?"

"There was no one around, Portia!" I say, throwing up my hands.

"Clearly, that's not true. I saw the pictures, *someone* was there."

I groan, cradling my head in my hands.

"It's not the end of the world," she says, rubbing my back.

"You sure about that?" I look up at her, eyebrows raised. "Because it looks like Austin got benched and I'm on leave."

"Well, no, I'm not sure. But it seemed like the right thing to say." She sighs, sweeping my braids over my shoulder so she can continue rubbing my back. "If I know one thing about you, Dani Marshall, is that you'll find a way. You always do."

I close my eyes, focusing my attention on Portia's long nails tracing circles over my back. I wish she was right—I wish I could find a way out of this, with Austin starting again and me with my job intact.

But, even if we had all of that back, where would that put Austin and me as a couple? I try to imagine a future with him, but all I can see when I close my eyes is the paparazzi crowding me as I stepped out of my condo. Embarrassment coils in my stomach as I squeeze my eyes tighter, trying to get the image to leave me alone.

That night, as I'm lying awake on Portia's couch when I should be sleeping, I try to come up with plays. But even that old faithful trick leaves me high and dry tonight. I pull out my phone and before I can overthink it, I text Austin.

> Me
> I'm sorry they benched you.

> Austin
> I'm sorry they put you on leave.

I stare at the screen, watching as the three dots come and go as Austin's contemplating saying something. I wait for so long that my screen goes black, without another text from Austin.

67

Austin

Playbook: In football, a playbook is a comprehensive collection of plays and strategies that a team uses during a game. It includes detailed diagrams and descriptions of offensive and defensive plays, as well as special teams' formations and tactics. Each play is designed to exploit the weaknesses of the opposing team while maximizing the strengths of the team executing it.

It's been two weeks since the pictures of Dani and me were spread around in the media. Two weeks since I've had her in my arms. And two weeks since I've heard her voice.

Well, except for when I listened to *The Fantasy Playbook* and heard her then. Me and 100,000 others.

I'm trying to honor her request and give her space, but it's hard not to lose my mind. I keep reaching out to Claire, trying to figure out where Dani's head is at, but she's not giving me much. I told myself I'd wait till the end of the day today to reach out to Claire again, but practice just ended and I can't wait a second longer.

> **Me**
> Any word for me?

> **Claire**
> Sorry, Austin. She's still on leave in Miami, I'm not sure when she'll be back.

I groan, pressing the tips of my fingers into the corners of my eyes. All of Dani's worst nightmares have come true from one evening with me—and I'm not sure I'll ever be able to convince her I'm a good bet ever again. Especially if she won't talk to me.

Even after I texted her back last night, she didn't respond. I debated saying more—typing out a few different messages—but ultimately decided to honor her request for space. "I miss you" remains typed in the text thread, unsent.

Malik sits next to me on the bench in the locker room. "Media problems, Drake problems, or girl problems?"

I scoff, not bothering to look up. "All of the above."

"Hey, I've got a tried and true method for forgetting all of the above—"

Liam comes up behind us and smacks Malik with the back of his towel. "And it involves ending up in the media even more than you already are."

"I'm just saying, man. If you want to forget what's going on . . ."

"I don't want to forget," I tell them. "I just want to fix it."

Liam throws on his clothes and sits on my other side. "Look, I know what you guys need."

I glance over at him warily. A night at the club and some top shelf liquor aren't going to solve my problems.

He holds up his hands, sensing my defensiveness. "I've been married to my wife for seven years. It's hard being married in the NFL, but we've figured out what we need."

"And what's that?"

"A playbook."

I raise an eyebrow. I don't know what playbooks have to do with me and Dani, but if Liam knows a way to fix all this mess, I'm here for it. "Okay, I'm game."

68

Dani

On average, my heart will grow approximately three sizes whenever I have a heart-to-heart with my dad.

I'm driving back from Miami when I get a call from my stepmom, Heather.

"Hey, sweetheart," she says in her Southern-sweet voice. "I just wanted to check on you to see how you're doing."

Like my heart's been ripped out of my chest and I'll never get it back. Like I'm returning to work with my tail tucked between my legs. Like I let my boundaries slide and look where it got me?

I don't say this to Heather, but I also don't say 'I'm fine' like I normally would. "It's been hard," I confess.

"I know it has been," she sighs, her sympathy clear through the phone line. "I'm so sorry for everything the media put you through."

"Thanks, Heather," I say, genuinely grateful for her empathy.

"You close to home? Want to stop by for breakfast tomorrow before your dad leaves for New Orleans?"

I've been avoiding my dad since the news dropped about Austin and me. But now that I'm going back to work after this week's game, I'll have to face him sooner rather than later. The team is heading to New Orleans today for the NFC South division title against the Saints, but my dad has some work he needs to finish up here so he's leaving tomorrow.

I agree to show up to breakfast and we chat for a few more minutes about this and that. When I get off the phone, I feel a mix of emotions: grateful—for the first time in a long while—for Heather and also terrified to face my dad.

When I arrive at my dad's house the next morning, I walk inside on shaking legs. I've braced myself for the worst—gone through what I'm going to say and how I'll never let it happen again. I find my dad in the kitchen, his hulking form huddled around the coffee maker. I hold my breath as he turns. But instead of his typical stern look, his eyes are soft as he holds open his arms to me.

I hesitantly step into his embrace. He squeezes me gently before releasing me. "I thought you were going to lecture me."

My dad chuckles, the sound a deep rumble in his barrel chest. "I'm still going to lecture you," he says, but he's got a smile playing on his mouth.

"You could've just summoned me to your office weeks ago, you know." I lean against the kitchen counter, grasping it with both hands to steady myself. "You are my boss."

My dad takes a sip of his coffee, looking thoughtful. "But I didn't want to be your boss when we talked about this." He puts his hands around his mug, completely dwarfing the cup. "I wanted to just be your dad."

"Well, *Dad*," I say, with more confidence than I actually feel. "There's not much to add to the media narrative except that it's over and won't happen again."

"Is that so?"

I nod solemnly, though my insides feel like they're splitting apart with the admission. How could I possibly be so cut to pieces by the ending of a relationship that wasn't even a relationship? We kissed a handful of times over the course of twenty-four hours. To most people, that would be a blip. Something they barely remember. And yet everything about Austin Taylor is seared into my memory, and I'm certain I'll never get over it. I'll never get over *him*.

"Is there a reason it's over?"

"Well, it was inappropriate."

My dad frowns at this, his forehead wrinkling as his gruff voice says, "Inappropriate, *how*?"

I want to sigh, to groan over this very Socratic method of discipline, but instead I say, "I shouldn't date someone on the team. I know this."

"So it was inappropriate from an HR perspective, not, say, a physical perspective?"

"What? Dad! No." I smooth my hands over my pants in an attempt to settle my nerves. "It was completely physically . . . appropriate."

My dad raises his brows. "I saw the pictures, Danielle."

I throw my hands up. "We kissed, Dad. That's it."

He sets his coffee cup down, folding his arms over his chest. "A very passionate kiss."

I cover my face with my hands, and this time, I do groan. But a moment later, my dad's before me, gently prying my hands away from my face. I'm afraid to meet his gaze, but what I find there is surprising. The eyes that meet mine aren't stern or threatening, they're sympathetic. "When I saw those pictures, I didn't think about it being inappropriate. I just thought it looked like you were . . . in love."

I breathe in, unable to comprehend the four-letter word he's saying so casually.

"Sweetheart, did you break up with Austin because of some misguided assumption that you shouldn't date a football player? Like it was somehow . . . against the rules?"

"Well, no," I swallow. "Not totally. But it's against *my* rules."

"Because of Jared?"

My dad holds my gaze for a long moment before I give a short nod.

"Is Taylor anything like Jared?"

I scoff, shaking my head. "Not even a little bit."

"Then what are you afraid of?"

The question catches me completely off guard, and the thought that surges to my mind is: *Everything. I'm afraid of everything I can't contain into a formula.* Tears prick my eyes with the realization. "Everyone leaves, Dad," my voice comes out in a sad croak, but I can't stop the confession from pouring out. "And I can't control it. I can't stop them. Mom left, Jared left. Even you left when you married Heather."

"Oh, Danielle," my dad reaches out, gently enveloping me in his strong arms once more.

As I let him hold me, the tears I've been holding back for weeks finally come. This time, I don't fight the tears, I open the floodgates.

My dad hugs me tight as I mourn the whole situation—the way things went down with Austin, the fact that my privacy was so violated, that people in the media are raking me over the coals and it's affected my work life.

But I'm also mourning the fact that I've distanced myself from my dad and Heather and the twins because of my hurt. Standing in my dad's arms, I'm convinced for the first time in a while that he loves me no matter what. And that his love for me never diminished when he married Heather or had the twins. I mourn the fact that I could've been closer to Heather, Lucas, and Layla, but I haven't.

After I've cried out all my tears, my dad leans back. "You know, I wouldn't change anything about my relationship with your mom. I wouldn't have changed the narrative just because it ended with her loss. Not least of all because it produced you." He runs a hand over my braids, affection blurring his brown eyes. "What is it that they say, 'It's better to have loved and lost than never to have loved at all'? It's true, Danielle. It's so, so true."

I sit quietly, absorbing my dad's words.

"And I'm sorry that you felt abandoned by me when I married Heather. I think that I was so eager to have a full family again that I didn't consider that you might not feel the same way."

"It wasn't the worst thing for me, when it was just the two of us."

It surprises me when my dad lets out a boisterous laugh. "We were eating ramen every night and you looked homeless because

I didn't know enough to do something with your hair. I was getting calls from your school all the time because they were concerned for you."

I shrug. "I was happy, Dad."

"I wish I would've known that."

"Would it have changed anything?"

He considers my question. "It wouldn't have changed the fact that I married Heather, but perhaps it would've influenced how I went about it. The speed with which we started a new family. I would've given you time to adjust, instead of simply assuming you needed this family as much as I thought you did."

I nod. Something about his words are like a balm on my hurting heart. For the first time, I see just how much my dad was looking out for me when he married Heather. "I appreciate that, Dad."

"Look, I know Heather's flaws as much as anyone, but she did help us."

I give a very ladylike snort. "She certainly helped my hair situation."

"She certainly did. Heaven help us, you needed it. Badly."

"Hey! It wasn't that bad."

"Rose colored glasses, Danielle. It was terrible."

We laugh, remembering my hot-mess hair—but I wouldn't change anything about those years spent by my dad's side in coaching staff meetings where I became who I am today. We busy ourselves in the kitchen, making breakfast for the twins. On a different day, I might begrudge my half-siblings that my dad is now the kind of father to make Mickey Mouse pancakes, but today, I don't. Instead, I'm grateful for the dad that he was for me during the hardest days of our lives, and how he's grown as a father now with Heather beside him.

I stay for breakfast, enjoying the bedhead on both Lucas and Layla. When Heather comes out with a brush and hair products for them, I take them from her and do their hair while she eats breakfast. It feels all very domestic in a way I've never truly experienced since my mom died. And today, I'm grateful for it.

When it's time to leave for work, my dad puts an arm around me and says, "Look, about Austin Taylor." I gaze at him, his dark eyes serious yet soft. "Don't let fear of loss keep you from living your fullest life right now."

I press my lips together, nodding as I take in his words. "Thanks, Dad."

"I love you, Danielle." He presses a soft kiss to my temple. "No matter what."

I surprise Heather with a quick hug and the twins with a kiss on each cheek before heading back home.

69

Dani

> In the NFL, teams may update or change their playbooks several times throughout a season to adapt to injuries, opponent tendencies, and player strengths. On average, significant changes can occur 3-4 times per season, with minor adjustments happening weekly based on game plans and scouting reports.

When I get home, there's something taped to my door. For a moment, my stomach twists, worried that someone in the media got through my condo building. But when I can see what's typed on the front, it says, "Austin + Dani's Playbook" with a QR code underneath. My heart races so fast it feels like it might burst from my chest and take flight.

I glance down the hall, hoping maybe Austin's waiting for me somewhere—but I know it's close to game time and he's off to New Orleans with the rest of the team. For all I know, he could've left this here two weeks ago—but this is the first time I've been home since being on leave, since I spent last night at

Claire's. I pull the paper off of my door and slide inside, not even making it to my couch before I scan the QR code.

A video pulls up, with Austin taking up the screen. He's in his practice jersey out on the field. He says, "Hey, Dani. I know you need space to figure this out—but I thought this playbook might help."

The shot zooms out to show some of the players running through a play—and it takes me a moment to realize, it's one of my plays. After the play runs through, Austin's back on the screen. "This is called the Can't Say No Blitz. Because whatever you ask for, I can't say no. Whether it's signing with a team or giving you space."

The next scene cuts to a bunch of the players in the gym at the Bucs Center. They're all on yoga mats, doing a vinyasa. I laugh out loud as I watch Jordan and Malik moving from a downward dog to a plank to a cobra. Austin shows up in the corner of the screen. "This play is called Losing My Dignity Formation." He grimaces playfully. "You were right about yoga . . . but maybe we could just do it from home now?"

Another shot shows a bunch of the players eating take out on Austin's couch. "This one's called the Ramsey Take-Out Fake-Out." Austin leans closer to the camera and faux-whispers, "Don't tell the guys, but they're not invited."

There's play after play of Austin showing me what it's like to have a relationship—and it looks an awful lot like the relationship we already have. There's the Fresh Kitchen Shake-n-Bake, where we order Fresh Kitchen to be picked up. There's the BFF Help Line—my jaw drops when Claire's on the screen and she says, "Daddy sent cease and desist letters to all the media that posted pictures of you. Take that, E!"

At the very end of the video, Austin takes the screen by himself again and says, "Sometimes, you have the perfect playbook and a defense still reads your routes or sacks your QB. But I know that if we can regroup and put our heads together, we can figure out anything, Dani."

For the second time that day, tears spring to my eyes. I put my phone down, checking the time again. It's too late to catch Austin before the game, but I'll be waiting for him after.

There's just one thing I have to buy first.

70

Austin

> Option Play: A versatile play where the quarterback has the choice to either hand off the ball to a running back, keep it and run himself, or pitch it to another back, depending on the defense's reaction.

The roar of the Superdome is ear-splitting, a cacophony of boos and cheers reverberating off the walls as the Saints and Bucs clash on the field. The NFC South division title is on the line, and the pressure is palpable. Sweat trickles down my back, the air thick with tension and anticipation.

Drake Blythe, our backup-turned-starting quarterback, is struggling. He's off his game, throwing errant passes and making critical mistakes. The Saints' defense is relentless, blitzing him at every opportunity and forcing him into bad decisions. It's painful to watch. Our offense stutters and stalls under his command. I can see the frustration etched on Coach Clive's face, mirrored in the eyes of my teammates.

The clock ticks down to halftime, and we head to the locker room trailing by fourteen points. The atmosphere is tense, the weight of the moment pressing down on everyone. I know this is it. This is my chance to prove myself, to show that I can lead this team to victory.

I approach Coach Clive as he paces near the whiteboard, his brow furrowed in thought. Taking a deep breath, I muster every ounce of courage I have. "Coach, we need to make a change," I say, my voice steady but urgent.

Clive stops, turning to face me. "What are you saying, Taylor?" His gaze sharpens, but there's a flicker of something—trust? hope?—as he studies me.

"I'm saying I can do this. Drake's off his game, and we can't afford any more mistakes. Put me in." The words spill out, fueled by a newfound confidence that I'm fairly certain is 87.6% Dani Marshall's fault . . . and my own growth. "The Saints are blitzing on almost every down. They're exploiting our weak spots. I've studied their defense. I know I can make the plays we need."

There's a moment of silence, the weight of my request hanging in the air. I can feel the eyes of my teammates on me, a mix of hope and doubt. Clive's eyes remain fixed on me, measuring my resolve. I've never felt more certain of anything in my life. This is my moment, my chance to show what I'm made of.

"Alright, Taylor." He gestures at the board. "Show me what you've got."

I take a deep breath and reach for a dry erase marker. "I've got a series of plays that can exploit their aggressiveness. Quick slants, bubble screens, and a couple of designed quarterback runs." I quickly sketch out a few plays on the whiteboard with several options.

Coach scans the board. "These are Dani's plays."

I nod, the familiar ache in my chest surfacing at the mention of her name. These are the plays we worked on together after London—Dani's signature flair woven into every move, with a touch of my precision in the pocket sprinkled throughout. Dani must not be as sneaky as she thinks when she slips her plays into Coach's office. I clear my throat, trying to dislodge the emotion that's stuck there as thoughts of Dani flood my mind.

"We start with a quick slant to Malik," I say, pointing at the play with my marker. "If the linebackers bite on the blitz, he'll be wide open in the middle. Then we hit them with a bubble screen to Jordan. It'll pull their corners out of position. And finally, a designed QB run to the right side. Their defensive end is crashing hard inside—we can catch him out of position."

Clive nods, rubbing his hands together. "Good. Real good. Let's make it happen."

As I walk back to my locker to grab my helmet, the reality of what just happened sinks in. I'm going in. I'm taking the reins. This is my chance to turn the game around, to prove that I belong here. The doubts and fears that have plagued me—that I'm not enough for the NFL, that I deserve to be on the bench—dissolve, replaced by a fierce determination.

I glance over at Drake, who's leaning against his locker downing a Gatorade, a towel draped over his head. We exchange a brief look as I pick up my helmet. It feels heavier in my hands, and the noise of the locker room fades into the background. All I can hear is the pounding of my heart, in sync with the roar of the stadium outside.

Coach Clive runs through the plays with the starting offense with only a few minutes to spare. As we go through the plays, the energy returns to the room, and with it, hope.

When halftime is over, I jog out onto the field, the world narrowing to the ball in my hands and the turf beneath my feet.

This is my chance.

My moment to show them who I am.

This is my time.

71

Dani

NFL jersey sales are a massive part of the league's revenue, with an average of 15 million jerseys sold each year. Star players often see their jerseys among the top sellers, with some of the most popular players moving over 100,000 units annually.

When I walk into the staff box seats in the Superdome wearing Austin Taylor's jersey, I hold my head high. Yes, I promised myself I'd never wear a jersey—but that was before I fell for Austin Taylor. And he changed everything.

And, honestly, things needed to change.

A few staffers flick their eyes at me, but I ignore them. Even wearing Austin's jersey, I'm still a professional—and I'm really good at my job. I can still excel, even while dating an NFL player.

Ethan's eyes brighten when he sees me. "I thought we sold out of Austin Taylor jerseys weeks ago," he says with a laugh.

"I know, I had to buy this secondhand."

"That's what you get for being a late adapter," he jokes. "I've been telling you since the beginning, Marshall. Taylor's where it's at. He's the future of this team."

I laugh with Ethan, appreciating the new camaraderie between us. "Unfortunately, I think we have to survive a little Drake Blythe first."

We both grimace as Drake gets sacked for the second time on this drive. "He's not looking hot out there."

"Apparently he was out all night partying."

"See, Dani, it's that decision making I keep telling you about," Ethan teases. "You see, there's this algorithm called CHOICE, a brilliant analyst came up with it—"

I smack his arm, but we both groan again when there's a turnover.

"Thanks for being a good friend, Ethan," I say—amazed that these words are sincerely coming out of my mouth.

Ethan smiles and gives me a quick nod before returning his attention to the game. The first half is brutal. Drake can't find his rhythm and the Saints defense is tearing through our offense like tissue paper. It's tough to watch. It feels like everyone in the staff box is holding their breath until the game is over. I just wish, for everyone's sakes, it were Austin out on that field right now.

At halftime, I turn back to Ethan, handing him a wrapped gift out of my purse. "By the way, I got you a Christmas present."

"Aww, Dani, you shouldn't have," he says dryly.

"It's nothing."

"No, really, you shouldn't have. I didn't get anything for you."

I wave a hand at him. "Just look at it already."

With a cheeky side eye at me, he unwraps the gift. He picks up the sheet of paper that I taped to the front of the gift—it says "To @FieldAnalyst From @GridironGeek."

"Wait a second." Ethan turns, gaping at me. "Are you . . . ?"

I smile, nodding.

"No freaking way." Ethan laughs, running a hand over his beard as he shakes his head. "I can't believe it. All this time."

He unfolds his gift and holds up his very own number seven Austin Taylor jersey. "No way." He cackles, the rest of the room turning to look at us.

"Now we can match," I tease.

"What I've always wanted," he quips before nudging me with his shoulder. "Thanks, Dani. Or, should I say, Gridiron Geek?"

I laugh, flipping my braids over my shoulder. "Hey, I think we should come up with something a little more clever for your handle. FieldAnalyst is just so blasé. I was thinking 'AustinTaylor4Ever' or maybe even 'DaniMarshallWasRight.'"

He rolls his eyes but my smile widens when Ethan actually pulls the jersey on. "We should take a picture or else it didn't happen," I tell him, gesturing between our jerseys.

"The podcast wasn't enough?" He scoffs. "Now you're just getting greedy, Dani."

"Fine, fine," I say, but when Ethan looks away, I snap a picture of him in the Austin Taylor jersey to use for blackmail whenever I need it.

When the Bucs take their position after halftime, I can hardly watch. It's Sandy, the secretary, who tugs on my jersey and says, "Look! It's your man!"

I press closer to the glass and sure enough—there's Austin Taylor, number 7, out on the field lining up in shotgun.

The Saints' defense lines up, ready to blitz as they have all game. My heart is in my throat as Austin snaps the ball. He immediately fires a quick slant to Malik, who catches it in stride and gains twelve yards before being brought down. A perfect start.

The next play, Austin executes a bubble screen to Jordan Ellis. The Saints' corners bite on the play, and Jordan weaves through traffic for a solid gain. I recognize these plays as surely as I recognize my own name. The staff box erupts in cheers. The plays are working. *Our* plays are working.

I watch, my pulse racing, as Austin surveys the defense. He's calm, focused, in control. He calls for a designed quarterback run—it's not his strength, but we've been working to loosen up his run all season long. The Saints' defensive end crashes inside, just as I predicted, and Austin takes off to the right, finding a seam and picking up a crucial first down. I can't help but cheer, my voice lost in the sea of noise from the other staffers.

Play after play, Austin chips away at the Saints' defense. He's precise, exploiting their aggressiveness with quick passes and calculated runs. The momentum shifts, and the Saints are on their heels.

While the Saints are on offense, I turn to Ethan. "I gotta get down there."

He gives me a quick salute. "Here's looking at you, kid," he says.

When I frown at him, he sighs. "Casablanca? Really?"

I shrug but tell him, "Look, old man, you can educate me on all of that later. I'm gonna go get my man."

"You go girl!" Sandy cheers.

I grab my staff badge and run down to the field. I have to be on the sidelines—I can't stand to be any farther away from Austin for a minute longer. I stay out of the way, though, standing beside the medical tent as I watch Austin take the field once more.

It's the fourth quarter, the clock ticking down with a minute left, and we're within striking distance. Austin takes the snap and drops back, scanning the field. The Saints bring the blitz, but he's ready. He lofts a beautiful pass to Jake Foster, our tight end, who reaches up at the goal line and—

Touchdown.

The stadium goes nuts with cheers from Bucs fans and boos from the Saints, and I can hardly breathe.

We've taken the lead, 24-21.

The scoreboard reflects the hard-fought battle, and I feel a surge of pride. Austin has done it. He's proven himself, and he's done it with *our* plays. Nothing in my life could prepare me for how beautiful this moment feels—to have created something so amazing with the man I've fallen for.

And that's when I realize it: I love Austin Taylor. And, if I'm being honest with myself, I've loved him for a while. Even before we kissed, even before it all fell apart, even before his playbook. The playbook may have helped me to have faith in my love for him—but that love was there all along. The realization ripples through me, filling me with a sense of peace and rightness. Because this is what matters: I love him and he loves me. I'm sure of it.

This is everything—this is life and breath and hope and joy. I can't believe that I shut this down for so long, choosing the lesser option instead of risking it all for greatness.

And I realize that this is why people love sports—why *I* love football—because we all love stories of endurance, hope, overcoming odds, and most of all, faith. Because that's what being a competitor is all about—believing in yourself enough to keep fighting for one more down, one more point.

But that's what life is about too: it's about getting up when you fall, it's about pushing through when the odds are stacked against you. It's about believing in yourself and believing in others. And when the person you love is lacking, you let them borrow your faith.

In the same way that Austin and the Bucs have fought for this season, Austin and I can fight as a team together through life. Because if there's one thing I've learned these past few weeks being away from Austin, it's this: I don't want to do life without him anymore.

As the final seconds tick away, the Saints make a desperate push, but our defense holds strong. The whistle blows, signaling the end of the game.

We've won.

The team erupts in celebration, and I'm swept up in the chaos. On the sideline, the coaches and staff are all high-fiving, cheering, and clapping each other on the back. I find myself hugging people in the medical tent that I've never seen before—but we're joined together by this team, this victory.

My heart hammers in my chest as I watch Austin stride across the field, shaking hands with Derek Carr and some of the other Saints players. I wait for my moment and it comes faster than

I anticipated. Austin turns back to the Bucs' sideline, his eyes finding me, lighting up when he sees me.

I can't hold back a minute longer—I run. But instead of running away from Austin like I've been doing for weeks, I run toward him. I sprint into his arms, and he catches me. His arms hold me tight against him as I wrap mine around his neck, holding him back.

And, even though we're in a crowded stadium filled with fans and reporters and teammates, I kiss him. I run my fingers through his hair and press my lips against his. I can feel Austin smile against my lips as he tugs me even closer, deepening the kiss.

"You're wearing my jersey," he says when we finally part. "I thought you didn't wear jerseys."

"Well, I added a new play to our playbook," I tell him.

"Is that so?"

"I may not wear *jerseys*—but I'll wear yours."

"I like that," he says. "I didn't know if you got my playbook."

"I just got it this morning when I got home. I came here as soon as I could." I press my forehead against his, soaking up his closeness, his breath against my skin. "And I've got one more play to add," I tell him.

"I would expect nothing less. You *are* the writer of plays, Miss Marshall," he laughs. "What's the play?"

Austin's still holding me in his arms and I tilt my head back so I can see his whole face. "The play is called Tandem Sweep. And it's the one where we face whatever comes at us, together."

Austin captures my lips with his and it's as if we're communicating everything we've experienced together this season: the ups and downs, the joys and trials. Austin pours all of his feelings into that kiss, and I match him, holding nothing back.

Something tells me Austin likes my play idea.

Dani

Sometimes in life, you don't need any statistics because some things aren't quantifiable.

Family dinners at Uncle Clive and Auntie Rox's house are always lively, and tonight is no exception. Myles Smith's song "Stargazing" plays on the radio as Austin and I pull into the driveway. Formally introducing Austin to my family feels monumental—I keep swinging back and forth between excitement and nerves— but I've never been more ready for something in my life.

Austin takes my hand as he parks his Jeep—my car is with Ethan for the weekend. A present from me for a hot date he has tonight. "You okay?"

I smile at him, his steady presence calming my jitters. "Yeah, just . . . you know, family stuff."

He leans over and kisses my forehead, sending shivers down my spine. I may never get used to the feel of Austin's lips on me—and I'm just fine with that.

"I have a better idea," I tell him, grabbing hold of the front of his shirt before he can get out of the car. "Something much more productive."

Austin groans, cracking open his car door. "Dani, I'm telling you, I already have the playbook memorized for the Super Bowl."

I tug him closer to me. "Not *that*," I say as I press my lips against his. I feel him smile beneath my lips and then he leans across the middle console, deepening the kiss. I get lost in Austin Taylor as Myles Smith continues to sing, "All this time I wasted/You were right there all along." And that's exactly how I feel now that I've made the jump with Austin—like I'm making up for lost time. I've only known him about nine months, and we've only officially dated for about a month, but I'm more certain about Austin Taylor than any stat I've ever recorded.

"Paparazzi!" a voice calls out from beyond the car. Austin and I shoot apart, my back banging against the passenger door.

Outside Austin's Jeep, Uncle Clive is rolling the trash can down the driveway, cackling. A quick glance around confirms there's no paparazzi.

Austin laughs good naturedly while I scowl at Uncle Clive. "I'm ready to meet the rest of your crazy clan," Austin says with a squeeze of my hand before exiting the car.

Uncle Clive kisses my cheek and slaps Austin on the back, still chuckling to himself. We walk up to the front door, and before we even reach it, Auntie Rox swings it open. "Dani, darling!" She pulls me into a warm hug before turning to Austin. "Austin Taylor." She says his name like it's a treat. "Welcome to our home."

Austin grins, shaking her hand. "Thank you, Mrs. Howard."

"Oh, none of that Mrs. nonsense. It's Auntie Rox to you."

We step inside, and the familiar sounds of laughter and chatter greet us. Uncle Clive heads to the backyard to man the grill, while my cousins Portia, Patrick, and Pierre gather around him, catching up. The twins, Lucas and Layla, are running through the yard, full of energy as always. My dad is deep in conversation with Heather in the kitchen, but he looks up and smiles when he sees us.

"Hey there, Dani girl," Dad says, pulling me into a hug. "Austin, good to see you again."

"Good to see you too, Mr. Marshall," Austin replies, shaking my dad's hand.

Heather comes over, giving me a quick hug. "You both look wonderful. Dinner's almost ready."

As we settle in, Auntie Rox hands Austin a beer and me a glass of wine. "Make yourselves at home. We're all family here."

Austin and I find a spot on the patio, and I take a moment to soak in the scene. The twinkling lights strung across the backyard, the smell of Uncle Clive's famous barbecue ribs, the sound of the twins' laughter—it's all so familiar and comforting. And now with Austin here, it's absolute perfection.

"Portia, Patrick, Pierre," I call out, waving them over. "Come meet Austin."

My cousins saunter over, each offering a handshake and a welcoming smile. Pierre, towering over everyone with his linebacker build, claps Austin on the back. "So, you're the guy who's been making all the headlines," he says, giving me a pointed look. I roll my eyes, though I'm wondering when my headlining kiss with Austin will become old news. "Nice to finally meet you."

Austin chuckles. "Nice to meet you too, Pierre. Heard you had a great season with the Packers."

We spend the next few hours eating, laughing, and sharing stories. The atmosphere is relaxed and joyful, and I can see Austin is going to fit right in. He even joins the twins on the trampoline for a while, making them giggle with his silly antics. Over the past few weeks, I've made more of an effort to get to know them—coming to their soccer games and taking an interest in what they're into. I never knew how much I was missing out on with Disney princesses, but Layla's doing her darnedest to fill me in.

It's wonderful.

At some point, Auntie Rox pulls me aside. "He's a good one, Dani. I can see why you fell in love with him."

I open my mouth to argue—it's too soon to use the L-word, at least with my family. But then I glance over at Austin, who's on the trampoline with the twins, making them giggle with his silly antics. "Yeah, he's pretty special." I bite my lip, attempting to hold back a smile. "I'm a goner," I confess. Auntie Rox reaches over, tugging me into a hug. I squeeze her tight and imagine that this is what it would be like if my mom were here too. She'd be happy for me. And, I'd like to think, somewhere out there, she *is* happy for me.

As the evening winds down, we all gather around the fire pit, toasting marshmallows and making s'mores. Austin sits next to me, our fingers intertwined.

"So, Austin," Uncle Clive begins, a twinkle in his eye. "What are your intentions with our Dani?"

Heat creeps up my neck, but Austin squeezes my hand and answers confidently. "I'm all in, Coach Clive." He runs a thumb over my hand. "I'm just biding my time until I'm at least 36.2 percent sure she'll say yes to spending the rest of her life with me." My jaw drops at his casual reference to getting married—and his callback to the stat I'd dropped on him when we first met. But my dad and Uncle Clive just laugh while Auntie Rox and Heather look like they've turned into a pair of heart eye emojis. Portia looks almost as scandalized as I do, while her brothers are just baffled.

"Well as long as the wedding is during the offseason," my dad says with a shrug—as if it's every day that a guy shows up declaring he's going to marry me.

"Dad!"

"Darius," Heather chides.

"Aren't we getting a little ahead of ourselves?" Portia says.

Austin places a tentative hand on my knee. "Are we?" he asks in a low voice.

I put my hand on top of his. "Maybe . . . " I glance up at him, his eyes dancing in the light of the fire. "Or maybe not."

Austin smiles, lighting up every nerve ending in me as he raises my hand to his mouth, pressing his lips to my knuckles. I can practically hear my stepmom and aunt swooning.

My dad clears his throat, breaking the moment. "Offseason," he says, pointing a stern finger at the two of us.

The warmth from the fire is nothing compared to the warmth spreading in my chest. This is my family, my home, and now Austin is a part of it.

Later, as Austin drives me home, I lean my head on Austin's shoulder. "Thanks for coming tonight. It means a lot to me."

He kisses the top of my head. "It means a lot to me too, Dani. I love being with you and your family."

I smile, feeling expansive and free. And I know this is just the beginning.

73

Dani

In Super Bowl history, the team that scores first has won approximately 66% of the games.

I'm in the staff box at Hard Rock Stadium in Miami, and my heart is pounding like a drumline. The energy is electric, palpable. It's coursing through the air and seeping into every corner of the stadium. It's the Super Bowl—an event I've dreamed of being a part of my whole life. And here I am, not just watching, but contributing. I glance down at my laptop, fingers flying over the keys as I input the latest data, tracking stats, and analyzing plays in real time.

Austin Taylor, our undrafted rookie sensation and the love of my life, is out there on the field, and I can't help but feel a surge of pride. He's come so far, and now he's leading the Tampa Bay Buccaneers against the Kansas City Chiefs. The odds were never in his favor, but he's proven himself time and time again. I scan the field, my eyes locking onto Austin as he commands the huddle. His confidence is unmistakable, and it's clear the team trusts him implicitly.

Mark, our lead analyst, leans over. "How's he looking, Dani?"

"His completion rate is at 72%," I reply, my voice steady despite the nerves. "He's reading their defense perfectly."

Mark nods, a rare smile crossing his usually stern face. "Good. We need to keep this momentum."

Momentum. It's one of those football buzz words that coaches love and analysts hate because it's not something you can measure. But I'm beginning to believe in it. Maybe not in the way that the coaches do.

Because to me, momentum is wherever Austin Taylor is.

I return my focus to the game. The Chiefs' defense is formidable, but Austin has been executing our game plan flawlessly. I watch as he drops back, scanning the field, and then delivers a perfect pass to Malik Washington, who dodges a tackle and sprints for a first down. The staff box erupts in cheers, and I allow myself a brief moment of celebration before diving back into my analysis.

Austin throws an incomplete, missing Mike Donnelly by centimeters.

"Fourth and two," Mark says, tension creeping into his voice. "What do you think?"

"Go for it," I reply without hesitation. "Our analytics show we've got a 65% chance of converting if we run it. Better odds than punting."

Mark nods, relaying the information to Coach Clive down on the field. Moments later, I see Austin signaling for the play. The ball is snapped, and Austin hands it off to Landon Mitchell, who barrels through the line, gaining just enough yards for the first down. Relief washes over me, but there's no time to relax.

The game isn't over yet.

74

Austin

> Bootleg: A play where the quarterback fakes a hand off to a running back, then rolls out to one side of the field to either pass or run with the ball, taking advantage of the defense's focus on the fake run.

The noise in Hard Rock Stadium is blaring, but all I can focus on is the ball in my hands. This is it—the moment every kid dreams of. The Super Bowl. I take a deep breath, feeling the weight of the game, the expectations, and the dreams of every fan resting on my shoulders. But I also feel the support of my teammates, my coaches, and Dani.

Especially Dani.

She's with me everywhere I go, as essential as my helmet or pads. Her faith propels me forward yard after yard.

We're down one touchdown with two minutes left in the game. I call the play and look around at my teammates in the huddle. "This is it, guys. Let's finish this. On three. One, two, three—Bucs!"

We break the huddle and line up. The Chiefs' defense is ready, but so are we. I take the snap, drop back, and search the field for an opening. Jake is running his route perfectly. I see a window and launch the ball. Jake catches it in stride and heads for the end zone. He's tackled just short, but it's enough for a first down. I pump my fist, the adrenaline surging through me.

Time is ticking away. We're in the final moments, and every play counts. The defense is giving us everything they've got, but we're pushing back just as hard. I take another snap, fake a hand off, and roll out to my right. I see Jordan Ellis breaking free downfield. I throw a dart, and he makes a spectacular catch, pulling us even closer to the goal line.

We're on the 2-yard line now, fourth down, and the tension is palpable. I look to the sidelines and see Coach Clive nodding. We're going for it. I line up, take a deep breath, and call the play. The ball is snapped, and I hand it off to Landon, who dives over the pile and into the end zone.

Touchdown.

The stadium erupts. I'm mobbed by my teammates, and we're all jumping and shouting, the realization hitting us—we've won the Super Bowl. I can hardly believe it. All the hard work, all the doubts, it's all worth it for this moment.

As the celebrations continue around me, my eyes roam the field, looking for one person in particular. Dani. I spot her making her way through the crowd, her face lit up with joy. I run to her, and without thinking, scoop her up in a hug, spinning her around.

"We did it!" I shout, the elation bubbling over.

"We did," she agrees, her voice choked with emotion. "You were amazing, Austin."

"No," I say, setting her down but not letting go. "*We* were amazing. This is our victory."

She smiles, and in that moment, surrounded by cheering fans and teammates, everything is right in the world. The road here was wild, but we faced it together. And together, we conquered.

Epilogue

Austin

It's a Tuesday morning, a few weeks after our Super Bowl win. After epic levels of celebration, we're finally returning to the grind.

Well, sort of.

After a couple weeks off, I told Dani it was time for us to go over game footage from the Super Bowl. She's meeting me here, in the film room, in five minutes. And if I know Dani Marshall, she won't be a minute late.

Which is why I need to get these candles lit ASAP.

I'm pretty sure what I'm doing is a fire hazard of the highest degree—I've packed this room with every candle I could get my hands on. Cued up on the screen is a video montage from the past few months—complete with highlights of the season, screenshots of Dani's tweets, along with pictures and videos of our past few months together. I've even included a few of the more tasteful news clips from when someone caught our first kiss on camera.

Dani may cringe—but, hey, I'm grateful for proof that Dani actually kissed me. Because sometimes I still can't believe that she's mine. I'm not sure what's more surreal, that or the fact that I won a Super Bowl as a starting quarterback for the Bucs.

One thing is certain: the latter wouldn't have happened without Dani's faith in me.

The soft glow of the candles casts flickering shadows on the walls, filling the room with warmth and a golden light that seems to make everything softer, more intimate. I've finally got them all lit and I'm going over my speech in my head when Dani walks in.

The shimmer of the candles reflects over Dani's face, making her look even more magical than the first time I saw her. My breath catches in my chest and I can't find a single word in my head, despite the fact that I practiced my speech a hundred times before this moment.

I was supposed to play the video first, supposed to say the speech I've been practicing. But as I see Dani standing there, lit up by the light of the candles, all those plans disappear. My heart is racing, my mind blank—except for one thought: *I can't wait any longer*. My knee hits the ground in front of Dani and I extend the ring box to her. "Marry me?" I manage to get out. Her eyes widen, filling with tears as she covers her mouth. For a second, she's frozen, like she's processing what's happening, and then she nods—quick and sure—before stepping into my arms.

I stand, pulling her close as I feel the steady rhythm of her heartbeat against mine, and in that moment, everything is perfect. I know, without a doubt, this is exactly where I'm meant to be.

Epilogue

Dani

Things I'm certain of:

The probability of winning the coin toss is 50%.

The success rate for field goals from 30-39 yards is approximately 85%.

A quarterback's average release time is roughly 2.5 seconds.

The two-point conversion success rate is about 47%.

And I am 1000% certain that I will love Austin Taylor all the days of my life.

End Zone Report ✓
@endzonereport

Bucs' QB Austin Taylor and data analyst Dani Marshall tied the knot in a private ceremony on Saturday, surrounded by their close friends and family.

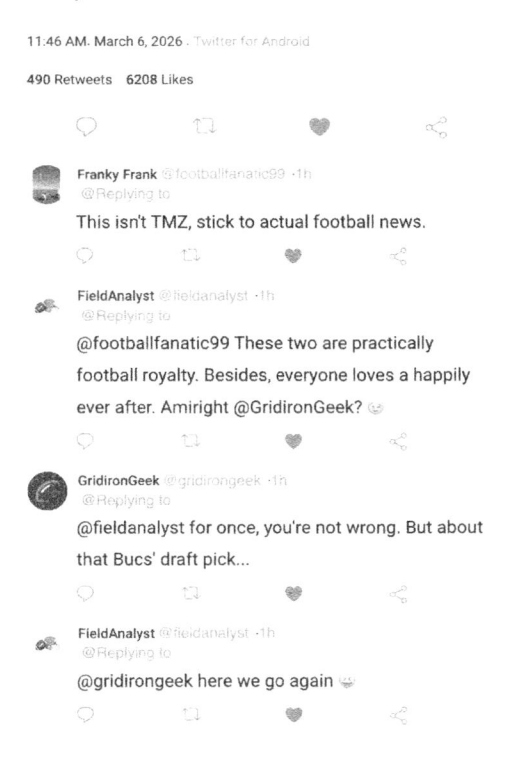

11:46 AM. March 6, 2026 . Twitter for Android

490 Retweets   6208 Likes

Franky Frank @footballfanatic99 ·1h
@Replying to

This isn't TMZ, stick to actual football news.

FieldAnalyst @fieldanalyst ·1h
@Replying to

@footballfanatic99 These two are practically football royalty. Besides, everyone loves a happily ever after. Amiright @GridironGeek? 😉

GridironGeek @gridirongeek ·1h
@Replying to

@fieldanalyst for once, you're not wrong. But about that Bucs' draft pick...

FieldAnalyst @fieldanalyst ·1h
@Replying to

@gridirongeek here we go again 😩

THE END

Did you enjoy Dani and Austin's story? Don't forget to leave a review or share with a friend!

Want to read Isabella and Elliot's story? Head here to pick up the free novella, Pucks & Pranks:

Bonus Scenes

More love, laughs, and football—get your exclusive bonus scenes now!

Step back into the world of *Off the Bench* with these exclusive bonus scenes! Celebrate the heartwarming, hilarious, and high-stakes moments of Austin and Dani's life after the final whistle. From championship games with their kids to Austin's first game on the sidelines with the Bucs, these scenes bring all the romance, humor, and family feels you love. Download now for an extra dose of sunshine-filled sports romance!

What's coming next in the Sports in the Sunshine State Rom-Com series...

Claire

"To Dani and Austin, the beginning of a dynasty!"

Glasses clink, a soft echo of champagne flutes fills the room. I'm smiling so hard my cheeks might just fall off, but watching my best friend newly engaged to Austin, both of them radiating happiness, it's worth the smile lines I'm earning today.

We're at Bern's Steakhouse, tucked away in the dessert room—Dani's favorite. It's a small, intimate group, mostly family and close friends, exactly what Dani wanted amidst the media frenzy swirling around her engagement to Austin. His family, in their sweet Midwestern way, has already started bombarding her with questions about wedding dates and dresses. I sip my champagne, certain I'll be the one doing most of Dani's wedding planning. She'll happily hand over the reins, and I'll gladly take them.

I lean over to Isabella, who's just weeks away from her own wedding. "Does this make you want to get married, like, tomorrow?"

She huffs, pushing her wild curls away from her forehead with one hand. "Girl, I tried to elope last week, but he—" she tilts her head toward her fiancé, famed hockey player Elliot Adler—"wouldn't let me."

"Well," I say, stifling a laugh. "It does take two to tango."

"That's the other thing I could do without. We're supposed to have our first dance lesson tomorrow. Choreographed, of course." She rolls her eyes, as if the whole idea wasn't hers. "And the instructor thinks I'll learn better by watching while *she* dances with Elliot."

"Yikes. Maybe it's time for a new instructor."

"You're tellin' me."

Our desserts arrive, and the conversation fades. I dig into my crème brûlée, savoring the rich custard topped with berries, paired with a honey lavender latte—perfect for a spring day. I've always been a seasonal creature. Living in Florida, you have to be intentional about embracing the seasons, or you'll blink and miss them. My art gallery reflects this: flowers in spring, beachy vibes in summer, pumpkins and autumn leaves in the fall, and a full-on North Pole in winter.

I never do things halfway.

So, why can't I seem to find a suitable guy? I've tried everything—dating apps, blind dates, and I even got a dog. Gronk's been a great companion, but so far, no husband.

Yet.

That night, as I lie in bed after Dani and Austin's celebration, I take one last desperate step toward finding love.

In a blur of impulsive clicks and forms, I apply to my favorite reality show: *Love is Blind*.

Is this something I'd do in the cold light of day, with all my logic intact?

Absolutely not.

Is it fueled by a twinge of melancholy seeing my best friends getting married?

You bet.

Am I backing out now?

Not a chance.

Want to find out what happens with Claire Beaumont's love life? Join my email list and be the first to hear about Claire's story!

Many Thanks To...

I'm so grateful to God for the written word and the power of faith and love.

This book wouldn't be here without my husband, Tyler. First of all, without him, I wouldn't be remotely interested in writing such a football-heavy book. And secondly, he did A LOT of work with me to make sure that the football scenes and all the stats are as accurate as possible. I also wouldn't be writing at all without his belief in me and encouragement. Tyler, I'm so grateful for you and I love you infinitely. You inspire me, motivate me, and love me unconditionally. No love story I'll ever write could match up to ours.

To Amanda: the Claire to my Dani. Thank you for your unerring belief in me and support for me. This book was written during a very challenging time in my life and I can't think of how many text messages you fielded during these past few months, always cheering me on and supporting me. Thank you. And thanks for always being willing to read the worst versions of all of my books and loving me and my characters anyway!

Endless thanks to my family, especially my parents and in-laws, for loving and supporting me.

To Auntie Roxi: I remember so vividly that first phone call we had where I asked your advice about writing a female main character who was a POC. Your belief in me and your advice on how to portray Dani and her family propelled me through writing this book. You are all over the pages of this novel and I'm so grateful for it.

My foster sister, Dorothy, beta read this book and was (and always is) a huge support to me. Thank you, big sis.

Jenn Fix, a dear friend and avid reader, also beta read this book and cheered me through this process. Thank you!!

Rachel Abril, my lovely friend, thank you for your support and for your feedback on the London scenes!

Another dear friend, my college roomie Paige Parnell, patiently answered approximately a bajillion questions about braids, and inspired the salon scene with Teetee and Bisi. Thank you, my friend.

Thanks so much to Rachel from Closed Door Romance who gave me advice on launching this book, the cover, and so many other things. Thank you for all the support you give to indie authors! I'm so grateful for you. I'm also grateful for my friends in the Bookstagram Academy (which Rachel formed to help authors and Bookstagrammers) for your friendship and collaboration as we journey through this indie author life together!

I'm so grateful for all the ARC readers, launch team members, Bookstagrammers or others who have supported me and other indie authors: you are amazing and you make this little indie publishing world go 'round! Cheers to you!

And to you, dear reader, thank you for picking up this book! Just by reading it, you're making this author's dreams come true.

XOXO,

Tiffany

About Tiffany

Tiffany LOVES love. Married to her middle school sweetheart, this award-winning novelist adores writing stories with heart, humor and depth. As a five-time national equestrian champion, she loves sports romances with heart-pounding action sequences and a whole lot of sweet romance. She received her Masters of Fine Arts in Creative Writing from the University of Tampa. A homeschooling mama, she lives in Tampa with her husband and their two wild and crazy sons. She loves hearing from readers and would love to connect with you on any social media platform at @authortiffanynoellechacon or on her website at tiffanynoellechacon.com.

Join Tiffany's Facebook readers' group here:

Made in United States
Orlando, FL
08 January 2025